Jacquie Tyler grew up in London and started writing mini-novels from age ten. After moving to leafy Hertfordshire and bringing up a family, she decided to pursue her dream of being a writer. During lockdown, she wrote short stories for an online magazine and completed a copywriting course, leading her to write the novel she had always wanted to read: *To Love, Honour and Betray*.

This book is dedicated to my Mum, who taught me the value of hard work and perseverance, and to my Dad, the wind beneath my wings. His unwavering support and belief in me have given me the courage to soar.

To the ones who challenged me, tested me and showed me the world in ways I never expected—you may not know it, but you helped me bring these characters to life and shaped this story.

Jacquie Tyler

TO LOVE, HONOUR AND BETRAY

AUSTIN MACAULEY PUBLISHERS
LONDON * CAMBRIDGE * NEW YORK * SHARJAH

Copyright © Jacquie Tyler 2025

The right of Jacquie Tyler to be identified as author of this work has been asserted by the author in accordance with sections 77 and 78 of the Copyright, Designs and Patents Act 1988.

All rights reserved. No part of this publication may be reproduced, stored in a retrieval system, or transmitted in any form or by any means, electronic, mechanical, photocopying, recording, or otherwise, without the prior permission of the publishers.

Any person who commits any unauthorised act in relation to this publication may be liable to criminal prosecution and civil claims for damages.

This is a work of fiction. Names, characters, businesses, places, events, locales, and incidents are either the products of the author's imagination or used in a fictitious manner. Any resemblance to actual persons, living or dead, or actual events is purely coincidental.

A CIP catalogue record for this title is available from the British Library.

ISBN 9781037101991 (Paperback)
ISBN 9781037102004 (ePub e-book)

www.austinmacauley.com

First Published 2025
Austin Macauley Publishers Ltd®
1 Canada Square
Canary Wharf
London
E14 5AA

I would like to thank Claire Petulengro, the strongest, most inspirational woman I have ever met. Without you, this book would have only ever been a dream. You swept into my life like a whirlwind and presented me with the opportunity to write from the heart.

To the one and only. Ted, who believed in me from day one. I hope I've done you proud.

Thanks to Jean Wallace, my power hour coach, who gave me the push to do more than just stare at the finished manuscript.

Em, my twin flame in Oz. Writing together for Lengro magazine during lockdown put the fire back in my belly. You always encouraged me and made me laugh out loud!

To my children, Ben and Annie, my greatest achievements. You taught me how to love.

Chapter 1
2016

Riley stared at the girls through the car window. They both had their hair tied in neat French plaits. She had never tied their hair that way. *It had to be Blair*, she thought; *Daniel wouldn't have a clue how to do French plaits.* Blair would be in her element, playing 'mummy'. She pictured the woman in her kitchen, tossing pancakes while Daniel sat in his battered-looking brown leather chair by the window, sipping his morning espresso.

The bright morning sun would be filtering in and shining directly onto Daniel, making his piercing blue eyes light up like sparkling sapphires that, when Blair glanced away from her perfectly round pancakes and looked up at him, would take her breath away; just like it used to do hers. He would, most probably, be on his phone, and her daughters would be sitting at the breakfast bar, eyes wide with excitement, waiting as the delicious sweet aroma of shop-bought batter mix and maple syrup wafted through the air. They would all be there, sitting in Riley's kitchen, a happy little family. Her happy little family!

The girls had grown so big. She wanted to grab hold of them, wrap them tightly in her arms, breathe in their sweet smell, and never let them go. For two long, miserable years, she had to rely on memories of her darling daughters to stop herself from going completely insane in her depressingly austere prison cell where life was grey—grey walls, grey food, grey clothes! Each night, she lay on the stiff, thin mattress and prayed for an early release. The days seemed to get longer, and her mind started playing tricks on her, confusing her and engulfing her, until one day she could no longer cope, so she shut down. She just melted away into nothingness. She was completely numb.

Apparently, she was told by the healthcare professionals that she had suffered a nervous breakdown. She was placed in psychiatric care for a short time, which she was actually grateful for. She welcomed the drugs that helped her switch off from reality and protected her from the excruciating 'lows' that hit her like a sledgehammer each morning as soon as she opened her eyes.

In the playground, Riley's daughter Patsy ran over to greet her friends. Riley noticed the slight limp as she ran. She had hoped that, by now, Patsy's limp would have gone. Guilt churned like bile in her stomach. She opened the window slightly to let some air in.

As she glanced in the rear-view mirror, she was shocked to see the dark circles that had developed under her eyes. She groaned at the state of her hair and quickly ran her fingers through it, trying to untangle the knots that had formed as a result of her tossing and turning restlessly all night. The familiar sound of laughter rang out from the din of excited playground chatter, and tears immediately sprang to her eyes, then a loud knock on the passenger side window quickly shook her from her thoughts and made her jump. "What the fuck!" she shouted and swung round to see a woman's face peering in at her.

Riley opened the car door and got out. "What are you doing here?" she asked the woman.

The woman stared at her coldly. "What are you doing here, Riley? You know this is completely against the rules," she said bluntly. Her steely grey eyes bore into Riley's, and Riley suddenly felt completely inadequate and self-conscious in her ripped jeans and vest top.

She noticed that the woman confronting her was immaculately dressed in a red fitted, expensive-looking jacket and matching skirt, emphasising her petite figure. Her salon-perfect, glossy, blonde hair was scooped up into a neat chignon, with not a single strand of hair out of place.

"You are not their mother, Blair!" Riley hissed at the woman.

"No, Riley, you are! It's a shame that didn't seem to be enough for you," she retorted flatly.

The woman averted her gaze from Riley to the footwell of the car and sniggered. Suddenly, Riley felt her face starting to redden as she noticed the top of a wine bottle poking out from under her seat. She carefully moved her foot to the left and gently pushed the bottle back underneath. The woman laughed out loud at the absurdity of Riley trying to hide the bottle.

Riley stared at the woman's face and for a split second contemplated slapping the smug, judgemental look off it, but instead, she bent down, quickly picked up the bottle, held it out in front of the woman, so she could see it was unopened, and then she got out of the car and threw it in the bin outside the school. She felt like a naughty schoolgirl who had just been told off by the headmistress. She almost expected Blair to send her to the naughty corner. As if reading her mind, Blair shook her head in disgust. "You haven't changed, Riley," she said condescendingly.

"Mummy, Mummy," a dark-haired girl called out from the school gate. Riley's heart leapt as she turned and walked towards her daughter. She put her hand through the bars, and the little girl reached up to grab hold of it.

"Rose! Come back here, please," called out the teacher on playground duty. Rushing up to the child, she gently pulled her away from the gate and her mother's grip. Rose's face crumbled as she reluctantly let go of her mother's hand and started to cry. The teacher gave Riley a scathing look. All the staff knew about Riley Fairgate and what she had done.

Blair walked victoriously over to speak to the teacher. "Hello, Mrs Davies. I'll be picking the girls up today. See you soon, Rose!" she said, blowing the little girl a big kiss. The clattering of her high heels on the pavement echoed as she walked away. Then she stopped. Riley's heart was in her mouth as she waited for another onslaught of hate to be hurled her way. Blair swung around and looked scornfully at Riley. "Oh, and sign the bloody divorce papers," she said.

Riley felt hot, angry tears rolling down her cheeks as she turned to her daughter. "Mummy will see you soon, darling. Be a big girl now; no crying," she said softly.

Chapter 2

Loud banging woke Riley from a deep sleep. She groaned as she lifted her head from the pillow and rubbed her eyes. She pushed back the dishevelled hair covering her face and looked over at the clock on her bedside table; it was twenty past ten. She sat still for a few seconds, giving her brain time to reload. The last thing she remembered was staring at the bottle; the one she had brought in from the car; the one that Blair hadn't seen.

There had been a special offer at the Co-op: two for the price of one. She bought them, but of course, she wasn't going to actually drink them! She slowly started to piece together the events of the day and remembered the disparaging looks at the school from Mrs Prim and Proper Davies who looked like she needed a good shag to soften the pursed lipped, furrowed brow look on her large angry-looking face and the way Blair had belittled her; well, that was just the icing on the cake. She had returned home feeling completely humiliated and ashamed.

The bottles had been tempting her every day since she had come out of prison, but it had been six months now, and she wanted to prove to herself and everyone else that she could do it; that she could resist the temptation. For years, she had used alcohol to block out her feelings. First, it had been to numb the pain of her dad's death. Her husband, Daniel, hadn't known how to support her properly during that time; he had been dealing with demons of his own and had always had a problem with showing his emotions. She had felt alone and abandoned.

One night, she had made a terrible, unforgivable mistake and lost the most precious people in her life, and she had been paying for it every day since, but she wasn't a bad person; anyone who knew her could vouch for that. That was in the past, though! She did her time and paid the price, and now, she was going to sort herself out and come back stronger and be the best friggin' mother in the world! Unfortunately, the urge had been too much for her this time. She had stared at the bottle for a good five minutes then thought, sod it!

"Riley!" a man called out.

"Oh god," she whispered to herself. She made her way downstairs, turned on the outside light and opened the door. Her husband stood on the doorstep, looking agitated. Riley stared at him and felt the familiar butterflies in her stomach. She hadn't seen him for a while, and the sight of him shook her.

"You know why I'm here," Daniel said. "You can only see the girls at arranged times, Riley."

She sighed and said, "I'm sorry, Daniel. I couldn't help it. I haven't seen them in so long. I miss them so much." She looked into his bright blue eyes and bit her lip to stop herself from admitting that she missed him too. Quickly pulling herself together, she said, "It won't happen again."

"Have you been drinking?" he asked her.

"No," she lied.

"Okay," he said, knowing full well she was lying.

"Are you on your way home?" she asked him.

"Yes. I had a meeting," he answered.

"Fancy a night cap?" Riley asked, cheekily. She knew, no matter how disappointed and angry he got with her, she was his 'weak spot'. No woman could ever make Daniel Fairgate feel the same way as Riley did. No matter how hard he tried to forget her and move on, Riley was always there, under his skin, in his head, running through his veins. He would always love her.

It amazed him how beautiful she looked. Daniel's mind flicked back to when they had been a couple. He had always looked forward to coming home to her after work. The girls would be in bed, and she would usually be in the kitchen, perched on the breakfast bar, scanning through emails with a glass of white wine beside her, while listening to old classics on Smooth Radio. Her hair would be tied up, and she would be wearing denim shorts and her favourite baggy off-the-shoulder sweatshirt but still managing to look sultry.

He remembered how he would put his arms around her waist and gently kiss her shoulder, working his way up her long, smooth neck; the smell of her would drive him wild. She would turn and wrap her long legs around his waist. Sometimes, they didn't make it to the bedroom and ended up making passionate love on the kitchen table, pushing whatever was on there onto a heap on the floor. Sex with Riley was always incredible.

When she looked into his eyes, it felt like she was looking right into his soul. But the drinking slowly became a problem, eventually causing an irreparable rift and leading to a heartbreaking parting. Realising that he was staring at her, Daniel quickly averted his gaze and said, "I should get back."

"Okay. Next time, maybe," Riley said suggestively, holding his gaze one more time. She then smiled and closed the door.

Daniel got into the car and glanced at his phone; five missed calls, then finally a message from his concerned girlfriend, 'Where on earth are you? It's late, I'm worried!' He looked up at the upstairs window. The light was on, and the blinds weren't fully closed. He watched as his wife slowly took off her jumper. Riley could see the car lights in her driveway and knew he would be watching her.

Chapter 3

Blair lay in bed with a million thoughts racing through her mind. It was the third time that week that Daniel had been late home. She knew what he was like after a few drinks; he was flirty and tactile although he never seemed to remember his behaviour the next day. She had fallen in love with Daniel the first time she had met him, but unfortunately, Riley met him at the same time, and as usual, after meeting Riley, no man would ever notice any other woman.

Blair knew she was no competition for Riley. Riley was stunning; a natural beauty with great bone structure, long slim legs and great breasts. Blair was plain in comparison. She was petite with a nice figure and shiny blonde hair but had never been the girl who got the wolf whistles from the builders. But she had won the war! She had Daniel now, and things were different.

He was the love of her life; her soul mate. She would do anything for Daniel, including helping him bring up his girls, and she would even give up her career if he decided they should have children of their own one day, but first, he would need to get divorced. Riley was stalling, but Blair was a patient woman; she could wait, and she looked forward to revelling in Riley Fairgate's downfall; it was something she had been waiting for, for years.

"Blair! Blair," screamed Patsy.

Blair threw off the duvet and leapt out of bed. She ran to Patsy's bedroom. "It's okay, darling," Blair said, wrapping her arms around the little girl. Patsy often had night terrors since the accident three years ago. Blair heard the front door open. She laid Patsy back down on the bed and gently stroked her hair for a few seconds until she was fully asleep.

Downstairs, Daniel walked into the large, open-plan kitchen. He threw his suit jacket onto the worktop and looked out at the night sky from the huge window that ran from the ceiling to the floor. It was a clear night, and the full moon lit up the whole room. He pulled out a bottle of whisky from the built-in bar in the lounge area. "Ice?" asked Blair, heading towards the fridge.

"Please!" he answered, as he turned to watch her glide into the kitchen in a silky kimono, loosely tied, so he could just see the outline of her small, pert breasts. Blair grabbed a couple of cubes of ice from the freezer and put them into a glass tumbler. She took the bottle from his hand and poured it out for him. Daniel was tempted to untie her robe and throw her down onto the velvet sofa beside them.

"Patsy had another nightmare," she told him, interrupting his lustful thoughts.

"Is she okay?" he asked, concerned.

"Yes," said Blair, still not looking up from her glass. "Were you with her?" she asked him, coldly.

"Who?" asked Daniel, feeling guilty even though he hadn't done anything wrong. Blair looked into his blue eyes, hoping they would reveal some telltale sign that would give him away.

"I'm not stupid, Daniel. I told you that she showed up at the school. It was obvious you would go straight round there to see her," she said.

Daniel turned back to the window. "I only popped in on the way home to warn her to stay away," he answered, trying to defend himself. He hated himself for lying.

Blair was an angel. She had saved him from the fallout of the accident and the effects of Riley going to prison. She was kind, loved him unconditionally, and he knew he could trust her. She was also brilliant with his two girls, too, but she wanted 'marriage'. As much as he tried, Daniel just couldn't commit to that. He kept telling her to wait and give him time, and she did; she had waited patiently for two years, but he wasn't sure if he would ever be able to commit to her.

"Let's go to bed," she said softly, taking the glass from his hand and leading him upstairs.

Chapter 4

Riley felt like she was in heaven. She groaned softly as she lay on her front, naked apart from a warm, fluffy white towel that covered her from the waist down. This was just what she needed! Each painful, tender knot deep within the tissues in her back was kneaded gently, and she felt a painful but pleasant crunch as each trapped nodule was released.

"Wow, lady, you have been under some intense stress lately," said Siobhan, Riley's therapist and good friend, as she finished off the massage with a firm rub down along both of Riley's legs.

"Nothing new there!" said Riley, turning over and covering herself with the towel. "I had a run-in at the school with Blair, then drank a bottle of wine and had a visit from Daniel," she said, sighing.

"Oh, Riley, love, you were doing so well. Why did you have the bloody bottle in the house?" asked Siobhan, gently helping Riley up from the massage table. Riley took a sip of water from the glass Siobhan handed her and shook her head.

"Because I'm an idiot!" she admitted.

Siobhan's phone beeped with a text message. "Oh sorry, honey, I thought I had it on silent," she said, glancing down to see who it was from.

Riley smiled and said, "No worries. I'll get dressed and pay at the desk. Don't come out."

"You're a star! I'll catch up with you later," Siobhan said, giving Riley a kiss on the cheek. She left Riley in the room and then closed the door behind her and opened up the message on her phone. *'I need to see you, Von. Can you fit me in this afternoon? D xx'.*

Chapter 5

Siobhan made herself a cup of mint green tea and quickly tidied the kitchen. She glanced in the mirror on the kitchen wall to check she was presentable and tucked a few stray auburn hairs behind her ears. She could have done without having to rush home from the salon, but luckily, she wasn't busy that afternoon and managed to juggle a few appointments to enable her to leave early. Daniel had wanted to see her for some reason, and she didn't want him coming to the salon.

A car pulled up outside. Damn! She thought. He was early. Daniel stood on the doorstep with a bunch of white roses wrapped beautifully in white tissue paper and floral print wrapping paper. She smiled and invited him inside. "They're beautiful, thank you," she said, lifting the flowers up, so she could smell the fresh, light scent. "This is a surprise. To what do I owe the pleasure?" she asked, giving him a quick peck on the cheek.

"Do I need an excuse to see you?" he asked, grabbing her waist and pulling her towards him. He looked into her eyes for a couple of seconds and then kissed her gently.

Siobhan put the flowers down and wrapped her arms around his neck and hungrily reciprocated the kiss. She pulled his t-shirt up over his head and threw it on the chair beside them. His body was warm and smelled delicious, and Siobhan quickly made her way down to the buckle of his belt while he fumbled around with her bra strap underneath the black tunic he had just unbuttoned. She moved him away carefully and took off her top and black lace bra and threw them on to the chair too. Daniel gazed at her sensuous body, admiringly.

Siobhan was extremely health-conscious. Her strict fitness regime was hard work, but the rewards were evident in her toned arms and legs and rock-solid abs. He was sure there weren't many sixty-year-old women with a body like Siobhan's. He stroked her tanned arms and cupped her warm breasts in his hands, then bent his head to kiss her neck. Siobhan felt warmth in her stomach that she hadn't felt for a while, and the desire for him was almost too much to bear. "Let's go upstairs," she whispered breathlessly.

Sex between Siobhan and Daniel was always quick but exciting. She got up and headed towards the shower, leaving Daniel to catch his breath. She didn't see the point of lying together afterwards and wasting time. She had had a good half an hour, but now she needed to get back to work.

Daniel wasn't in love with Siobhan but was in awe of her. She was attractive in an elegant, regal kind of way. Her short, layered hair framed her heart-shaped face, which was covered in light-coloured freckles. Daniel had been fascinated by her the first time he met her at Riley's house, all those years ago. She had later become his masseuse and ran the spa in the country club her husband owned.

As he slowly got to know her, Daniel found he enjoyed her company even though it was only for an hour during a massage. Daniel wasn't one of those clients who liked to chill out, close their eyes and listen to soothing bird chirps and pan flute music. He liked to chat. At first, it had irritated Siobhan; she liked to concentrate when she was working and create a peaceful atmosphere, so she could really tune in to her client's body and feel where all the tension points were, but Daniel had a great sense of humour which she loved, and she also got the feeling he was troubled. Being the empath that she was, she liked to try and help people whenever she could, and she wanted to help Daniel.

For the first time in Daniel's life, he felt like he could open up to someone. He loved Riley with all his heart but didn't feel like he could share all his deep, dark secrets with her. He was her husband and protector, and he didn't want her to be disappointed or think less of him if he revealed his vulnerabilities. But with Siobhan, there was no commitment or expectation. She was just his friend who was a great listener, calm, strong, intellectual, gave great advice and was also ten years older and wiser than him.

It was not long after Daniel started having regular treatments with Siobhan that they both realised there was chemistry between them. One afternoon, Siobhan had been working on the muscles in his back, and Daniel had become quiet. She moved her hands lower towards his waist, and she heard him moan softly. She felt the need in him and gently pulled the towel down and stroked his firm buttocks. She carried on all the way down his legs until he groaned louder and turned over.

Siobhan sometimes provided 'extras' if she thought a client really needed it. Usually, the added extras didn't faze her, but with Daniel, she felt herself becoming aroused. It became apparent to both of them that their relationship was more than just that of therapist and client.

Siobhan was happily married to Jeff; she enjoyed her life with him but sometimes found sex with Jeff boring. She had been known to have had a couple of lovers during her marriage. Her husband had had his suspicions but had never confronted her. He accepted that she had *needs* he couldn't always meet, and she was always discreet with her actions, respected him and had never treated him any differently; Siobhan was a loving, caring wife, and he adored her, but he had found out a long time ago, his wife was a free spirit who didn't follow rules. She made up her own rules, and he knew if he tried to tie her down, she would leave, and he couldn't bear to lose her.

Siobhan and Daniel agreed that they would meet at her house when her husband was out. She never gave a second thought to the wife or partner when she began a tryst with anyone; as far as she was concerned, it wasn't normal to be expected to be monogamous with one person for your whole life. She believed everyone should do what makes them happy, as long as they weren't hurting anyone, and if Riley never found out, she would never be hurt. Daniel hadn't been happy cheating on his wife, but he didn't want to give Siobhan up either. She made him feel safe and understood. She was his little bit of respite from his often complicated, sometimes confusing, life.

Chapter 6
2011

Daniel found it hard to escape from the demons in his head and the constant voices that tortured him. He was also always under pressure from clients and staff at work and found it difficult to unwind. Riley was out at races a lot in the evenings with the greyhounds that she trained, and often he would find himself on his own when the children were in bed. Daniel knew his wife had to attend the races; it was part and parcel of the job. He started stopping off at the pub after work, so he wouldn't have to be on his own with his thoughts. Their neighbour, Mary, loved babysitting for them as she had lost her husband and was bored most of the time as she didn't go out much, so she was always willing to watch the girls for them.

Blair loved her job, but she was lonely. Going home after work was such an anti-climax. A ready meal for one wasn't exactly something to look forward to, and she was usually too tired to get absorbed into a TV drama, so she usually settled for having the soaps on. They were easy to watch and didn't require much concentration, mainly because they were mind-numbingly boring, but it was a distraction until it was time to go to bed.

One evening, she decided to be brave and stop off at the White Horse on her way home from work. She fancied a gin and tonic but hated drinking on her own at home; it was so depressing and just emphasised the fact that she didn't have a partner or children, making her feel even more lonely. She had never been for a drink on her own and didn't want people to think she was Billy-no-mates, but she had just finished reading a self-help book about 'venturing out of your comfort zone' and she had vowed to try something new each month to push herself. She took a deep breath and sheepishly walked through the door. As she walked to the bar, she was surprised to see Daniel there.

After that evening, stopping off at the pub became a regular Monday evening event for Blair that she really looked forward to. Daniel was always in there on a Monday evening, too. They started off just having a chat at the bar; then after a few weeks, whoever got to the pub first would grab a table for two. Daniel enjoyed listening to her stories about work. She was a managing editor for an online magazine, and her job sounded incredibly interesting.

On their first meeting, she told him about a salacious, well-known celebrity that she had interviewed that day. What she was about to reveal the next morning would shock the public and ruin the man's career. Blair had mixed feelings about it being published, but she was under pressure from the chief editor to report the story, or it would go to someone else. Daniel was impressed with her empathy but, at the same time, turned on by her ambition. A bitch with a heart; he liked that!

The greyhounds and kennels were in Riley's blood; it was her passion, like her father's and grandfather's. The Mulligan family were well-known and highly established in Hertfordshire. They had an impressive track record of wins over the decades, and the welfare of the dogs was just as important as the races. Greyhound racing had received bad press over the years regarding misconduct and ill treatment of the animals, but the Mulligans did everything by the book. Terry Mulligan was an honest, family man and was respected by everyone who knew him.

Riley adored her father and had spent every spare minute when she was younger, helping him in the kennels after her mother died. As soon as she left school, Riley worked full-time at Mulligan's Racing Kennels. Her father insisted she start at the bottom and work her way up, and soon, she became an assistant trainer, and her days were full and happy. There wasn't time for any kind of social life, but Riley didn't care. She had always been popular at school and was the cool girl every boy wanted to go out with and every girl wanted to be friends with, but her life was centred around her job and her family and only a close-knit group of friends, which included Blair Matthews.

Chapter 7
1986

When Blair first joined St James School, she had felt completely out of place. Her mother had walked out on them, leaving her father alone to bring them up. Not being able to cope with the memories, her father decided they would have to relocate and apply for a job transfer. Blair felt angry and resentful at being dragged away from her small village in West Sussex and everything that was familiar to her and forced to live in a completely new county where they didn't know anyone.

The school she was enrolled in was much bigger than her previous school, and she found it completely daunting. Her uniform consisted of a blue pleated skirt, which was much too big for her so needed to be rolled up a couple of times, an unflattering pale yellow blouse which hung limply over her flat teenage chest, and as she was so petite, the school blazer didn't even come in her size, so she had to settle for the smallest one, which completely swamped her.

On her first day at school, Blair was assigned a single wooden desk in the centre of an uncomfortably overly warm form room. She sat in-between two girls who had seemed friendly and made the effort to talk to her, which she was relieved about.

"Write your name on the front of your workbook," one of the girls instructed her.

"Thank you," Blair replied gratefully. She felt hot and stupid in her ill-fitting clothes but didn't dare take off her blazer in case everyone saw the sweat marks which would have, by now, formed on her blouse underneath her armpits. She had the feeling that the two girls who had befriended her were the 'nerdy' girls of the class. The trendier, louder girls were crowded around another very pretty dark-haired girl. They giggled as they examined a red, angry-looking love bite on the girl's neck.

Outside, the teacher's footsteps could be heard coming along the corridor, and the girls quickly separated and went to their own desks. The pretty girl with the love bite pulled her collar up and slid into the chair behind her desk. The boys were all looking in her direction, and she smiled, pretending to be shy, but Blair could see the girl was lapping up the attention. Blair was mesmerised by her. She was the most beautiful girl she had ever seen and was also confident, but not in an arrogant way.

A boy sitting at the back of the class had caught Blair's eye. He had short, spiky, almost white hair and an angular face with deep-set green eyes. His shirt button was undone, and his tie wasn't up as far as it was supposed to be. He had pulled his blazer sleeves up slightly, which Blair thought looked really cool. He reminded her of a rock star. He was the most gorgeous boy she had ever clapped eyes on. He looked up slightly from something he was sketching with a pencil and caught her watching him.

She turned away quickly; her cheeks burned and turned a light shade of scarlet. One of the nerdy girls seemed to read her mind. "That's Ricky. He's very handsome, isn't he?" she whispered. Blair shrugged, completely mortified that he had seen her staring. He smiled to himself and put his artwork away on his desk.

Blair learned that the nerdy girls were called Colette and Gabriella. They had decided to take her under their wings and gave her a tour of the school at lunchtime to show her where everything was. The three of them sat in the school canteen after deciding on hot dogs and chips from the hot counter for lunch. Blair watched the other girls from her form sitting outside in the sunshine with their packed lunches.

Colette informed her that the 'cool girl' with the love bite was called Riley Mulligan. She wore her skirt just above the knee and her blouse was slightly too small, showing off her already well-formed breasts. She wore dark eyeliner and mascara, which emphasised her huge brown eyes. The boys swarmed around her like bees around the queen. Out of nowhere, Blair saw Ricky appear. He glided across the grass like a god.

As Blair watched him, it felt like she was watching him in slow motion; her heart was beating so fast she thought she might have a heart attack. He walked over to the bench where Riley was sitting and put his hands over her eyes.

Riley jumped and pulled his hands away, and then, realising it was him, she pulled him down next to her, and they kissed.

Fuck! thought Blair. The hottest girl in the school is dating the Rock God! Blair decided then and there that even though Colette and Gabriella were sweet and kind, she wanted to hang out with the cool girl.

Chapter 8

Mrs Donegan, the art teacher, had placed Blair next to Riley, and Blair could not have been happier, especially when Riley introduced herself. "I'm Riley, by the way," she told Blair.

"Yeah, as if I didn't know," said Blair.

"Pardon?" Riley said, confused. Blair couldn't believe she had just said that out loud.

"Oh, I mean, Mrs Donegan said your name when she told me to sit next to you," she said.

"I hate this class. I'm rubbish at art," Riley told Blair.

"Yes, me too," said Blair.

Their common dislike for the subject was the beginning of a special friendship for Riley and Blair, and they discovered they had a lot in common. One of the things they had in common was their attraction to Ricky Berg; although Blair didn't disclose that bit of information to Riley or anyone else. Ricky was brilliant at art, and Mrs Donegan had high hopes for him.

Blair was convinced Mrs Donegan had a crush on him. He sat in front of Blair and was a complete distraction for her. She could never complete any of her assignments as she found herself either staring at the mole on his neck, which she thought was really cute, or becoming mesmerised every time he ran his long, slim fingers through his spiky hair.

One Friday afternoon, Riley had been absent from art class, and Blair had been concerned. She would miss her new friend; they had such a laugh when they sat together. They would mostly spend the time making fun of Mrs Donegan, who was about sixtyish with a mass of salt and pepper coloured hair that wasn't in any particular style but just stuck out at all angles. Her favoured uniform was wide-legged brown trousers, which were just a bit too short, which she wore with brown brogues, stripy socks and a pale blue velvet blazer. Blair wondered where Ricky was that day; as he too hadn't turned up, then she spotted him through the small window of the classroom door, and she noticed that he looked agitated.

They would be going outside this afternoon, Mrs Donegan informed them. They would be doing some landscape drawings of the views from the field behind the school. Blair was beside herself with excitement, especially when Ricky walked out of the school gate beside her. She had rolled her skirt up like Riley did and even put on a bit of mascara, which she did in the school toilets, so her dad wouldn't know about it. "This is different!" he told Blair.

Blair looked around to see who he was talking to and then realised he was talking to her, and she blushed, yet again. Why did she always go red when he spoke to her? It was so embarrassing. "Yes, it makes a nice change," she said, wondering where her high-pitched voice had suddenly come from and feeling annoyed with herself for not being able to say something more profound.

The pupils were instructed to sit anywhere they liked on the grass and sketch anything they wanted. Ricky walked over to some of the boys, and they all sat together in the shade of a large oak tree overlooking a rundown, empty barn. Ricky stared at the barn. That was where the magic had happened; where he had had sex with Riley Mulligan.

Riley had decided that she was ready. It would be the first time for both of them, and she was simultaneously excited and nervous. Deciding where to 'do it' had been difficult as neither of their houses was an option as their families were always there. "What about the barn?" Riley suggested.

Ricky raised his eyebrows in surprise. "You know it's haunted, right?" he asked.

Riley rolled her eyes. "Well, that will make it even more fun then," she said with a giggle.

The barn belonged to a local landowner who owned practically all the land in the area and was far too busy developing houses and extending his already successful hotel to worry about an old, dilapidated barn and certainly wouldn't be going round to check if anyone was in there having underage sex. Ricky knew there were some haystacks in there as he and his friends sometimes went there to have a cheeky smoke after school, but he knew that when it got dark, no one dared to go in there as it was apparently haunted by its previous owner, a notorious old woman called Mildred Mayles, who used to live in the area and hated children.

Ricky and Riley held hands as they walked through the school grounds, past the oak tree and down a little steep path to the barn. Riley pulled her scarf tightly around her neck as the wind was quite fierce that afternoon. Neither of them said a word. They were just about to do something momentously life-changing, but what if they got naked and then didn't know what to do? None of their friends had had sex yet, so it's not as if they could have asked anyone for advice.

Riley knew her sister, Eden, had had sex with her boyfriend, as she heard her boasting about her 'first time' on the phone to her friends. However, Eden was two years older than Riley, so it was legal. She couldn't possibly tell Eden what she and Ricky were about to do, as Eden would have been horrified. As if reading her thoughts, Ricky asked, "Are you sure you want to do this?" All doubts left Riley's mind at that precise moment. She loved Ricky and wanted to be with him forever; after all, he had carved their initials and the word 'forever' on the trunk of the oak tree.

There was no door on the barn, and inside, it was freezing cold. Riley shivered, and Ricky stopped and hugged her tightly. There was no going back now, he thought. He just hoped she wouldn't be disappointed. She felt her body relax in the warmth of Ricky's embrace, and as his hands moved up towards her breasts, she closed her eyes and let him kiss her. He had touched her breasts before, and she had enjoyed it, but this time, they were going to go further, and suddenly, she got that excited feeling again in her stomach that she usually got when Ricky touched her breasts, and she now felt completely ready and couldn't wait.

Ricky paused for a moment to lay his jacket on the haystack behind them so Riley would be comfortable. It was too cold to undress completely, so he undid her bra underneath her blouse and pulled her school skirt up to her waist. Riley fumbled about with the zip on Ricky's trousers until she managed to pull it down and undo his button, and he then manoeuvred himself into position. Next, came a lot of thrusting and body shifting until they both found a comfortable position. Riley kept her eyes firmly shut, which Ricky was pleased about as it gave him the chance to glance down a few times without her seeing, to re-position himself as he wasn't exactly confident about what he was doing.

When it was finally over, Riley felt relieved. She got off the haystack and rearranged her uniform. She hadn't expected it to hurt so much. "Are you okay?" Ricky asked.

"Fabulous," Riley lied and managed a half-smile. Ricky was pleased. He couldn't say he really enjoyed the experience as he was worrying about Riley all the way through it. She wasn't making the usual noises they made in the movies; hers were more like those of a wounded animal. She was also pulling some weird faces. Obviously, he wouldn't tell all his mates that. He would tell them it was unbelievable and that they did it three times.

Thankfully, the next few times they had sex in the barn were much better than the first. They even took a blanket with them to put on the haystack. Riley didn't find it painful anymore, and Ricky seemed to know what to do without having to look down so often.

Blair watched as Ricky, the Rock God, took off his tie, unbuttoned the top two buttons of his shirt and rolled up his sleeves. He looked happy and relaxed, and she was totally in love with him. Colette grabbed Blair's hand. "Come and sit with us," she said.

Blair smiled. She didn't mind being with them today as Riley wasn't there to chat with. Gabriella was an even worse artist than Blair, and the three girls laughed at her attempts to draw some sheep that were grazing in the field. "Oh my god, Gabby, they look like beetles on stilts," said Colette, causing Blair to choke with laughter and spit out a mouthful of orange juice.

After an hour of hysterical laughter and not a lot of work accomplished, the girls heard Mrs Donegan shout out, "Right, guys, pack up your things and let's head back to class."

"I won't have time to look at your work today, so just get your belongings and head home, and we'll talk about the pictures next time. Thank you." Blair walked with Colette and Gabriella back to the classroom. Blair couldn't help staring at Gabriella's hairy legs. *Did she not realise she had hairy legs?* wondered Blair.

It made her an easy target for the boys to make fun of. Luckily, no one made fun of her to her face as she was such a nice, kind girl who also happened to be the cleverest student in their year. She used this fact to her advantage as she was also very shrewd. She started up a little private business aimed at the pupils who were struggling with their homework. She would do their homework for them, for a price! "I saw a gap in the market, so I thought I'd exploit it," she told Blair one afternoon. Blair was impressed. Gabriella was hairy but awesome!

Blair started to clear her desk in the classroom when Ricky turned around from the desk in front and handed her a sheet of rolled-up paper. She stared at it, not knowing what it was and looked at him. "For you!" he told her.

"Thank you," she said.

He smiled, slung his rucksack over his shoulder and walked out of the room.

Blair's hands trembled, and she felt a bead of sweat form on her top lip as she waited for everyone to leave the room. She carefully unrolled the paper. It was his drawing from their lesson outside. It was a pencil drawing of a girl sitting cross-legged, looking out towards the woods; her straight shoulder-length hair was blowing in the breeze, and she looked relaxed and happy and was laughing. She looked beautiful. Oh my god, it was a picture of her!

Chapter 9

Blair had been awake all night; she couldn't stop thinking about the drawing Ricky had given her and what she was going to do about the situation. Obviously, she and Ricky would want to go out with each other, but how would they tell Riley? She had been so desperate to be friends with Riley when she first arrived at St James's, and now, she finally was; this had to happen. She didn't want to lose Riley; she was the most exciting friend she had ever had. If Riley decided to stop talking to her, she would have to hang around with Colette and Gabriella again. Blair turned over on the lumpy mattress and then turned back again. This was no good; she would have to get up.

The phone rang, startling Blair and her dad. "Who on earth is that ringing at this time of the morning?" he asked.

"I don't know, Dad; why don't you answer it and find out," Blair said, shaking her head. People didn't phone them very often since they had moved to Hertfordshire, mainly because Malcolm hadn't given the number out to many people. He didn't like speaking on the phone; he would rather speak to people face to face. Since his wife, Carrie, had walked out on him, he didn't much like speaking to anyone and tended to keep himself to himself. Blair worried about him constantly. She and Brett had been able to carry on with their lives, but her dad seemed to be stuck in memory lane, not knowing how to get out.

One day, Blair and her brother had returned home from school to find their father sitting alone at the kitchen table. His face was ashen. When they asked him what was wrong, he just sat there and didn't answer. Blair immediately thought their mum had died. "Is it Mum?" she asked, panic-stricken.

Her father nodded slowly.

"Oh my god, is she dead?" she asked.

He remained completely still for a few seconds, then shook his head. Finally, he opened his mouth to speak but could only manage a whisper. "She's left me," he said.

Blair and her brother, Brett, both looked at him, confused. "What do you mean?" asked Brett.

"She's gone, Brett! She's gone," said Malcolm Matthews. He then got up and calmly walked out of the room.

Carrie and Malcolm Matthews had got married in a small registry office with just a couple of witnesses. It was a low-key affair due to the fact that Carrie was three months pregnant. Her parents had insisted that Malcolm did the right thing for their only child. The couple were young and had only been dating for a few months.

The newly married couple couldn't afford a reception, let alone a honeymoon, so they celebrated their nuptials by going to the local pub with a handful of friends for a few beers and chicken-in-a-basket. They managed to find a small flat to rent and welcomed baby Brett into the world six months later. Carrie tried her best but found motherhood daunting. She cried most days, and Malcolm would usually find her slumped on the sofa, still in her dressing gown, when he got home from work.

Two years later, Carrie fell pregnant again with Blair. When she held her newborn daughter in her arms for the first time, she stared into her half-open eyes but felt nothing. She wasn't able to bond with Blair at all. It seemed like the depression that had begun when she had Brett had worsened as the years went by.

Malcolm's mother, Betty, started helping them out, then seeing how incapable her daughter-in-law had become, ended up having them move in with her, so she could look after the children. "I know what you need," she told her daughter-in-law one morning. "You need 'mother's little helper'."

Betty took Carrie to see the doctor, where she was promptly prescribed Valium; the miracle pick-me-up for stressed housewives. Carrie eventually started to take an interest in her looks, visited the hairdressers regularly and enjoyed shopping once again. She had discovered a new lease of life and felt like she could breathe again. Of course, she loved her children and husband but had no real interest in them; preferring to meet up with friends in the evenings and go to the local pub or go dancing.

Jimmy, the landlord at the pub, took a shine to Carrie and offered her a job behind the bar. He could see she had a natural rapport with the regulars down there and was convinced she would make a great barmaid.

Carrie jumped at the offer. Having her own money would give her some independence, and she knew Malcolm's mum would look after the children for her while she was at work.

One day, when Carrie had come home after an afternoon's shopping trip, she found her mother-in-law sitting in her chair with her head slumped over her shoulder. She had passed away in her sleep. The family was devastated; the matriarch and rock of the family was gone. Naturally, Malcolm was crushed, so it fell on his wife's shoulders to pick up the pieces and hold the family together. She gave up her job at the pub to play the dutiful wife and mother, begrudgingly, and became depressed again.

Blair tried desperately but couldn't seem to wean even a fraction of affection from her mother. She didn't know what she had done wrong to make her mother dislike her so much. Carrie was never cruel to her daughter and made sure she was fed and had clean clothes to wear and even tucked her into bed every night, but she couldn't bring herself to kiss or hug her. She hated herself for it, but it was something she just couldn't control. The needier Blair became, the more Carrie pulled away.

Rumours soon started circulating that Carrie was having an affair with Jimmy, the landlord. Malcolm had heard the gossip but refused to believe it; in his eyes, his wife could do no wrong.

"Hello, Malcolm Matthews speaking," Malcolm said in his best telephone voice. "Yes, just a minute please." He beckoned Blair to come to the phone.

She quickly chewed the last bit of her toast and wiped her hands on her skirt. "Riley! Where have you been?" asked Blair, surprised to be hearing from her friend.

"I'm in a bit of trouble. Blair and I can't come to school. I need you to do me a favour," she said.

"Of course," Blair replied.

"Go and find Ricky before registration. He'll be with his mates by the bike shed. Tell him to come over to my house just after 9 o'clock," she said.

"Are you okay?" asked Blair.

"I can't talk now; my dad and his girlfriend are here, but they'll be gone just before nine. Got to go! Thanks, Blair," Riley said and then hung up.

Ricky wasn't by the bike shed when Blair got to school. Her stomach had been in knots all morning since she had got the phone call. She looked around but couldn't see him, and then she began to panic; what if she didn't find him before registration? Finally, she spotted him; he was having a sneaky cigarette by the houses near the school. She made a dash for the gates before the bell went. "Ricky," she called out as she ran towards the houses. "Riley phoned me. She wants you to go to her house just after nine," she told him.

He nodded and started to walk away.

"Is everything okay?" she asked, concerned.

"Yeah, fine," he said bluntly.

"Oh, and thank you for the picture, it's lovely," she said, feeling herself blush.

He frowned, not knowing what she was talking about.

Her heart dropped. "You know, from art yesterday?" she said.

"Oh yeah," he said, remembering. "No problem," he said and walked away.

Blair's heart sank. How could he have forgotten? It hadn't even been 24 hours. She felt completely stupid. Of course, the picture had meant nothing to him. He was probably just bored and couldn't think of anything else to draw. Blair couldn't believe she had practically planned their future together and was even prepared to dump the amazing Riley Mulligan for him. She wouldn't make that mistake ever again, she told herself, trying hard not to cry.

Chapter 10

Blair sat on the bus and stared out of the smeared window beside her. As the houses and shops went whizzing by, she watched all their colours blur into one. She was wondering what Riley wanted to speak to her about. She hadn't been in school for 3 days now. Ricky had been there, but he had seemed subdued. Blair had tried to speak to him, but he was despondent and reluctant to talk to her.

The bus pulled up abruptly, and Blair banged her head hard on the glass. She realised it was her stop, and she quickly got up from her seat and squeezed past the lady beside her. She jumped off the bus and glared at the driver as she rubbed her forehead. Riley's house wasn't far from the bus stop, and Blair started to feel nervous.

When she got to the front door, she stood for a while trying to prepare herself for whatever her friend was about to tell her. Riley spotted Blair as she looked out of the downstairs window and rushed to open the door to let her in. Blair could see that Riley had been crying; her red-rimmed eyes revealed a look of hopelessness. Blair reached out to her and hugged her tightly. "What's wrong, Riley?" she asked.

"I'm pregnant!" said Riley.

"Oh my god! But you're only 15," exclaimed Blair.

"No one knows except you and Ricky," Riley said, in-between sobs.

"What are you going to do?" Blair asked her.

"Ricky's sister knows someone in Cambridge who can sort this out. I have to go there this weekend. And, I was wondering if you would come with me?" Riley asked her.

"What about Ricky? Won't he go with you?" asked Blair. Riley shook her head.

"He's dumped me! He said he can't deal with this. He told me he'd pay, but he can't go with me. If his parents found out, they would disown him."

Blair felt the anger rise up in her body. Ricky had turned his back on his pregnant girlfriend, and to think, she was prepared to lose Riley to go out with him. "Yes, of course, I'll go with you. I'll have to tell my dad, though, but I promise he won't tell anyone; he's cool," Blair assured her.

"I won't be able to go home afterwards, Blair, so I was also wondering if I could stay at your house for a few days. My dad doesn't know you, so he wouldn't be able to contact us and it's half term that week too, so it'll work out well."

Blair's dad was shocked but saddened to hear about his daughter's friend and the trouble she was in. He wasn't comfortable with keeping the news from Riley's father, but he understood that she didn't want to upset him. The thought of the two girls going to Cambridge on their own concerned him, so he offered to drive them. He would wait in the car and bring them both home afterwards. It was the least he could do for the poor girl.

Chapter 11

A week after the operation, Riley packed her bag and got ready to leave Blair's house. She felt stronger and slightly less emotional. The whole experience had been terrifying and heartbreaking. Even though she was so young, the loss she felt was almost unbearable at times. Her mixed emotions were confusing, and Ricky just abandoning her made her feel even more worthless and bereft. She was so grateful to Blair and her family for looking after her.

If her aunts or her dad had found out, there would have been hell to pay, and Ricky would have felt the wrath of her dad, which would not have been a pretty sight. Riley missed her mother so much that week. What she would have given to have felt her warm arms around her and her gentle kiss on her forehead. She didn't often think about her anymore as she had developed a coping mechanism which enabled her to block her mother out of her mind, but every now and then, as is the case when you tend to block things out, the memories had a way of creeping back in when you least expected them.

Riley went downstairs and found the family in the kitchen having breakfast. "Hi, Riley. Where are you off to?" asked Blair. "I have to go home sometime," she said.

"But thank you all so much for everything you've done for me," Riley said gratefully. Blair and Riley both knew that after what they had just been through together, they would be friends for life and nothing and no one would ever come between them. Riley glanced at Malcolm Matthew's bottles in the glass cabinet in the dining room and hoped he wouldn't notice there was less rum in one of the bottles at the back.

Chapter 12

Riley was surprised to see that her dad's girlfriend, Siobhan, had come to pick her up. "Hello, darling. I told your dad I'd pick you up; hope that's okay?" Siobhan asked her.

"Yeah, sure," said Riley.

Siobhan smiled and gave Riley's knee an affectionate squeeze. "I'm going past Kentucky on the way home, do you fancy some chicken?" she asked, knowing it was Riley's favourite.

"Oh, yes, please," Riley said gratefully. She had loved every minute of her stay at Blair's house, but cooking wasn't Blair's strong point; not that Kentucky Fried Chicken was proper cooking, but it beat Findus crispy pancakes, beans and chips every night of the week.

Riley's life was very different to Blair's. She came from a big, Irish family that all helped each other out, even when they didn't need help. When her mum died, she never had to take on the same responsibilities as Blair did. She always came home to a home-cooked meal that one of her aunts or her sister, Eden, had cooked, and the house was always tidy and clean. Riley certainly wasn't domesticated. She was like her dad; they loved to be in the kennels all day with the dogs.

"Is everything alright, Riley?" Siobhan asked her. She knew something was wrong. Riley knew she couldn't pull the wool over Siobhan's eyes; she was way too smart.

"I suppose," she said, sheepishly.

"Do you want to talk about it? I know I'm not your mum, and I'm not trying to be, but I do care about you, and you know you can tell me anything," she told her.

Riley swallowed back tears and told Siobhan the whole story.

Siobhan swore she would keep Riley's secret and never tell Terry. As far as she was concerned, Riley might be his daughter, but she was a person in her own right and was entitled to her privacy, and Riley was grateful to Siobhan for not only keeping her secret but being a good friend and helping her through the experience. She had mixed feelings about what she had been through, but Siobhan talked her through the confusion and guilt she felt and helped her get on with her life.

>Siobhan had worked as a Bereavement Counsellor in St Andrew's Hospice in Ballinasloe, in County Galway, when she first met Terry. She had been new to the position and was still finding her feet, but she was enjoying it. She loved being able to talk to the bereaved and giving end-of-life care to the patients. She had always been good with advice, and people seemed to gravitate towards her when they had a problem or needed to be uplifted.
>
>One Wednesday afternoon, she had been called in to work. A lovely lady, who had been in the hospice for a while, had passed away in the early hours of the morning. Her family had been by her bedside all night, but one of her sons, Terry, had flown over from England to be with her and was taking her death quite badly. The rest of his family had eventually gone home, but he refused to leave. The nurses were, therefore, unable to prepare his mother's body to be returned to her home.
>
>Siobhan entered the room where Mary Mulligan had passed away and saw the heartbreaking sight of her son, with his head in his hands, sobbing. "Mr Mulligan?" she said softly. Terry looked up and saw the most beautiful woman he had ever seen, looking down at him. Her long auburn hair fell in curls down her back and was lit up by the sun shining in from between the curtains, making her look as if she was encompassed by a golden aura. For a second, Terry felt disorientated and thought he was looking at an angel. "I'm Siobhan, the bereavement counsellor."
>
>Terry and Siobhan became close as she tried to help him come to terms with the loss of his mum. He had to return to England to look after his children, and he felt torn by having to leave Galway, but he had been there for a while, taking care of his mother's affairs and catching up with his huge family. "Come with me?" Terry asked Siobhan.
>
>"What? I can't just give up everything here, Terry," she said, in disbelief.

"There are hospices in England, Siobhan," he said as he took both her hands in his. "Come out and visit, at least?" he asked her.

"Now, that I can do," she said, putting her arms lovingly around his neck and kissing him gently.

A few months later, Siobhan turned up on Terry's doorstep with a battered old suitcase and a rucksack. It was the first time she had ever left Ireland, and she was buzzing with exhilaration. The look of astonishment on Terry's face, when he opened the door, made Siobhan howl with laughter. "Surprise!" she shouted. Terry blinked a couple of times to make sure he wasn't hallucinating and then grabbed hold of her and lifted her up off her feet. Siobhan giggled as her long auburn curls fell in front of her face. Peering from the kitchen door, Eden wondered, for a moment, if her dad had lost his marbles. She knew straight away who the woman was, as he had not stopped talking about her since he had come home.

Riley ran down the stairs to see what the commotion was all about, and her eyes lit up when she saw the woman in denim dungarees hugging her dad. "Who's this?" she asked her dad.

Terry dropped Siobhan as he realised both his daughters were watching. "Oh erm, er…" he stuttered.

"Hi, I'm Siobhan," said the woman, picking herself up off the ground where she had just landed. "I'm a friend of your dad's. I hope you girls don't mind me dropping in?" she said in a strong Irish accent.

Riley smiled; she decided at that very moment that she liked Siobhan a lot!

Chapter 13
1990

It had been a long day, and Daniel was looking forward to getting home, having a beer and switching off. He owned Hertfordshire's biggest and most successful flying centre. He knew from the age of eight that he wanted to be a pilot. On the way to a family holiday in the Algarve, he visited the flight deck of the plane with his father and was allowed to sit with the pilot, and from the moment he looked out of the window, his passion was born.

The feeling he got from seeing the world from above the ground and feeling the power of the aircraft was indescribable. His father saw the desire in his son's eyes and decided he would do everything he could to help him fulfil his dream. He sent him to one of the top pilot training centres in the country, where he earned his Private Pilot's Licence and then went on to work at a training school in Elstree. After finishing his training at the age of 24, Daniel worked his way up to general manager, and his father couldn't have been prouder.

"So what's next for you, Daniel?" his father asked him.

"Well, Dad, I'd like to eventually have my own flying school," he told him as they sat outside on the patio one summer's evening. The sky was lit up with shades of red, like a decorator's paint chart, and Daniel watched as a tiny plane in the distance was cutting through it.

"Tell me more," his father said, lighting up a cigar.

Daniel sat up enthusiastically. "I know aviation is a challenging market, but I have so many ideas, Dad, and I know I could be different and better than anyone else out there. I want to show first-time flyers or people just considering the experience that it can be fun and easy. I want a team of the best operations staff and instructors who are professional, loyal, friendly and personable. There would be no 'minimum hours' requirements for customers; if they want the plane for the day to take their wife to Paris for lunch, they can do that, or if they want to go away for the weekend, they could do that too, but just pay for flying time. I know a great Class Rating Instructor called Andy and a Medical Examiner who would come on board with me," Daniel said.

"You've really thought about this, haven't you? I like your attitude and your enthusiasm, son," said his father. He then got up from his chair and went into the house. He returned shortly afterwards with a large manila envelope which he handed to Daniel. Gordon Fairgate had bought his son a flying school.

Daniel looked shocked. "But when...?" he said, confused.

"I knew when you were a little lad that you could do this; I was just waiting for the right time. I had a chat with the right people about a month ago, and we did a deal. But this is your business, Daniel; nothing to do with me," Gordon told him.

"I don't know what to say, Dad," Daniel said, wiping the tears from his eyes.

"No need to say anything, son. You have brought nothing but joy to our lives, Daniel. You have always been like a son to me, and I've never treated you any differently from Kate and Joe. What is money for, if it's not to help the ones you love?" Gordon got up and hugged him tightly. Daniel had a lot to be thankful for, if the Fairgates had not adopted him all those years ago, who knows how his life would have turned out.

The first two years of the Fairgate Flying Centre were tough for Daniel. It was the wettest summer in over 50 years, and he found it difficult getting his name established or making any money whatsoever, but he didn't give up. Daniel Fairgate wasn't scared of a challenge; he was building an empire, and nothing was going to get in his way. He convinced some of the friends he had trained with to come and work part-time for him, and soon, he built up a great little team. He wanted to make the business work on his own merits without any more help from his father, and he worked day and night and didn't let anything abate his belief that he would be a millionaire in his own right by the age of 30.

Incredulously, two of his competitors closed down, leaving the door wide open for Daniel to headhunt their staff and poach their clients. One of *those clients happened to be Terry Mulligan, one of the most successful greyhound trainers in the country.*

Daniel had a quick look round to check that everything was in order before locking up and heading towards his car. He had just bought himself a brand new Porsche 911 in guards red with a cream leather interior. His father had been with him when it was delivered to their house; it was a proud moment for both of them. However, he didn't notice his older brother, Joe, standing by the tree nearby, silently seething.

Their father never looked at him in the same way he looked at Daniel, which was rich, considering Daniel wasn't even Gordon Fairgate's biological son, thought Joe. He was Gordon's nephew, brought into the family after his dad disappeared and his mum died. But Daniel was the golden child who could do no wrong as far as Gordon Fairgate was concerned.

Gordon's brother, Douglas, had walked out on his wife, Elizabeth, when their twin boys were toddlers. Gordon had stepped in and taken pity on the family and helped his sister-in-law financially as he knew she was struggling; however, he wasn't allowed to have any contact with the boys. Elizabeth had insisted on it. She didn't want anything to do with the Fairgate family when Douglas left, especially Gordon's wife, Diana, whom she despised. Diana could be a tyrant when she wanted to, and when she took a dislike to someone, she made sure they knew about it.

Diana thought Elizabeth was common and didn't fit in with the Fairgate family, but Gordon had always liked Elizabeth. She was quiet and good-natured, not particularly pretty but kind, nevertheless. The disrespectful way his brother spoke to Elizabeth made Gordon feel uncomfortable. He didn't want to interfere in their marriage, yet he felt sorry for his sister-in-law and felt strangely protective towards her.

Daniel froze when he approached his car. Sitting on the bonnet were two sinister-looking men; one in a long black leather coat, smoking a cigarette, the other in a denim jacket and jeans wearing a cap pulled down to his eyelids. Daniel had no idea who they were, but the one in the black coat looked slightly familiar. The man slowly stood up and threw the cigarette on the floor. "Well, well, well. Daniel Fairgate, haven't you done well for yourself?" he said.

The other man then stood up, grinning. "Remember us, Danny?" It eventually dawned on Daniel just who these two men were: the Dooley brothers. He felt his throat closing up, and he swallowed hard. "What do you want?" he whispered.

"Money!" said one of the men, now standing in front of him, glaring into his eyes. Daniel broke out in a sweat as the banks of the dam in his head started crumbling, and his carefully concealed nightmare started pouring in.

Chapter 14
1995

Blair took a fresh croissant from the plate which had just been placed on the table in the conference room. "Thanks, Marie," she said to the editor's secretary, who had picked up the pastries from a little bakery on the high street on her way to work, as she did every Monday morning.

Caroline Rogers, the editor of *Today* magazine, liked to make sure her staff were fed before all her meetings; it was her motherly instinct coming to the fore. She wasn't one of those slave-driver bosses who threw commands at her staff constantly, she was more of a gentle, nurturing kind of editor who thought being encouraging and supportive was a more productive method of extracting great ideas and obtaining effective writing rather than being intimidating and minacious. Blair was always early to the meetings as she liked to go over her notes and ideas for upcoming editions of the magazine before the others arrived.

"Morning gang," Caroline said breezily as she walked into the meeting, laden with folders. "How are we all today?" she asked, grabbing a pain au chocolat as she sat down. The tall blonde woman reminded Blair of the Danish actress, Brigitte Nielsen, with her angular features and severe, short platinum-blonde hair. Marie appeared with a cafetiere of coffee and placed it beside Caroline.

"Will that be all?" Marie asked.

"Yes, thank you, Marie. If you could just collect the faxes and leave them on my desk, I'll go through them when I come out," she said, crossing her long athletic legs at the side of the table.

Caroline opened her Dior glasses case and took out her elegant, black rimmed spectacles; she then opened her notebook and looked at Blair. "Blair, I have a great story for you for our *Women of Today* feature. I met with an acquaintance at the weekend who happens to be managing a new pop group called The Spice Girls. He said they are young, opinionated and sassy, and he thinks they could be the next big thing in the music industry. One of them, Victoria Adams, lives in your neck of the woods, Hertfordshire, so I thought you could arrange to interview her. If I think there could be some interest there, I'll get them in, and we'll do a photo shoot afterwards. Does that sound good?" she asked.

Caroline liked Blair and was impressed with the articles she produced. Blair was young, enthusiastic and willing to learn, and her writing was edgy and refreshing.

"Absolutely!" Blair said, excitedly. She loved working for Caroline; she was inspirational, and she had an uncanny sixth sense about her staff and knew as soon as she met them where their strengths were, even before looking through their CVs.

"Also, another one for you, Blair; Riley Mulligan has been on my radar lately. She also lives near you. She is creating a name for herself in the greyhound racing industry. She is young and sexy, so I think we have a great story there. Her dad is a bigwig in the racing circles. Could you get in touch and find out all you can?" Caroline said, not looking up from her notes.

Blair felt her cheeks burning. After they had left school, she and Riley had drifted apart. Their careers had taken them on different paths, and sadly, they had lost touch with one another, even though they had promised to be best friends forever. "Is there a problem, Blair?" Caroline asked, looking up at her.

"Erm, no, no, not at all. I'll get on to it straight away," Blair assured her.

"Great! I want you to really capture all these women's personalities; compelling, passionate, playful and ambitious," she added.

"No problem, boss," said Blair, feeling elated about the feature but also numb with shock.

Chapter 15

Terry Mulligan showed Daniel around the kennels. He loved his job but had dreams of retiring and moving back to Ireland. He was getting older and started yearning for a slower pace of life. He wasn't sure if Siobhan would want to move back, though, as she was enjoying life in England. She had never given him the impression that she wanted to settle down, though, and Terry wasn't sure if he was just a pleasant interlude rather than someone she could see her future with, but whatever he was to her, was fine with him.

Losing his wife was the worst thing that had ever happened to him, so wherever and whoever he could grab a bit of happiness with was very much appreciated. He had a feeling deep down that one day, Siobhan would leave. He had learned that she was like a bird who liked to spread her wings and be free.

Terry liked Daniel; he often required Daniel's services to fly him and his clients to destinations in the UK and Ireland. He was a nervous passenger and always requested that Daniel piloted the plane when he was travelling. During his first flight with him, Daniel had sensed his client was terrified, even though he would never admit it, but Daniel was an expert at making people feel calm and confident and explained every detail of the flight for the whole duration so that Terry felt safe.

Terry trusted Daniel, and the two men found they both had a lot in common and soon became firm friends. Daniel was contemplating buying a greyhound after Terry had introduced him to the thrill of greyhound racing and taken him to a few races with him. He was young with money to burn and still lived at home, so life was just one big adventure for him.

Blair waited in the yard for Riley. She had been asked to take a seat in the office, but she was too nervous; she needed to be out in the fresh air. She had been to the kennels many times when she was younger and had loved playing with the dogs and had sometimes helped Riley prepare their meals and sweep out the kennels. They were fun times. She was starting to wonder whether this interview was a good idea; she hadn't spoken to Riley in eight years.

Riley stood by the wash basin and looked in the mirror; her stomach was churning. The last time she saw Blair was at the School Leavers' Disco. Thinking about it now, Riley couldn't believe they had just let their friendship die. She should have made more effort and got in touch with Blair years ago. She closed the tap and pulled a paper towel out from the holder and dried her hands. She ran her fingers through her freshly blow-dried hair and wiped a smudge of mascara from under her eye. Here goes, she thought to herself, and headed out to the yard.

As she walked out of the door, Riley bumped straight into an extremely handsome man walking past. "Oh, I'm so sorry," she said.

The man stared at her. "No. It's my fault," he insisted as he looked into the huge brown eyes of the most beautiful woman he had ever seen.

She smiled when she saw her dad beside him. "Hey, Dad," she said, putting her arms around him.

"Hi, darling. Let me introduce you. This is Daniel Fairgate," he told her.

"Oh, the pilot?" Riley asked. She had heard her father mention him many times.

"Yes! Pleased to meet you," Daniel said, holding out his hand to shake hers. He couldn't take his eyes off her; even her smile was electrifying.

"Honey, I want you to show Daniel around; he is interested in a dog," Terry told his daughter.

"Sure, Dad. I've got an interview booked in, but if you like, Daniel, you can come along, and I can kill two birds with one stone," she said.

Daniel loved her confidence. "I'd love to," he told her.

Terry patted Daniel on the back. "I'll leave you to it. Riley will look after you. Come and catch me when you're finished," he said, walking off towards his office.

Riley caught sight of Blair, and her heart melted. She looked exactly the same. Her blonde hair was straight and shiny, just like it always had been, and her figure-hugging black trouser suit accentuated her petite frame perfectly. As she got closer, Riley felt tears well up in her eyes, and she noticed Blair also had tears in hers. Riley grabbed hold of her old friend and hugged her tightly.

Overwhelming emotion completely took over Blair as she lifted her arms up to embrace her friend, and all the memories came flooding back. Images of them laughing hysterically at things that wouldn't be funny to anyone else, secret underage drinking binges in the garden shed when Riley's dad had gone to bed and the time they held hands tightly while they waited for Riley to be called in for her termination procedure and then afterwards, stroking her friend's hair gently as she lay her head in her lap as her dad drove them home.

Riley suddenly remembered that Daniel was there. "Oh, this is Daniel, the pilot. He's thinking about buying a dog," Riley explained. Daniel smiled awkwardly. He felt as if he was intruding on something important and didn't know whether to politely excuse himself and go and find Terry or pretend he hadn't noticed both women crying.

"Sorry, Daniel. We haven't seen each other in years," Riley explained.

"Oh, okay," he replied, not quite knowing what to say. "Would you like me to leave you ladies to it? I can always come back another time," he said.

"No, don't be silly. Come on, let me give you a tour. Blair, shall we talk as we walk?" she asked.

"Fine by me," Blair replied. Blair smiled at Daniel. Wow, so this was Daniel Fairgate? Blair had heard his name mentioned in the local media circles she moved in. He had been described as one of Hertfordshire's richest young businessmen. She hadn't realised that he was also extremely good-looking too. This was going to be an interesting afternoon! She had been reunited with her friend and met an intriguing stranger. She couldn't wait to find out more about him.

Blair knew the background story already, so all she needed to do was fill in the gaps with the parts of Riley's life that she had missed out on. She couldn't help but feel proud of her friend. She had worked hard, breeding and rearing 3 litters of pups and had built a good team of dogs. She spent hours working with the dogs individually, deciphering their traits and trying hard to get into their heads, so she could get the best out of each one of them. It had paid off, as Riley had some classy runners and achieved an amazing run of victories. Even her father, the infamous Terry Mulligan, hadn't achieved that many wins at such a young age.

Daniel was also impressed; not only was this woman incredibly beautiful, but she was intelligent and ambitious. He couldn't get enough of hearing about her achievements, and the more he heard, the more he was attracted to her. Once Blair had finished the interview, she put her notebook and pen into her bag and glanced at her watch. "Guys, I've got to love you and leave you. I've got a meeting to get to," she said, feeling disappointed that she had to rush off.

She would have liked to have been able to get to know Daniel a bit better. As she was asking Riley questions, she had only been half-listening most of the time, as she was so distracted by Daniel's presence. He was handsome, in a rugged sort of way. His messy dark hair and the casual way he dressed made him look more like a male model than a pilot. And he smelt divine!

She had no idea what aftershave he was wearing, but she could tell it was expensive. She needed to see this man again. She had to think quickly; then an idea popped into her head. "Hey, Daniel, do you fancy having a feature about your flying centre in the magazine sometime? Caroline, my editor, loves young entrepreneur stories. I'm sure she would love to hear about you," she said, trying not to sound excited.

"That sounds good. I'll give you my card," he said, reaching inside his leather jacket.

"Thanks. I'll be in touch. Speak soon, Riley," she said as she hurried out of the yard.

Daniel was relieved to finally be alone with Riley. "I'm so sorry, Daniel. Time has just flown by. It's time to feed the dogs and get them paddocked and exercised," Riley said, apologetically, feeling guilty for talking to Blair for so long.

Daniel had never been able to put on a good poker face, and the disappointment was written all over him.

Riley noticed and said, "Listen, are you free later this week? If you came over in the morning, I would have more time to show you around properly and go over everything with you," she said.

"No, I can't this week, I've got so much on, but how about the weekend?" he asked, hopefully.

"Okay, how about Sunday?" she said.

"Sunday is perfect. And maybe we could go to lunch after?" said Daniel.

"Great! It's a date!" Riley said, and then, realising what she had just said, she backtracked, "I mean, not a date-date obviously, but a date in the diary, date-type thing," she said, blushing, and then they both burst out laughing.

"Okay, it's a date-type thing. See you Sunday," he said, and he leant over and gave her a kiss on the cheek. Riley was surprised but secretly quite glad.

There was no doubt Daniel was hot, but there was something sweet about him, too. Riley couldn't wait to get to know him better.

Chapter 16

Riley was in the paddocks with some of the dogs. She had one dog on a lead, and she was walking slowly beside him. Daniel stopped at the gate and watched her. Her face was bare apart from an outline of dark eyeliner around her eyes, which made her warm gypsy-brown eyes look even more enormous.

Her high cheekbones gave her face a sculptured look, and her perfect, pale pink lips slowly opened into a wide grin when she saw him in the distance. She strolled towards him, looking incredibly sexy in denim shorts, a white vest top and wellies. Her hair was blowing to one side, and Daniel knew, at that moment, that she was the woman he was going to marry. "Hi, Daniel," Riley called out.

"So who have you got here?" Daniel asked, pointing to the dog beside her.

"This is Finley," Riley said, patting the dog on the head. "I'm afraid he's got a slight injury, so it's just a gentle walk on the lead for him for a while. He's got a trip to the vet tomorrow for a scan," she told him.

"Oh, I hope it's nothing serious," Daniel said.

"He'll be fine. He won't be able to race for a while, but once he starts healing, I'll get him on the treadmill and in the pool for a bit of physio," she said.

"Then he can race again?" asked Daniel.

"Well, I won't race him straight away. He'll be galloped for a while first, along the track to build up his strength and fitness."

Daniel was very impressed at how knowledgeable Riley was and listened intently to every word. "Wow, this training business is full on, isn't it? Do you ever get time off?" he asked Riley.

She laughed, "Yes, but I love being here. I love the dogs and love getting them ready for bed in the evening."

"You mean you're here all night?" Daniel asked, surprised.

"Oh no! If they're not racing, they get fed at 4:00 pm. I take them out in the paddock for a pee and a poo, they have their feet washed, teeth brushed, and then I give them a quick check over for any injuries. My dad insists that the kennel assistants put them to bed; otherwise, I *would* be here all night, and he would never see me," she said.

"Remind me to come back as a greyhound in my next life," Daniel said, cheekily.

Riley laughed, and Daniel had a strong urge to kiss the cute dimples on each side of her face. He knew one day he would!

Riley showed Daniel around the kennels and let him meet the dogs. "You must get a real buzz when one of your dogs wins a race," said Daniel, slowly beginning to understand Riley's passion for the dogs and racing.

"Well, it's more about seeing a homebred dog all the way through their career, which includes training them and understanding them and then seeing them win a race is the ultimate reward. I can't explain the feeling of pride I get. I suppose it's like watching your child win a race at sports day," she said, laughing.

"Yes, I suppose it is," he said. "So do you have a dog in mind for me?" he asked her.

"Well, I do actually, Balyard Ronnie. He's got a couple of big races under his belt. He's not the fastest out of the box, but he's a stayer and manages to get to his top speed and keeps it all the way to the line while the others are burning out. I trained him myself," she said proudly. "He's a Blue Brindle by the way, in case you were wondering what colour he is," she told Daniel.

Daniel didn't care if he was Sky Blue Pink; if Riley Mulligan said he was the perfect dog for him, that was good enough. "Sold!" he told her. "Now, how about that lunch?" he asked.

"Sounds good!" Riley told him. "I'll get changed and meet you at your car."

Chapter 17

Riley was so hungry, she absentmindedly demolished all the breadsticks in the basket while they waited for their meal to be served. The butter was so salty and moreish that once she had dipped the first stick in, she couldn't stop. She was also talking non-stop at breakneck speed without realising. "Oh god, I'm so sorry, Daniel; I haven't stopped talking since we got here," she apologised.

Daniel laughed. "It's fine. Oh, and it's okay; I didn't want any breadsticks," he said, teasing her. Riley was mortified, but Daniel enjoyed seeing her blush and watching her scrunch her cute, turned-up nose in embarrassment. He could listen to her all day; she was so captivating, and he was genuinely interested in everything she had to say.

"Okay, so tell me about yourself. Dad thinks you're wonderful, by the way. You know, he's really nervous about flying, but he said he feels really safe with you," Riley told him.

Daniel was chuffed to hear that, and he explained how he created the flying centre, and soon, he found himself revealing all his plans and ambitions for the future. Riley loved his enthusiasm, and she could feel the fire raging inside his belly, willing him to succeed. She could also identify with what he was saying. She was fiercely ambitious, too.

"So have you got a boyfriend?" Daniel asked as she started tucking into her Steak Diane.

"Nope," she told him. "And I don't want one either," she added, picking up the serviette and wiping away the sauce dripping down her chin.

Daniel was slightly taken aback by her reply. "Oh. Why is that?" he asked. He knew he was prying, but he was intrigued.

"I haven't got the time, to be honest with you," she said, putting her knife and fork down. "My life is my dogs. How about you?" she asked him.

Daniel shook his head. "I feel the same as you. Too busy!" he lied. It wasn't a complete lie; he had been too preoccupied with his career to think about a relationship, but after meeting Riley, he had changed his mind. He had to see this woman again; there was no doubt about that. And when Daniel Fairgate wanted something, he usually got it.

Chapter 18

"Thank you so much for a lovely afternoon," Riley said, as Daniel pulled up outside her house. She couldn't remember the last time she had actually been out for a meal, let alone been taken out for lunch to the poshest restaurant she had ever been to. She hadn't really been suitably dressed in her jeans and oversized jumper, but she had been expecting to be taken to a pub, not a Michelin-star restaurant.

Daniel didn't seem to have been bothered, though, and she could tell he liked her by the way she caught him gazing at her throughout the meal.

"Give the office a call when you're ready, and they'll deal with the paperwork for Balyard Ronnie," she said, opening the door.

Daniel felt his heart sink. He wasn't quite sure what to expect next, but he thought she might have at least leant over for a kiss. He watched as she swung her ridiculously long legs out of the door and stepped out of the car.

Riley turned around to shut the door and smiled, and Daniel felt something stir inside him. She held his gaze for just a little too long, confirming what he had hoped. "This is a great car, by the way," she said.

Not wanting the date to end, Daniel leapt out of the car. "I'll walk you to your door," he insisted.

Riley raised her eyebrows in surprise. "Oh, okay, Thanks," she said.

Just then, the front door opened in front of them, and Daniel found himself face to face with a red-haired woman standing in her underwear. Riley read his mind, "She always irons in her underwear; she gets hot," she said, trying not to laugh.

"Siobhan, this is Daniel," Riley said, introducing them.

"Nice to meet you, Daniel," Siobhan said, shaking his hand.

"Likewise," said Daniel, not knowing where to look.

Riley waved goodbye to Daniel, and Siobhan closed the door. "He's hot," she told Riley.

"Hmm, he's okay," Riley replied with a wink.

Chapter 19

The building was empty apart from a cleaner vacuuming one of the offices and a couple of security guards eating their sandwiches and comparing notes on the previous night's football match. Blair had stayed late to finish the Riley article; she wanted it to be perfect and capture the Riley she knew so well. She was proud of her friend's success, and she wanted Riley to be proud of her too, so the copy had to be just right! Caroline rushed back into the office and looked surprised to see Blair still at her desk. Her head was down, and she was in deep concentration. "What are you doing here so late?" Caroline asked, making Blair jump.

"Just finishing off this piece," Blair said, as her hand flew up to her chest. "You gave me a fright," she laughed. She could have done without the distraction, but it was Caroline, so she didn't have a choice.

"How much longer will you be?" Caroline asked. Blair looked worried; she hadn't realised it would be a problem to stay late and finish it.

"Um, about fifteen minutes," she said.

"Okay, I'll wait and go over it with you, if you like. I came back to get my camera so a few more minutes won't make much difference," she told her, taking off her coat and slinging it on the back of the chair in her office. She kicked off her cream Jimmy Choo's and stretched out on the white leather sofa in her office.

"Come in with it when you've finished," Caroline told her.

Blair had never seen this side of Caroline; she was so calm and relaxed. She was grateful that Caroline had offered to look at her piece but also felt a bit intimidated. She could feel her watching her as she carried on typing. She tried hard not to let it put her off.

Blair swivelled slowly but nervously in the chair while Caroline read through her article. "This is great, Blair; well done! It feels like you really know this woman," Caroline said enthusiastically, sitting beside Blair at the desk in her office.

"Well, actually, I do," Blair said.

"Really, tell me more?" Caroline said, moving the chair closer to Blair.

"Well, we were best friends in secondary school," began Blair.

"Hold on! Do you have to rush off this evening?" Caroline asked.

"No," said Blair, wondering what she was going to suggest.

"Good," Caroline said, opening her drawer and pulling out a bottle of Jack Daniel's. "Grab those glasses from the tray over there," she told Blair.

Blair did as she was told, feeling a little apprehensive but excited.

Caroline was not known to fraternise with the staff; she liked to keep things professional at all times, so Blair felt privileged. She didn't even care that she wasn't keen on whisky; she felt like she had just been rewarded with an A Star by her teacher. Caroline poured out two generous measures of whisky for both of them and sat back in the chair to listen to what Blair had to say. Caroline was fascinated by Riley Mulligan and wanted to know more about her, so Blair told her the story of how they first met. She explained how her mum left and her family had to move to a new town.

Caroline poured some more whisky. Blair then explained about having to start at a new school and how she met Riley, the most popular girl in her year. Caroline topped up their glasses yet again, and as they both got a bit tipsier, they went off track at times, talking about different things, but Caroline always managed to bring it back to the subject in hand; she wanted to know more about the beautiful Riley Mulligan. Blair then went on to tell her about Ricky and the secret pregnancy.

Blair started feeling a bit sick. "I think I need to get something to eat," she said.

"How about we go out for some dinner?" Caroline asked, laying her hand gently on Blair's knee.

Blair tried to focus on the woman in front of her, but the room was starting to spin. "Where do you want to go?" she asked, trying to speak clearly and not tumble off her chair. Caroline's eyes started to glaze over, and she moved in even closer to Blair.

Blair could feel her warm, boozy breath on her face. Her hand didn't leave Blair's leg, and slowly, she started moving it up under her skirt. She stopped at Blair's bare thigh and stroked it gently, gasping quietly at the softness of her skin. Blair didn't quite know what was happening, but she didn't care either. She felt herself becoming unexpectedly aroused.

Instinctively, Caroline reached higher up Blair's petite but shapely leg until she reached the edge of her pants. *Oh god*, thought Blair; how she wished she was wearing something silky and sexy instead of her old faithful M&S hipsters. Caroline slipped her fingers underneath and pulled them down slowly. Blair moaned in anticipation as Caroline moved her hand back up again, exploring her crotch with her fingers. She kissed Blair's neck and then, with her other hand, undid the buttons of her blouse.

Blair gasped and felt like she was about to explode. She threw her arms around Caroline's neck, and the two women started kissing each other passionately. Blair quickly lifted Caroline's cashmere jumper up over her head and threw it across the floor. She then undid her bra and grabbed hold of her huge, warm breasts. This was a completely new experience for Blair.

Both women groaned with pleasure as their hands explored each other's bodies. Caroline sensed it was going to be a new experience for Blair, which excited her even more.

"Lie back," she instructed.

Blair did as she was told as Caroline moved down and ran her tongue down Blair's stomach. Soon, she was between Blair's legs, and Blair shouted out with pleasure as she gripped the cushion behind her tightly with both hands.

Chapter 20

Blair opened her eyes and threw her hands up to her face. She blinked as the blinding sunlight poured in, hurting her eyes. Her head was pounding, and she had no idea where she was. She heard someone breathing next to her. She turned her head and saw the smooth naked back of someone with short platinum-blonde hair. Her confusion slowly turned to horror. "Oh my god!" Blair said under her breath. She was in bed with Caroline Rogers.

Not wanting to wake Caroline up and feeling completely embarrassed as well as seriously hung over, Blair quietly picked up her clothes and shoes and tiptoed out into the hallway, where she quickly got dressed. She then searched for her bag and ran out of the apartment as quickly as she could. It was only when she got outside and the fresh morning air hit her in the face like a cold, hard slap did it dawn on her that she had no idea where she was. She needed to call a taxi, so she rushed to the top of the road to find a board with the street name on it. She just hoped the cab company would know where to find her.

Chapter 21

Blair was going through the final copy of her article one more time when suddenly her grey eyes froze on the first line of the second paragraph: *It hasn't all been plain sailing for the up-and-coming Riley Mulligan; at the age of fifteen she had a secret abortion...* Blair felt like she was going to vomit! She looked over at Caroline's office. She could see the editor through the full-length glass window, laughing and gesticulating wildly with her hands. The fury was boiling up inside Blair as she got up and marched towards the office. Caroline saw her approaching but carried on talking on the phone.

What the fuck was she playing at? thought Blair. She didn't bother knocking on the door but stormed straight in and stared over the desk at Caroline. Blair's presence didn't faze Caroline in the slightest as she continued her conversation. Her eyes slowly panned downwards and stopped at Blair's legs. Feeling even angrier, Blair quickly sat down and tucked them under the desk.

"Yes, Blair, what can I do for you?" Caroline asked, sighing like she was talking to an annoying child.

"I think you know why I'm here," said Blair, her voice quivering with rage.

"Enlighten me!" said Caroline coolly, folding her arms in front of her large chest.

"The stuff about Riley's abortion was off the record, and you know it," hissed Blair.

"I asked you to tell me about her, and you did. If you didn't want me to use that information, why tell me?" Caroline asked, deriding Blair's remarks.

"I was coerced into it. You got me drunk and then tricked me," Blair said, adamantly. "Oh, so now you're fourteen years old and didn't know what you were doing, and I was a monster who tied you up and poured booze down your throat?" she asked, sarcastically.

"I remember you quite enjoying our little night together," Caroline said seductively, moving her arms away so Blair could see her ample cleavage in her low-cut, tight-fitting silk blouse.

"The other night was a mistake," Blair blurted out. She was confused as to what their rendezvous meant and was ashamed that she had enjoyed it so much, but she liked men, so surely she couldn't be gay?

Caroline threw back her head and roared with laughter. "Okay, Blair; whatever you say. I know you enjoyed me, though," she said seductively. Blair's cheeks were scarlet by now. She had to pull herself together.

"You tricked me. I want it taken out; it's my piece, and I don't want to be associated with slander," Blair said, averting her eyes away from Caroline's chest and back to her face. Beads of perspiration formed on Blair's top lip, and she felt the uncomfortable wetness under her armpits. She felt intimidated, like she did when she was the new kid at school.

"Well, Blair, darling, I think you'll find I'm the editor, so it's my call!" Caroline told her coldly.

"Please close the door on your way out!" she said, looking down at the pile of invoices in front of her. She put her glasses on and began to flick through them. Blair shook her head in disbelief and walked out, slamming the door behind her. The rest of the staff in the open-plan office looked up from their computer screens and stopped their conversations in mid-flow to find out what had just happened. Blair walked to the lift, being careful not to make eye contact with anyone. She needed to get out of the building quickly before she burst into tears.

Chapter 22

"Wow, that smells good! What are you cooking, Von?" asked Riley as she threw her bag onto the kitchen worktop. Siobhan wasn't in the kitchen, but there was a big covered pot on the cooker. Riley opened it and inhaled the rich, meaty aroma. She could have jumped for joy; Siobhan had made her special Irish Stew that they all loved so much.

Terry walked in, looking distracted. "Dad? You okay?" asked Riley.

At first, he didn't seem to hear her, and then he saw her looking at him in confusion. "I'm just on my way out, love. Siobhan had to go back to Ireland; her dad passed away this morning," he told her. Terry had a sinking feeling in his stomach as he wondered if that would be the last time he saw her.

The phone in the hallway rang; it was Blair. The phone call was short. Riley felt her legs buckle beneath her, and she slumped down onto the floor. How the hell could this have happened? She had managed to keep this quiet for all these years, and now, it was going to be unleashed like a secret from Pandora's Box.

A knock at the door interrupted her thoughts. She glanced out of the window; it was Daniel. He was the last person she wanted to see right now. Her eyes were puffy from crying, and she looked an utter state. Too late; he had seen her at the window. She had no choice but to let him in.

"Hey," he said brightly.

"Hello," she said, trying to sound chirpy.

"You've been crying," he said, concerned.

"Oh, it's nothing," Riley said, trying to laugh it off.

"Would you like to talk about it?" he asked.

Something about the tone of his voice and the way his crystal blue eyes were filled with warmth and concern made Riley burst into tears. She beckoned for him to come in, and she told him the whole story. When she had finished, she felt strangely relieved. She had pushed it to the back of her mind for so long and thought she was over it, but every time she saw a newborn baby, something would stir inside her and a mixture of guilt and yearning would sweep over her. It felt good to finally let it all out.

Daniel reached over and held her hand tenderly. She moved closer to him and lay her head on his chest. He felt an overwhelming urge to protect this woman. She had been through so much pain; he didn't want her to hurt all over again. He kissed her gently on the head, and she looked up at him. Her big brown eyes searched his eyes for comfort, and he slowly moved his lips to hers and kissed her tenderly.

He wanted to do so much more, but he was aware how vulnerable she was at this time, so he pulled away gently. "Don't worry about anything, Riley. Leave this with me; I'll sort it out," he said confidently. Daniel got up and made his way to the door. Riley remained seated, feeling slightly bewildered. What had just happened? One minute she was kissing this gorgeous man, and the next he got up to leave. "I'll be in touch," he told her before he left.

"Okay," she said, not knowing what else to say. Maybe what she had just told him had completely freaked him out, and he didn't want anything more to do with her. She felt herself spiralling, so she went to the drinks cabinet and pulled out an unopened bottle of vodka. She poured it into a tall tumbler and topped it up with ice from the freezer and then took the glass and the bottle up to her bedroom.

Daniel sat in his car and phoned his lawyer. "Hey, Jack. I need a favour," he said.

Chapter 23

Marie walked into the meeting room, juggling her handbag and a large tray of pastries. Today, they weren't lovingly placed into pretty boxes and tied with string, as they usually were on a Monday morning; instead, they were plonked in a big foil container. Her hair was soaking wet, and her coat was dripping. Blair was already there, as per usual. "Marie," she said sympathetically.

"Don't ask, Blair," Marie warned.

"You're pissed off; I can tell," said Blair.

"Too fucking right! I've had to walk all the way down to Great Portland Street to get caramel muffins," she retorted.

The *Today* magazine was on the top floor of the Diamond Publishing building in New Cavendish Street. There was a lovely, family run bakery just across the road where Marie had been buying the breakfast pastries for all of Caroline's morning meetings for the past three years but, all of a sudden, Caroline decided that caramel muffins should be included, which Giorgio's bakery, across the road, didn't supply.

Blair convinced Marie to go and dry off and took over arranging the pastries on the large oval plate on the table. The room slowly started filling up. Blair looked forward to the Monday meetings; she loved catching up with the team and brainstorming for future issues. Caroline made her usual grand entrance into the room like a whirlwind about to blow them all into shape. However, today the chatting slowly fizzled out when they saw the stony look on her face. Her bleached blond hair had recently been layered, and that, together with her Amazonian figure, sharp features and prominent jaw line made her look even more powerful and dominant.

"Right! First things first; Blair, your article is going to go to print exactly as you wrote it. Martin, your piece on Hollywood News needs padding out a bit; it's a tad too short. Claire Petulengro's horoscopes for the month were great. Joan, your TV round-up was good, but who played Jake in Melrose Place? You need to put his name in! I shouldn't have to tell you that Joan, that's common sense, and we're nearly passed the deadline, so you need to get your arse into gear. And Selena, great news for you; you've been assigned to London Fashion Week. That means I want interviews with Kate Moss and the other supermodels."

Blair's ears pricked up with that bombshell. "Hang on, Caroline. That was going to be mine," she protested.

"Yes, Blair, 'was' being the operative word!" she said bluntly.

"Now, let's move on," Caroline said and carried on zooming through the rest of the morning's business. She ended the meeting saying, "Tina, did you get all that?"

"Yes, Caroline," her PA said, furiously scribbling away in shorthand.

"Great! Type up the minutes and get them to me by the end of play," she added and then waltzed out of the room, with her bag, folders and cup of tea.

Blair waited a few minutes and then knocked on Caroline's door. Caroline glanced up at her and rolled her eyes. Blair didn't wait for a reply. "Can I sit down?" she asked her as she walked in.

Caroline sighed and leant back in her chair.

"So why the change of heart? London Fashion Week was mine," Blair reminded her.

"You know, Blair, I don't actually have to explain every decision I make to you?" she said, getting even more irritated.

"No, but it's common courtesy," Blair said. "Selena is the better writer for the job. Sorry, if that offends you, but it's true," she said apathetically. Blair tried not to show her how offended she was. "And Riley's interview? Why did you decide to go with my version?" she asked, curiously.

"Because your friend's boyfriend got the lawyers involved, so thanks to you, we've lost a great scoop. Oh, and that is also why I took you off fashion week. Just so we are clear, I don't trust you, Blair," she said vehemently. Blair turned and hurriedly walked away so that Caroline wouldn't see the angry tears in her eyes.

"The feeling is mutual, Caroline," she said, not looking back.

Chapter 24

The familiar throaty acoustics of the sports car made Riley shiver as she watched Daniel drive round the corner. He frowned to get a better look at the woman in the distance. She was leaning up against one of his planes, wearing a red, knee-length, off-the-shoulder dress. As he drove closer, he recognised the long, tanned legs; it was Riley. His heart started thumping wildly in his chest.

She was holding something in her hand. He pulled up abruptly beside her at an angle and saw her face break out into a smile. She held a magazine out in front of her to show him. She was pictured on the cover in the shortest shorts he had ever seen, with her beloved greyhounds all around her. "So I'm the sexiest greyhound trainer in the country, and I bring glamour to the tracks, you know," she told him, with a sultry, playful look in her eyes.

"Oh, I knew that the minute I set eyes on you, Riley Mulligan," he said as he moved closer to her. They stood for a few seconds and stared into each other's eyes and the energy began to flow like an electric current ping-ponging between them. They both knew what they wanted! Riley put her arms around Daniel's neck and gently placed her lips on his; she was surprised at how soft they were.

The kiss lasted for what seemed like ages. He wrapped his arms around her waist and pressed his body against hers, and she could feel every part of him. She then slipped her hands underneath his pale blue shirt and felt the warmth of his ripped stomach. She wanted him so badly, more than she had wanted anyone in her life. They both suddenly became aware of people watching them, breaking the lustful spell they had both been under.

Riley pulled away, and they both giggled. "So, Mr Fairgate, are you going to take me up in this beauty or are you just going to stare at me all day?" she asked. Daniel smiled and then opened the door.

"Your carriage awaits," he told her as he held out his hand to her.

Chapter 25
1997

To: Jeff and Siobhan Deakin
Mr Terence Mulligan requests the pleasure of your company at the marriage of his daughter, Riley Mulligan, to Daniel Fairgate at St Andrews Church, Beddington Road, St Albans, on Saturday, 5 September 1997, at 2.30 pm and afterwards at Roebuck Country Club, Redbourn.

R.S.V.P

Siobhan smiled to herself; she was so happy to have been allowed back into their lives, let alone be invited to Riley's wedding and to top it all off, Riley and her husband-to-be had decided to have the reception at Siobhan's husband's country club. After she left to go back to Ireland for her father's funeral, she had planned on staying in Ireland, but then she met Jeff Deakin who was out there on business. For the first time in her life, she felt a strong desire to settle down, and Jeff seemed the perfect person to do it with. Siobhan liked him straight away; he was charming, kind and incredibly intelligent. Jeff wasn't spiritual or into alternative therapies like her; he was a businessman and grounded, which Siobhan loved.

Siobhan married Jeff after a few months of first meeting each other, and she moved back to England to live with him. Her new husband owned a country club and as a wedding present to his wife, he arranged for a spa to be built in the grounds as a new business venture for her. He knew she could never be a housewife, so this way, she would be doing what she loved as well as being near him, so they could have lunches together and spend time together at work, especially as most of the time Jeff worked long hours.

Siobhan decided to get in contact with Terry Mulligan. He didn't know she had got married and returned to England. May be he wouldn't even care; he had probably moved on himself but the fact that she had lost touch with him and the family weighed heavily on her mind. She had loved the time she spent with them, and she had also loved Terry. It was a different kind of love with Jeff, though; a more mature, grown-up type of love. She also missed Riley a lot. She had become like a daughter, and she had felt very protective over her. She wanted desperately to see Riley again and find out how her life had panned out.

Terry was shocked to hear from Siobhan and even more shocked to hear she was married. He had known Siobhan would never have considered marriage to him, and he was sad to hear she had settled down with someone else, probably because his ego was a bit wounded, but he had always only wanted Siobhan to be happy; she was a special lady. If Jeff made her happy, then Terry was happy for them both, and there were no hard feelings on his part.

Riley held the phone away from her ear and roared with laughter. She had just told Blair the news, and Blair was screaming and running a lap around the room. "Oh, Riley, that's fantastic news. I'm so happy for you. When is it again?" she asked, grabbing her diary to write the date in. Riley told her it was 5 September, and Blair gasped.

"What's wrong?" asked Riley.

"I can't come!" Blair was crestfallen.

She had recently been promoted to Hollywood Gossip Correspondent for *Today* magazine; a new position created especially for her on the back of her successful article with Riley. She had been designated a swish rented apartment in the Hollywood Hills which was described by Caroline as 'one of the most exciting places to live in LA'. Blair knew that it wouldn't have been Caroline's idea to relocate her to the US, it would have come from higher up, but Caroline would have been delighted as it meant she could get rid of Blair. Caroline had never forgiven Blair for her being threatened with legal action over the Riley Mulligan story.

At Blair's leaving party, during her 'goodbyes' to all her colleagues, Caroline had hugged Blair tightly; a little too tightly so Blair could feel her hardened nipples through her satin camisole top. Blair had blushed and pulled away gently, she didn't want the others seeing Caroline's uncharacteristic display of affection. "Watch out for those badass mountain lions out there,

Blair. Or should we say lionesses? We wouldn't want anything happening to you," Caroline told her.

Blair laughed, and then their eyes locked, and Blair felt butterflies in her stomach. She had a desperate urge to kiss Caroline. She remembered how it felt when Caroline's hands were all over her. It had all been so new to her but also so exciting.

Blair had never had a proper boyfriend or been in a relationship. She had lost her virginity on a drunken night out when she was at University, but it had been a major disappointment, and then she had a few flings over the years but nothing serious. She was attracted to men, though, so she couldn't quite understand why she had feelings for Caroline. Anyway, none of that mattered now; she was going to Hollywood, and it didn't get much better than that!

Chapter 26

Blair settled in well to life in LA; there was so much to do. Not only did she live near all the celebrities, but she was also able to go hiking and horseback riding. The first time she saw the famous Hollywood sign, she felt herself become emotional. She had memories of her and her mother watching old Marilyn Monroe and Audrey Hepburn movies. Her mother was a frustrated wannabe actress and blamed her husband and children for holding her back in life. She had starred in a few semi-professional theatre plays but believed she could have gone far if she hadn't become pregnant.

"Oh my god, Blair, you were supposed to be my matron of honour!" exclaimed Riley.

"I know. I'm so sorry," said Blair, trying not to cry. They had promised each other when they were fifteen that they would be each other's matron of honour when they tied the knot. "I've got the Julia Roberts interview the day before and the film premiere to go to." Blair was truly gutted she couldn't attend her best friend's wedding.

"I'll make it up to you somehow," she promised.

"Oh well, look on the bright side; there's always Eden to take my place," Blair said cheekily.

"Great! Thanks for that, Blair. I owe you one!" Riley said sarcastically. She loved her sister dearly, but if Eden was matron of honour, Riley would be lucky to get a say in anything as Eden would no doubt take her role to the extreme.

Chapter 27

Riley closed her bedroom door for the last time and walked down the stairs. Each step she took brought back a memory from her childhood. As she reached the last step, she saw her dad gazing up at her with tears of pride in his eyes. His little girl had grown up into a beautiful woman. She was the image of her mother as she stood in front of him in her wedding dress.

Patsy Rose had written both her daughters letters before she died telling them that whoever married first was welcome to wear her dress, and she hoped it would bring them as much luck as it had brought her. She also wrote that she would be there looking down on them and smiling.

As Daniel waited at the altar in his pale grey bespoke Saville Row morning suit, his mother, Diana, gazed at him while dabbing her eyes carefully, not wanting to smudge her professionally applied mascara. She was also bereft that she was losing him to a woman she didn't feel was worthy of him. Riley was beautiful, there was no question about that, but as far as Diana was concerned, she was 'rough round the edges and had a wild look in her eyes'. Like everything else his mother said, Daniel took it with a pinch of salt. He was sure she wouldn't approve of any woman he decided to marry, that's just the way she was.

The organist began to play the bridal processional song, and Riley's aunts in the front row of the church promptly got their hankies out. Daniel straightened his tie and pulled down his cuffs so that they neatly sat just below his wrists. Riley glided down the aisle with her arm linked into Terry's, trying to steady herself in her Dolce & Gabbana bejewelled slingbacks which Blair had sent her as a wedding gift. Her diamante shoulder straps sparkled as she moved along the pews, and her hair was pulled back into a low bun. She wore her trademark black eyeliner and dark mascara which coated her thick long lashes emphasising her deep brown eyes and a pale peach-coloured lipstick outlining her perfectly shaped lips.

Daniel gazed at his wife-to-be. He had never felt such infinite, immeasurable love and adoration for anyone, and he couldn't stop the tears of joy that rolled down his cheeks.

Riley didn't take her eyes off Daniel for a second. Her nerves dissipated the second she saw him and everyone else in the church seemed to fade into a blur as the magnetic gaze of his crystal blue eyes drew her towards him. When she reached the altar, she turned towards her dad and felt a pang of sadness at the thought of leaving him; he was the most amazing father, and it felt like their special father/daughter journey was finally coming to an end. Sensing what she was thinking, Terry gave her arm a squeeze. "I'm always here for you, baby," he told her.

"Thank you, Dad. I love you!" she said, swallowing her sobs.

Terry then took her hand, stroked it gently and handed it to Daniel. "Guard her with your life," he told him.

"Always," Daniel promised.

Chapter 28

Confetti rained down from all directions as the newly wedded couple stepped out of the ribbon draped white Bentley and walked up the path to the Roebuck Country Club to loud cheers and clapping. Inside the Cowshed Barn, the tables were decorated with yellow and white flowers intertwined and huge cream bows were tied on the back of the chairs. Eden had taken care of, or rather taken over, the entire decor after scouring all the wedding magazines for the latest trends. She would have chosen the menus too if Diana Fairgate hadn't stepped in; the queen of entertaining was determined to leave her stamp on the day and not be outdone by a young, novice, so she insisted on choosing the menus. It hadn't bothered Riley, If she had had her way they would have got married barefoot on a beach somewhere in secret.

Siobhan congratulated Riley. "I'm so proud of you, darling," she told her. "You look so radiant."

"I've never been happier, Von. I'm so glad you're here," Riley said, holding Siobhan's hands in hers.

"Are you serious? I wouldn't have missed this for all the tea in China," she said.

"Oh, the speeches are about to begin, we'd better sit down." Riley took her place in-between her husband and her dad. Daniel smiled proudly, kissed her tenderly on the lips and stood up to a round of applause.

Terry was next, he thanked all the appropriate people and gave a special mention to Siobhan and Jeff for gifting the venue, and then he toasted absent friends and relatives. Emotion got the better of him when he talked about his wife and how proud she would have been, so he paused to regain his composure and then finished off with a special announcement. "Here is a special message from Blair Matthews, Riley's best friend, all the way from America."

The guests turned to look at a screen that was set up in front of the wedding party. Blair appeared on the screen, and Riley screamed with excitement. Blair looked the same, but different; more polished and sophisticated. "Hi, my beautiful girl. I'm so sorry I can't be there with you and your amazing husband, but you know my heart is with you. As you can see, I'm standing with Julia Roberts, who is busy signing autographs," Blair said, moving to the side so that everyone could see the stunning actress. She turned and smiled, her famous wide smile, and waved at the camera.

"Congratulations!" the actress called out.

"We are at the premiere of My Best Friend's Wedding," continued Blair. "So how ironic that I am actually talking to you at My Best Friend's Wedding." The guests laughed and broke out in applause.

Riley could hardly see out of the tears in her eyes. "I wish you health, love and happiness. Enjoy your day and your life together, and I'll see you very soon," she said, raising a glass of champagne to them both.

"Right everyone; it's now time for the first dance," announced Eden, beckoning Daniel and Riley to make their way to the dance floor.

"I love you, Mrs Fairgate," Daniel told his new wife, "more than I've loved any other woman in my life."

"I love you too, Daniel," Riley replied as she blinked the tears away, then for one split second, she thought about Ricky.

Chapter 29

Daniel and his new wife spent their honeymoon in Italy in a private, secluded nineteenth-century villa away from everyone and everything. The stunning property was cosy and comfortably furnished throughout, painted in a warm shade of burnt orange with high ceilings and terracotta floors. Riley admired the fresco paintings and mosaic artwork on the walls. She had never been abroad, only to Ireland, but that was her sort-of second home, so it didn't count.

One hot humid evening, Riley was enjoying herself just sitting out on the balcony overlooking the stunning flowering plants and shrubs and breathing in the fragrances of the lemon trees. She sipped an espresso and smiled as she listened to the loud crows of excited male pheasants trying to attract the attention of their partners. "This is the life, babe!" she shouted out to Daniel, who was in the kitchen cooking dinner.

"Taste this," Daniel said, bringing out a spoonful of puttanesca pasta sauce.

Riley laughed playfully as she watched the expression of concentration on his face. "I'd rather taste you, it's too hot for food," she said as she wrapped her arms around his waist and followed him into the kitchen.

Daniel turned down the fire on the stove and scooped his wife up into his arms and laid her gently down on the wooden kitchen table. "Ouch!" she cried out as she felt a fork prick her back. "I think you better concentrate on the dinner sweetie; you obviously aren't very good at multi-tasking," she said, cheekily.

After a delicious meal, they sat together outside on the porch and then made love in the evening under the sun-drenched Tuscan Sky. In the morning, they lay in bed and looked out at the beautiful Italian countryside as they watched the sunrise, wrapped in each other's arms. "This is so beautiful, darling. Thank you so much," Riley said, feeling ridiculously content and very grateful.

Daniel couldn't imagine life being any better than it was now.

Chapter 30

After two blissful weeks together, the couple landed early morning at Luton airport, tanned and relaxed. The airport was starting to get busy with people bustling around, rushing for flights and trying to find the correct gates. Riley was surprised to see her sister at the entrance of the Arrivals point. She looked pale and anxious. Riley had a bad feeling in the pit of her stomach.

Firstly, if Eden had come to pick them up, it meant something terrible must have happened because she would never put herself out for her sister unless it was an emergency. Daniel felt Riley's hand tighten in his, and he also had a sinking feeling in his stomach.

As the sisters walked towards each other, Riley noticed Eden had been crying. "What's wrong?" Riley asked, feeling panicky.

"It's Dad," Eden sobbed. "He had a heart attack. He didn't make it, Riley."

Riley felt her legs give way, and the next thing she knew, she was on the floor. Daniel dropped his case and fell to his knees to help her. Everything started to spin, and the sounds around Riley blurred into white noise. One member of the airport staff saw what had happened and rushed towards her, talking quickly but calmly into his walkie-talkie. He carried out first aid procedures on her, and soon, Riley found herself sitting on a chair, wrapped in a blanket, drinking a cup of very sweet tea. Eden sat beside her in silence. "Is he really dead?" Riley whispered.

Eden nodded. Riley turned to her sister, and they held each other tightly and sobbed.

Chapter 31

The period between the honeymoon and the funeral was a blur to Riley. Her depression came back with a vengeance. Most days, she felt exhausted and inert and hardly had the strength to pull herself up from the sofa. Everyone assumed she was just grieving, which of course she was, but it was more than that. The answer to her problems seemed to lie in the bottom of a wine bottle, or so she thought, until she woke up the next day with a banging hangover.

The drinking had to be done in secret, which was difficult, as she was back living in her family home with her sister. Eden went to work during the day and was busy making funeral plans with her aunts in the evening, so she didn't really have time to take much notice of Riley. Riley refused to begin married life in her new home with her husband; she wanted to be near her dad's belongings, so she could still feel him around her. She needed time and space to grieve, which Daniel understood completely, but mostly, it was an excuse to drink herself into oblivion.

The only way Riley could squeeze any comfort out of the vacuum of despair she in was to sit in her dad's unmade bed and imagine his last night there, over and over again. His glasses had been clumsily tossed on the side table; there was a half drunk glass of water beside his phone charger and a framed photo of her mother which took pride of place in the middle of the table. His clothes from the night before he died had been slung over the chair by the window, and his slippers were neatly placed under the chair. Everything was untouched and exactly as he had left it. Seeing all his familiar things made Riley's chest hurt like she had never felt pain before.

One night, she woke up as she had heard him calling out to her. She opened her eyes and saw him sitting on the edge of the bed wearing his best clothes with a big smile on his face. "You've no need to worry about me, love. I'm grand! I'm with your mammy, and she wants you to know we're both happy, and you've got to move on now."

Riley couldn't answer him. She tried to speak. Her mouth was open, but there was no sound coming out. She was getting more and more frustrated with herself because she couldn't talk to him even though she was trying so hard. He then slowly started to fade. She was mouthing the word 'dad' and begging him with her eyes not to go. She started to shake her head furiously, but he couldn't understand what she was trying to say, and he started to disintegrate into small pieces then slowly started to vanish until there was just an empty space on the end of the bed.

Riley woke up with a start. Her head throbbed, and her eyes were sore from crying. She remembered the vision of her dad but wasn't sure if it had been real or a dream. Whatever it had been, it had brought some reassurance that her parents were together and happy; she was certain in her heart about that.

Reality then hit her like a brick. She would never see her dad again, never feel his strong arms around her shoulders, and never be able to talk about the dogs or the races again. There was only one other person who was passionate about the greyhounds and understood them apart from her and that was her dad, and now, he was gone forever. No one could make her laugh like him, with his silly Irish jokes. She would never hear his booming, rip-roaring belly laughs again.

Oh god, what was she going to do without him? She couldn't live without him. An overwhelming deep sense of hopelessness and emptiness enveloped her; she needed more wine to numb the pain, so she pulled out a bottle of white wine from under the bed which was next to the two empty ones from the day before. The wine was warm, but Riley didn't care; it would do the job. She unscrewed the top and drank it straight from the bottle and then replaced the top with shaky hands and placed it back under the bed to finish off later. Now, she was tired again, so she snuggled under the duvet, lay her head on the pillow and went back to sleep.

Chapter 32

"Are you drunk?" Eden asked her sister on the morning of their father's funeral. Riley rolled her eyes in irritation.

"No," she said, her words slurring slightly. She was talking slowly, trying to sound coherent. She had had a drink earlier, but surely, it was allowed. It was her father's funeral after all, and it made her feel calm and numb, which is what she needed to be to get through the day.

"For god's sake, Riley, can't you go one day without a drink? I know you're upset, I am too, but you don't see me downing bottles of wine," Eden said angrily.

"I haven't been downing bottles of wine," Riley protested.

"So what are all those bottles under Dad's bed then?" her sister asked.

"Why have you been snooping in Dad's room?" Riley asked. The effects of the alcohol had kicked in, so she wasn't too bothered that Eden had found the bottles; she was more annoyed she had been in their dad's room.

"He was my dad too! You don't get the monopoly on pain or the right to be the only one allowed in his bedroom," Eden said, breaking down in tears. Riley felt slightly guilty.

"I'm sorry," she said, putting her arms around her sister.

"It's okay, Riley. Now, can we just get on with the day? I've got to speak to Father O'Brien to check the pianist and choir are all there."

"Sure!" Riley said, feeling a bit unsteady on her feet. She decided she had better go to the kitchen and eat a banana to soak up the alcohol, so she didn't make an idiot of herself at the funeral.

Daniel held Riley's hand tightly as they followed the coffin down the aisle. Only a few weeks ago, she had been walking down the very same aisle with her dad, smiling and joyous on the happiest day of her life. Now, he was lying in a box being carried down the aisle with his family sobbing behind him; how very cruel life could be, thought Riley. Eden followed behind Riley, even though she was the eldest. She knew how badly Riley was taking their father's death, so she thought letting her lead would make her feel a bit better.

Riley had snuck in a few more swigs of whisky from a small hip flask of her dad's that she had in her handbag and was finding it a bit difficult to focus. Daniel guided her into the pew at the front of the church, but she refused to go in. "I want to sit near Dad," she said.

"I think we have to sit here, darling; Eden said," Daniel whispered awkwardly. He didn't know how to handle his wife when she was like this.

Since her dad had died, she seemed to be inebriated most of the time, and Daniel tried but seemed to fail at comforting her or being any help to her. "Well, I don't fucking care what Eden said; I want to sit next to my dad," she said, raising her voice. The congregation looked away, embarrassed. Eden was fuming. "You have to sit there, Riley," she said, pointing to the front pew. "Dad will be up by the altar where Father O'Brien will be. You can still see him clearly," she told her, sternly.

"Fine!" Riley snapped back and sat down like a scolded child. Daniel's parents were also in the church, and Diana Fairgate had a look of disgust etched across her heavily Botox-ed face. She leant over to her husband and whispered, "I can't believe she's drunk at her father's funeral. Poor Daniel is so embarrassed."

"I think we should cut her a little slack, Diana; she was very close to her father; this must be extremely painful for her," Gordon replied.

Father O'Brien conducted the mass exactly as Eden had requested. Terry's favourite hymns were sung, and the readings were perfect. Riley hadn't wanted to do a reading as she knew she would be far too emotional. "Hang on a minute," she called out from the pew. "I want to say a few words," she said.

"No, Riley," Eden warned. "You agreed not to."

"Well, I've changed my mind. I'm allowed to change my mind, aren't I, Miss goody-two-shoes?" Riley said, blinking a few times to focus on her sister properly as she swayed in her seat. Tears welled up in Eden's eyes. "Please don't do this, Riley. Not today," she begged.

"Then let me speak," Riley demanded.

Daniel closed his eyes in despair. He had no idea what to do or say. Terry's sister, Shirley, stepped in and said, "Right, lady, let's get you out of the church, you need some fresh air." Siobhan, who was seated in the next row with her husband, interrupted, "It's okay, why don't I take her outside," she said.

Riley looked over at Siobhan. "Oh yes, why don't you take me outside, Von? I mean, you dumped my dad and left when he loved you so much. It makes sense you want to leave the funeral too," Riley spat the words out venomously.

"Come on, love," Siobhan said calmly. She took Riley's arm and gently led her out of the church.

"How can I help you, Riley?" Siobhan asked when they were outside together.

The force of the cold, fresh air on Riley's face forced her to sober up quickly, and a mixture of emotions seemed to consume her. She felt bereft over her father, ashamed at the way she had treated her sister and embarrassed at the look in her husband's eyes. "I don't know if anyone can, Von," Riley said, sadly.

"Try me," Siobhan told her. Siobhan loved this family, and she would not let Riley self-destruct in front of her eyes. She owed it to Terry.

Chapter 33
1999

With Siobhan's help and some regular counselling, Riley got her life back on track. She and Daniel concentrated on building their businesses and making their home comfortable. They were both in love and happy and everything was alright with the world again, as far as Riley was concerned. Eden carried on living in the family house after their dad passed away, which Riley had no objection to. The kennel was starting to pick up prizes, and Riley managed to secure some lucrative contracts with some of the country's premier tracks.

The press was always interested in her movements, so she took part in photoshoots and gave interviews from time to time; anything that could be positive for Mulligan's. She divided her time between caring for her dogs and spending time with her husband. She encouraged Daniel to go with her to races, and he loved going to the track with her and meeting the other trainers. He experienced a different side of his wife at the track. Riley was one of the best young greyhound trainers in the country.

The media referred to her as 'one of the sport's leading lights'. She was hugely savvy, and when she said a dog would win, they usually did. Riley also had a special sixth sense when it came to the dogs and ensured each greyhound ran at the correct track and over the most suitable distance. Her attention to detail in every aspect of the business was incredible, from the welfare and care of the dogs to making sure all her staff were appreciated and rewarded. Daniel was hugely proud of his wife and gushingly sang her praises at every opportunity.

Greyhound racing was a very sociable sport too, and after races, they would often go to Charlie Chan's nightclub at the Walthamstow greyhound stadium. It was the place to be seen, especially if you were a footballer or a gangster.

Occasionally, Daniel had to work late or had functions of his own to attend and wasn't able to go to races with Riley.

After one of the races, some of the new kennel hands had decided to go on to the club afterwards. "Come with us, boss," they begged Riley. "I'd love to, honestly, but I'm shattered. I need a hot bath and my bed," she said. They pretended to cry, and their wailing got louder and louder until she reluctantly gave in. "Okay, okay, you win," she said holding up her hands, "but I'm only staying for an hour, and then I'm driving home, so if any of you want lifts home, you'll have to leave at the same time."

When they arrived at Charlie Chan's, the group sidled into one of the booths at the far end of the club, which Riley was pleased about as she could sit out of the way and be incognito while the others all went off to dance. Dancing wasn't Riley's thing as she had absolutely no rhythm whatsoever, but she was pleased to see her employees having such a good time. She watched them and laughed as they waved their arms around and pointed at her while doing silly dances, trying to embarrass her, and then she noticed someone standing near the table. She averted her gaze past the scantily clad bodies moving around provocatively on the dance floor, trying to attract the attention of the Tottenham Hotspur football team, who were celebrating their win that day, and looked up at the man standing in front of her. Riley gasped and dropped her glass of diet coke!

"Ricky?" she exclaimed.

"Hello, Riley," he replied apprehensively. He quickly grabbed some discarded serviettes on the table and mopped up the spilt drink before it trickled down into Riley's lap.

She hastily moved along the bench to avoid the drips. The familiar sound of his voice sent shivers down her spine. It had been such a long time ago, but seeing him again brought all the memories back; the heady rush of first love, the shock pregnancy, bewilderment at being abandoned and the guilt for the baby that she mourned for. Ricky saw in her eyes the pain he had caused by the way she looked at him. Even after all these years, he still missed her deep, infectious laugh, the mischievous twinkle in her eyes, and her cute turned-up nose, but he knew he would never see that Riley again. He had lost the right to a place in her heart a long time ago, and there was no way he could ever fix what he had broken.

"Do you want to sit down?" she asked.

"Thanks," he said, sitting down opposite her.

Riley gave him a half-smile. She wasn't quite sure what to say to him; she was still reeling from the shock of seeing him again.

He was still good-looking with his moss-green eyes and chiselled face with the addition of a few lines around his eyes. He had also filled out a bit. He used to be tall and skinny when they were teenagers, but he had grown into his body well. His pale blond hair had turned a few shades darker, and he had grown it long and tied it up in a messy man bun, tucking the shorter wispy bits behind his ears. Riley thought how much the style suited him. "I've never seen you here before," Riley said.

"I've been here a few times, but I was hoping to see you," he said, honestly.

Riley frowned. "Why?" she asked.

"I read about you in the papers. You're doing really well, and I'm so proud of you. You mentioned you come here sometimes. I was just sort of curious, I suppose," he said, reaching for her hand.

Riley pulled her hand away swiftly. How dare he waltz into her life out of the blue like this? They hadn't seen each other in thirteen years. He hadn't bothered to contact her to find out how she was in all that time, and now, all of a sudden, he decided they should meet; never mind about her feelings. "Well, now you've seen me," she said matter-of-factly.

"Look, I don't want to upset you, Riley; that was never my intention. Maybe this was a bad idea, but I've never stopped caring about you. I'm so sorry for running away from the situation like I did."

"The situation?" Riley retorted. "You mean our baby!"

Ricky sat back on the red, leather bench and felt completely defeated. He had no words for Riley that could make her feel better or forgive him. A part of Riley felt sorry for him; it was his baby too, and he was young and had panicked. She put her anger aside and asked him what he was doing with himself now. "I've got a small art gallery in Camden," he continued. "You should come down and have a look." He was relieved that she had changed the subject.

"Yes, maybe," Riley said, knowing that was never going to happen.

"Here," Ricky said, pulling a card out from the back pocket of his jeans. "This is my card. Give me a call if you are ever in the area, and I'll show you around, and maybe we could go out for a drink after," he said, not sure whether he had overstepped the mark.

Riley smiled and took the card. "Can I get you a drink?" Ricky asked her, looking at her empty glass. Riley knew she shouldn't, but she also didn't want to leave just yet. For some strange reason, she was curious about what Ricky's life was like now, and she was glad they had bumped into each other again, but if she was going to spend any more time with him, she would need a drink; a proper drink.

One drink led to a few more, and before Riley knew it, they were laughing and reminiscing about their school days. Ricky was filling her in on what their friends were all doing now, as he had kept in touch with most of their old gang. Riley glanced over at the dance floor, and the others were all having such a good time, she didn't want to have to drag them away. "So, you're married now," Ricky said.

Riley paused for a second and looked down at her wedding ring. "Yes, I am," she said, thinking about Daniel and suddenly feeling guilty. "I actually better get going now," she told him.

Ricky's face fell. "Can't you stay for just one more?" he asked.

Riley shook her head. "It's late. I told Daniel I wouldn't be late home," she said, picking up her bag and looking inside for her phone.

"Can I give you a lift?" Ricky asked.

"No, it's fine, I'll get a taxi back with the others," she replied. Riley desperately wanted to be with her husband and feel his arms around her. This encounter was starting to unnerve her, and she was beginning to feel the anxiety creeping in. She needed to get home.

Chapter 34
2009

"Hey, Mumma!" Blair called from outside the door.

"You found us!" Riley shrieked.

"Er, yeah! I think the 2000 huge pink balloons were a bit of a giveaway, don't you?" laughed Blair.

"Don't exaggerate; there're only 30," Riley said, rolling her eyes.

Both friends giggled and hugged each other. "Well, here's another one, so it's 31 now!" said Blair, tying the balloon to the end of the bed. "Right, where are they? Let Aunty Blair get her hands on them," Blair said, looking around the room.

"The nurse has just taken them to get weighed. They were slightly underweight when they were born, and the paediatrician wanted to check them over, apparently it's common in twins," Riley told her.

"Why are you dressed?" asked Blair.

"Oh, I'm going home. I can't stay in here any longer, Blair; it's been nearly a week, and the girls are doing well, and it's costing a fortune," grumbled Riley. "I just want to get home and into a routine."

Daniel walked into the room and looked surprised to see Blair. "Hi, Blair," he said.

"Hello, Daniel," Blair said, blushing. She had liked him from the first time she had met him when she was interviewing Riley at the kennels and had secretly hoped to get to know him better, but of course, that idea was shelved once she found out Riley and Daniel were dating. He was extremely good-looking with his hypnotic blue eyes and dark hair, which was greying slightly at the sides now, making him look more mature and sexy. He was also charismatic and personable and seemed to get on well with everyone. But he was Riley's husband, Blair reminded herself, as her mind shifted back to reality.

The nurses brought the babies back into the room, and Blair felt her heart melt. She had never understood why people fussed and cooed over newborn babies, saying they were beautiful; most of them had little shrivelled-up faces, and frankly, they all looked the same to Blair. But these two were actually beautiful. They both had Daniel's eyes and Riley's turned-up noses. Neither of them had much hair. Riley saw the emotion on Blair's face and said, "I hope your Aunty Blair isn't going to cry all over you both, you've both already had one bath today."

Blair laughed as she picked up one of the babies and gently put her nose to the baby's head and inhaled the delicious, sweet baby aroma. "I could sit here and sniff this baby all day," said Blair.

"This is Patricia," said Riley.

Daniel picked up their other daughter and said, "This is Rose."

"After your mum! Welcome to the world, Patricia and Rose. I'm afraid I'm going to be in your lives forever, whether your mum and dad like it or not," Blair told them.

During the short drive home, Riley glanced at Daniel and then at the twins asleep in the back of the car. Up until now, her wedding day had been the best day of her life, but having these babies and being married to such an incredible husband was beyond perfect.

Today was the happiest day of her life, the day she was taking her healthy, precious daughters home where they would be kept safe and happy until they were ready to spread their wings in the big wide world. She closed her eyes for a few seconds, and Daniel glanced over to check she was okay. She was impossibly beautiful; motherhood had added something to her whole demeanour. She looked serene and content, and it suited her. He still found it hard to believe she was his wife. He squeezed her hand. "I love you so much, Riley. Thank you for my beautiful girls," he told her.

Tears rolled down her exhausted, but happy face. "I love you too," she said.

Chapter 35
2013

"Von?" Jeff called out as he walked through the door. He threw his car keys on the table and sprinted up the stairs, two at a time. He was in a good mood; he'd won at golf, the club had been heaving that day, and the takings had gone through the roof, and to top it all off, there hadn't been any problems with the staff to deal with.

He walked into the bedroom and saw Siobhan packing a small case. He knew exactly what that meant. "Oh, are you off to the marina?" he asked.

"Hi, darling. Yes, I need a couple of days away, so I thought I'd go to the boat," she told him as she packed her case. Jeff's heart sank!

There was a new addition to the harbour staff at the marina: a lad called Jordan. He was a 29-year-old bodybuilder. He helped maintain the site and was responsible for boat services, which included getting the boats to and from the water and also driving and returning the boats. Siobhan and Jordan had clicked straight away after Siobhan suggested Jordan drive the boat for them on one occasion when Jeff had been feeling unwell.

The boat was a large, spacious, 8-berth; big enough to take family and friends out with them. Siobhan had kitted out the interior using her bold, eclectic taste and the result was a stylish, opulent cruiser which she absolutely adored and so did everyone who travelled in it. It was perfect for entertaining, lounging and having fun. Siobhan had suggested they buy a motorboat as she loved speed and fancied travelling around the French Riviera.

Jeff had noticed a subtle chemistry between his wife and Jordan, which made him feel slightly inadequate and a bit nervous. He reminded himself that his wife was nearly 30 years older than the boy, and he was probably worrying unnecessarily. However, Siobhan was incredibly fit and attractive, and some young men loved older women for their sophistication and experience.

"Will you ask the harbour boy to drive the boat?" Jeff asked, trying to sound casual.

"You mean Jordan?" Siobhan said, raising her eyebrows at the inappropriate reference.

"Yes, I think I will. I just want to chill out and relax," she told him as she zipped up her case. Jeff wanted to ask where they would be taking the boat but stopped himself; Siobhan wasn't stupid, she would suspect he was jealous, and Jeff knew that was one thing Siobhan could not abide.

Chapter 36

James' frightened eyes bore into Daniel's as he begged for his life. His little arms waved around frantically in a vain attempt to keep himself above the water. "Help me, Daniel! Help me!" he cried. Daniel was frozen to the spot as he watched his brother sink below the surface. He couldn't do anything to help him. It was like a spell had been cast, turning Daniel into stone. He felt numb, and his brain had shut off. "Help me. Help me. Help me."

Daniel woke up shouting.

Riley sat up, startled. "Daniel! It's okay. You're having a nightmare," she said, putting her arms protectively around him.

He hadn't had one of those nightmares for a long time, she thought, and it always disturbed her when they crept up on him like that. The nightmares usually left him reeling for days afterwards. They were always the same; his twin brother drowning and begging him to help him, but like a coward, Daniel just sat there on the raft and watched him sink to his death. He hated himself for not being brave enough to help him. James had looked up to him and relied on him his whole life, but just when he needed him the most, Daniel had let him down.

Riley hated seeing her husband so distressed. She gently stroked his hair, and Daniel hugged her tightly until his breathing had slowed down, and he felt calm. Riley's body was warm in his arms, and she smelled so good. He then threw the duvet off them both and fumbled for her camisole; he pulled it up over her head and threw it across the room. Riley felt her skin tingle with anticipation as she pulled her pyjama shorts down quickly.

Daniel grabbed her breasts. Her skin was soft, and her nipples were hard. As he worked his way down her body, she held her breath and then cried out in ecstasy as his tongue hit the spot that made her whole body shudder. Giving his wife so much pleasure made Daniel feel like a man, not the wimp that had let his brother die.

When Riley had caught her breath, she pushed him back on the bed and climbed on top of him. Daniel felt himself completely relax for the first time in ages, and soon, he was crying out with pleasure as Riley took control. The stress from the past few weeks trickled away, and the images from the nightmares that had plagued him slowly disintegrated.

Riley kissed Daniel goodbye as she hurried the girls into the car. "Bye, Daddy," the twins said in unison as they ran down the stairs.

"Bye, girls; see you this evening," Daniel said, kissing them both on the head as they rushed off.

After he had closed the door behind them, he went upstairs to his office and walked over to the window. He opened it and breathed in the crisp morning air; it was still slightly misty and damp. Daniel rubbed the stubble on his chin. He would need a shave before he went into the office, he thought. He glanced at the photos on the wall and smiled.

There was a picture of his girls hugging each other, looking mischievous with their big cheesy grins and next to it was a large framed photo of Riley that she had given him for his birthday. She was sprawled across the rounded nose of one of his planes, looking sexy and suggestive. A few of the buttons of her white blouse were undone, showing off her ample cleavage, and she was sitting cross-legged wearing a tiny black leather skirt, black stilettos and a pilot's cap. He smiled to himself, but his thoughts once again flicked back to dreams about his brother.

Daniel opened the middle drawer of his filing cabinet and took out one of the folders. He pulled out the small clear plastic bag hidden inside it and then sat down at his desk and pulled out a credit card from his wallet and an old train ticket. He carefully rolled up the ticket and then tipped the white powder out from the packet and carefully arranged it into a straight line, which he then bent down and inhaled. He rubbed the remaining powder into his gums and squirmed slightly at the bitter taste, and then he sat back and waited for it to take effect.

Chapter 37

Siobhan found Brighton particularly appealing this Saturday morning. Pedestrians walking by smiled happily at her; some greeted her with a pleasant 'good morning'. A cute Labrador puppy was bounding along on the pebbles, nearing the sea tentatively, but then running away when the white frothy water swept in and touched his chubby paws. Two teenage boys skateboarding along the boardwalk were singing and laughing as they whizzed past.

Siobhan wondered if she had been transported into a diet coke commercial when she had stepped off the train, where everyone in the world seemed to be happy and having a great time. She wasn't entirely sure if it was the bustling energy of the city combined with the warm summer sunshine or the bubbling excitement of seeing Jordan that was making her feel like a giddy teenager. Jeff liked to call Jordan 'The harbour boy' even though he wasn't actually a boy. He helped manage the family business, which his father had started up over 30 years ago. Once Jordan had met Siobhan, these services extended to out-of-hour services as well.

The marina looked glorious. The reflection of the clear blue sky on the water made it look almost like the Mediterranean Sea. All the yachts and motorboats were lined up, gleaming and ready to go. Jordan was waiting patiently for Siobhan beside *Venus Von*, looking like a tanned Adonis. His long, dark, shoulder-length hair fell loosely, just touching his shoulders, and his tattooed arms were bulging out from beneath his white t-shirt. He watched Siobhan sashaying towards him in a floaty, tiered cheesecloth skirt and a tight-fitting turquoise vest top.

She moved her Ray-Bans to the top of her head, pushing her short auburn hair away from her face. Her face looked sun-kissed and glowing, revealing a scattering of light freckles. Siobhan saw him watching her. His light hazel eyes were framed by incredibly long dark lashes, which Siobhan thought were completely wasted on a man but very appealing, nevertheless. "Hello, Mrs

Deakin," he said. His deep, husky voice sent shivers down Siobhan's spine. "Well, hello, handsome," she said, playfully as she wrapped her arms around his waist. Jordan bent down and kissed her hard on the lips, then picked up her case and led her onto the boat.

"I'm just going to freshen up," Siobhan said.

Jordan smiled and got the champagne out of the fridge. He popped the cork and poured the pink bubbly liquid into a chilled champagne glass that he had ready for her.

After a short time, Siobhan emerged in a tiny white bikini. She was pleased that her years of healthy living and exercise regimes had paid off, resulting in a youthful appearance and an incredibly toned body.

Jordan wolf-whistled his approval at the sight of her, and Siobhan laughed loudly. "You look fucking amazing," he said, putting the glass down and walking over to her. His hands started exploring her body, eagerly. He gently lifted her up, and she wrapped her legs tightly around his waist. He was hungry for her and buried his face in her neck, biting her gently.

Siobhan gasped as she felt the tingling sensations cascading down her body. Jeff never made her feel like this. Her young lover carried her to the bedroom and threw her down on the bed. His t-shirt was swiftly pulled up over his head and discarded, and he bent down towards her. Siobhan ran her fingertips slowly up his back and gently caressed his huge biceps; then she moved her fingers tenderly down his chest to the waistband of his shorts and pulled them down slowly.

She loved a man who looked after himself. She gazed at his body, just long enough to store the image and intoxicating smell of him away, safely, in her brain, where it would remain until she needed to retrieve it when she was having boring sex with her husband. The look on Siobhan's face told Jordan she was pleased with what she saw, which excited him even more. He expertly whipped her bikini bottoms off with one hand. She couldn't wait any longer and pulled him into her, arching her back in total desire.

The mobile phone on the counter, which was switched to silent, vibrated for the third time; it was Jeff checking to make sure his wife had arrived safely. It went to voicemail, yet again, and he hung up. The sinking feeling returned in the pit of his stomach.

Chapter 38

An emergency meeting was called at *Today* magazine headquarters. Blair knew it was something serious when she saw the Head of HR walking down the corridor with Caroline. The Editor-in-Chief's normally unflappable persona was replaced with a distracted, almost shocked demeanour. Her usually pristine platinum-blonde hair looked messy and dishevelled where she had been running her hands through it in frustration. There was no sign of a smile on her worried face.

Caroline waited impatiently for everyone to be seated. She, however, remained standing in an attempt to assert what little authority she had left. She cleared her throat, ready to deliver a speech that, for once, wasn't rehearsed. Some big changes had been made at the magazine without any prior consultation with Caroline, and she was livid. She was a professional, first and foremost, so she wasn't about to let her feelings spill out during a meeting with her staff.

"Thank you all for coming," Caroline began. "It has come to my knowledge recently that *Today* magazine has been having some financial difficulties. That is, categorically, not a reflection on any of your performances, it's just the way of the world, I'm afraid," Caroline continued, "The powers that be have decided that they want to try a new way of working. *Today* magazine will be going digital."

There were gasps all around the room. Blair was stunned. "What exactly does that mean?" Blair asked.

"It means the workforce will be halved, basically," Caroline said, brutally. "Going digital will mean fewer overheads, and hopefully, it will also mean we could target a greater proportion of readers."

John, Head of Advertising, interrupted, "Hang on, so what does that mean for advertising?".

"Well, John, it means your job is safe! We will be relying on advertising to keep the magazine afloat," she said, a little too enthusiastically. Blair could sense that Caroline wasn't entirely happy with the decision. "However," Caroline added, with a dramatic pause, causing the rest of the team to silently panic. "I am handing in my notice, as of today."

The Head of HR looked at her, confused. It was the first he had heard about it.

"I have been offered a new position in Australia for an up-and-coming, up-market glossy magazine, and I have accepted," she said. No one guessed that she had just made up her mind, ten minutes ago, after being told that she would have to take a substantial drop in salary if she stayed on at *Today* magazine.

After the initial shock had worn off, Blair started to get excited. If Caroline resigned, then her position would naturally be offered to her as she was the managing editor and Caroline's protégé. She had worked so hard to climb the ladder over the years. She had even gone to America when they asked her, even though she was heartbroken to have to leave her family. "I'm pleased to announce your new Editor-in-Chief will be…" Caroline paused, as if she were announcing the winner of Britain's Got Talent.

Blair was secretly jumping for joy.

"Selena," Caroline announced, while clapping madly.

The rest of the staff followed suit and gave her a round of applause even though they were completely stunned.

Blair sat motionless, her hands remaining firmly in her lap. She looked at Selena, who was grinning like a Cheshire cat, and then at Caroline, who was gazing at Selena like a love-sick puppy. *Holy Shit, Selena was sleeping with Caroline*, thought Blair.

Blair wasn't going to let anyone see her palpable disappointment, so she quickly congratulated Selena with the warmest smile she could muster up, then hugged Caroline and pretended she was really excited for her. Caroline hugged her back and then casually brushed her hand slowly across Blair's breast as she released her. Blair felt a familiar tingle run through her body. She had to get out of there quickly before she did something she would regret.

Chapter 39

Siobhan was glad to finally get home. The 1800 hrs train from Brighton to St Albans had been delayed for over an hour, and all thoughts of Jordan had faded. All she wanted to do was to get into a hot bath and relax. Hearing the taxi pull up, Jeff opened the front door for his wife. Siobhan smiled at him as she walked into the house. *Good old, dependable Jeff*, she thought.

Jordan was sexy and fun, but Jeff brought safety and security to her life. She loved their lifestyle and their family and didn't want to lose that. She hugged her husband happily. "Hello, darling," she said.

Siobhan never felt guilty about her dalliances away from home. 'Guilt' was a word she never used or thought about. Her little rendezvous helped keep her marriage alive, for her, anyway! She didn't find her husband sexually attractive anymore, and sex with him was mundane and monotonous, but she did love him. He was a good companion, which might be enough for her if she were in her 80s, but she was a red-blooded woman with needs, and unfortunately, she had no choice but to look to other men to fulfil those needs. Jeff had turned a blind eye to her infidelity, which she was pleased about, but she had given him the option to play away too; she called it an 'open marriage'.

Siobhan sighed as she picked up her wine glass and stepped into her sunken marble soaking tub, which had been filled with the most heavenly scented Hermes – Eau d'orange verte foam bath. Just as she sank into the warm, fluffy suds, her phone started ringing. She was just about to ignore it when she noticed it was Riley. "Riley?" she asked.

"Hi, Von, sorry to bother you, but I just wondered if you could fit Daniel in tomorrow for a massage, his back is really bad at the moment," she said.

"Of course, love, tell him to come about five-ish, I'll squeeze him in at the end of the day," Siobhan told her.

"Great, thanks. Love you!" said Riley.

"You too," said Siobhan.

Riley cleared away the dishes, singing along to Whitney Houston on the radio. Daniel sat watching her with his feet up on the footstool and a hot water bottle wedged between his back and the cushion behind him. It was astonishing how his wife could make so much mess and use almost every pot, pan and cooking utensil in the drawer to create one meal. It took his mind off the meeting he had had earlier with Darren Dooley and his insistence that Daniel pay him more money.

Daniel was being blackmailed, and he felt like he was being chased down a rabbit hole with no way out. His life felt like a pendulum going back and forth; one moment he was the successful businessman, husband and father, and then the next, he was frightened and weak and being blackmailed. Would he ever be able to unload this burden that he was carrying, he wondered?

"Are you listening to me, Daniel?" Riley asked as she loaded the last plate into the dishwasher and threw herself onto the sofa beside Dudley. The greyhound opened one eye to see what was going on and then stretched his long limbs out over Riley and went back to sleep.

"Sorry, babe, what were you saying?" he asked.

"I was just talking about Blair and her position at the magazine. She's worked her butt off; she should have been promoted," Riley said.

"Oh, really?" he murmured.

"Is everything okay? You seem really distracted lately," she asked, concerned. Daniel couldn't tell her about his 'problem'. He didn't want to drag her into it. It was his secret; his deep, dark secret that was only known by three people, and he wanted to keep it that way.

That night, Daniel opened his eyes in terror, yet again. The perspiration was dripping down his face, and his breathing was rapid. That was the third night in a row his nightmare had woken him. He didn't know how much more of this he could take. He sat on the edge of the bed and put his head in his hands in despair. There wasn't anyone he could talk to about this, and there wasn't any way out of the mess with Darren and Dean Dooley.

Chapter 40

"Siobhan?" Daniel said as he knocked on the door of the treatment room.

"Come in, Daniel," she told him. Siobhan smiled as he walked towards her. *God, he was handsome*, she thought. There was something wrong, though; she could tell straight away. He looked pale, and there was an empty look in his piercing blue eyes today. "Is the pain very bad?" she asked, putting her hand on his back and guiding him to the chair next to the massage table.

"It has actually eased a bit this afternoon, but it comes and goes," he told her. Siobhan asked him some more questions, taking notes as he spoke. Daniel felt himself relax for the first time in a very long while. Siobhan's soft, warm Irish lilt was sensuous and soothing. Daniel found her mesmerising. No wonder Riley loved her so much.

Her light strokes across Daniel's back helped her work out where the problem areas were. She sent tingles down his spine, and he closed his eyes as he felt the pain easing slightly. She decided he needed a Sports Massage, so she moved her hands slowly around him and then increased the pressure. She could feel the tension in one particular area, and using her thumbs and elbows, she deliberately focussed on individual parts of the muscle with firmer pressure. Daniel felt confident that Siobhan knew exactly what she was doing with her hands, and he surrendered to every painful penetration and prod, and in a funny sort of way, he was enjoying the sensations.

An hour later, and after some stretching exercises which Siobhan recommended after the massage, Daniel felt like a new man. "You'll need a few more sessions. You'll probably be a bit sore for a couple of days too," she told him. "But you know where I am; call me anytime if you are in pain again."

Daniel liked the way her eyes twinkled when she smiled. "Thanks, Siobhan. You have no idea how much you've helped me," he told her as their eyes locked. The massage had not only helped him physically, but it was like his brain had been rewired with a huge shot of dopamine, and he could finally think straight again. As Siobhan followed Daniel out of the room, she could feel the blood pulsating madly around her body. Daniel had unnerved her and left her wanting him badly.

Chapter 41

Blair watched Patsy and Rose running around in the play area, and for the first time, she felt a strange stirring deep inside her. The feeling took her by surprise. Could this be what it feels like to feel 'broody'? Blair had never wanted children; her mother had well and truly been responsible for that! She couldn't have asked for a worse mother. She couldn't recall one time when she felt or had received any love from her. She supposed the woman must have loved her in her own way; surely, it wouldn't be natural to be completely emotionless, but she didn't remember her ever hugging her or showing her much affection.

Thank god she had her father. He may not be the most 'on the ball' father and missed his fair share of sports days and school plays in the past, but he never missed a parents' evening or birthday; the most important days. He also always knew what course of action to take if either of his children were poorly or bullied at school or had a blocked drain or an unwanted swarm of flying ants squatting in their flat as Blair had, not so long ago. She remembered when Riley's dad, Terry, had died and the impact it had had on the family, especially Riley. The thought of her own dad not being around anymore was simply unthinkable.

Blair wondered what the girls would have looked like if they had been hers and Daniel's children. She could imagine them having her dimples and maybe one of them inheriting her blonde hair.

An elderly lady standing nearby watched over her grandchildren as they played. She glanced over at Blair and smiled. "Your girls are little beauties, aren't they?" she said.

Blair was about to explain that they weren't hers but then stopped herself. "Thank you. They have my husband's good looks," she replied.

"Well, he must be very handsome," the woman said.

"Yes, he is," Blair said and smiled back at her. "He is a great dad and a marvellous husband," she continued.

"You are very lucky, dear. My husband cheated on me when we were first married. It broke my heart, even though I forgave him. I never forgot, though," she said, sadly.

"Oh, I'm so sorry to hear that. My husband, Daniel, would never cheat on me. He adores me," Blair lied.

"Well, you hang on to him. There aren't many like him around," the woman told her as she walked away.

"Sorry, I'm late again!" Riley said, flopping down on the bench next to Blair. "Have they been good?" she asked, distractedly, while fumbling around in her bag for her phone.

"They've been great," Blair reassured her.

"So how are things with my bestie?" Riley asked.

"Fine," lied Blair.

Riley sensed by the tone of her voice that she was definitely not 'fine'. Blair was annoyed with Riley for coming back and shattering her fairytale. She looked at her best friend's confused face and instantly felt ashamed and guilty for having inappropriate thoughts about her husband, yet again.

"Aunty Blair! Come and push me," Rose shouted. Patsy was already flying through the air on the swing beside her. Blair laughed and walked across the grass to the tarmacked playground. She bent down to give the little girl a kiss on the cheek before taking hold of the steel chains of the swing and carefully pushing her forward. Riley smiled at the sight. She would make a wonderful wife and mother one day, thought Riley.

Blair gave Riley an extra-long hug before she left the park as a secret apology. She decided she would pick up some doughnuts and drop in and surprise her dad on her way home. Seeing the girls had lifted her out of the sombre mood she had been in all day. Riley was always rushing between work and her family. Blair wished she would slow down a bit and spend more time with them.

Did she not realise how lucky she was to have the perfect life? She had an incredible husband, two beautiful daughters and a fabulous home. Blair understood how much the kennels meant to Riley, but her family should come first. She would give anything to have that life and would treasure every single minute of it; life was so unfair.

There was something different about her dad's house. At first, Blair couldn't work out what it was. It wasn't until she got to the gate that she noticed the new flower beds and hanging baskets beside the front door. Wow! Blair had never imagined her dad would take up gardening. She was pleased he had a hobby, though; it was better than sitting on his own, night after night, watching TV.

Blair let herself in and was surprised at how quiet the house was. The back door was open, and she could hear voices coming from the garden. She hadn't thought to ask if her dad was having company that evening. Maybe one of his work friends had popped round.

As she walked towards the kitchen, she could smell grilled meat wafting in from the barbecue outside, which made her stomach rumble. She hoped there would be extra for her; she hadn't eaten all day. Blair stopped suddenly when she saw a blonde-haired woman with her back to her. Her dad had a woman round! Blair didn't know whether to turn and walk back out, but before she had the chance to decide, the woman turned round, and their identical grey eyes froze when they saw each other.

Blair couldn't move. She was paralysed with shock.

Malcolm leapt up from the garden chair, spilling his beer down his shorts. That was another surprise to Blair. She hadn't seen her dad in shorts since they were children. "Blair," he called out. He waved his hand to her, beckoning her to come outside. She went through the motion of walking through the kitchen and out into the garden without actually feeling her legs move.

"Hello, Blair," said the woman, who had now regained her composure.

"Mum?" said Blair.

Shock soon turned to anger, and Blair looked at her dad questioningly.

"Your mum is back," he said, trying to sound jolly, like she had just been out shopping for the day.

"What the fuck is she doing here?" hissed Blair.

"Blair!" Malcolm continued, "Don't be disrespectful."

"Are you serious?" Blair asked, shaking her head. "Why is she here? Has she run out of money or can't she find any more poor suckers to take her in now she's past her prime?"

"Blair, if you can't be civil, I suggest you leave," her dad's voice became shaky. He didn't want to upset his daughter, but he also didn't want her behaviour to cause his wife to run away again. Tears sprang to Blair's eyes.

She was dumbfounded. Her dad was choosing the woman who betrayed him and walked out on her children, before his own daughter.

Angrily, she threw the bag of doughnuts at him and ran back through the kitchen and out of the door, slamming it hard behind her. She ran down the road, sobbing, until she finally ran out of breath. Leaning on the nearest wall, she felt completely drained and exhausted and clutched her bag to her chest for comfort. She slid down the wall and sat on the cold, hard ground for what seemed like an eternity, until she noticed it had suddenly got dark. She shivered as she realised she was actually freezing cold. A man walking his dog walked over to her. "Are you okay, love?" he asked.

"Yes, yes, I'm fine," Blair said, embarrassed and then quickly got up and ran to her car.

Blair finally returned to her flat, had a shower, got into her pyjamas and poured herself a brandy. She curled up on the sofa and started to call Riley, then changed her mind. The last thing she needed was a reminder of her friend's perfect life, emphasising just how tragic hers was in comparison. Instead, she texted Tom. She had met him online on an internet dating site, and they had been texting each other for a few weeks.

Blair had no intentions of meeting up with him, but he made her laugh and was a good distraction. After a few texts back and forth, she ended the chat. She was exhausted and didn't want to have to think about her mother again that night, so she turned off her phone and went to bed.

Chapter 42

Blair's alarm went off, and she rolled onto her back and pulled the eye mask off her face. She blearily rubbed her eyes and looked at the time. She knew it was 7:30 am; the alarm went off at the same time every day, but she still looked at it every day just the same. The events of the evening before flooded through her mind, and she put her hands up to face in despair.

Why did her mother come back? Why now? Didn't she realise they had adjusted to life just fine without her? They had cried for her, they had grieved for her, and they had laid her to rest and moved on with their lives. She turned on her phone and message after message pinged at her. Three were from her brother, and one was from Riley. She read her brother's first.

Apparently, their dad wanted her and Brett to come over to the house that evening. Blair immediately phoned her brother. "I can't go tonight. Why are we going anyway?" she asked, frustrated.

"Because he's our dad Blair, and we need to hear what he has to say," her brother said, trying to reason with her.

"Well, I don't give a damn what he says, I don't want anything to do with her," Blair said angrily.

Brett knew his sister would react this way, so he said, diplomatically, "I understand, Blair, I feel the same way. But I'm going for Dad's sake. I'll let you know what he says."

Blair ended the call abruptly. She knew she was being completely childish, but wasn't she entitled to be angry?

Jeff woke up beside his wife and rolled over so that he was facing her. He slipped off his pyjama bottoms and gently started to stroke her cheek, then moved his hand down her long, elegant neck. She was so beautiful, even when she was asleep. He had half an hour before he had to get ready for work, and he was feeling horny. As he was getting older, it started to take him a while to feel amorous, and when he did, he sometimes struggled to keep an erection.

Siobhan had always understood, but it played heavily on his mind. It was because of this situation that he turned a blind eye to his wife's wandering ways. How could he expect her to stay with him if he couldn't even get it up? He stroked her breast, and Siobhan stirred. Realising what he wanted, she opened her eyes and inwardly sighed. Here we go again, she thought. She kept her eyes closed and reached for his groin.

Before long, Jeff was thrusting away on top of her. Siobhan moaned and groaned in the all the right places while she compiled a shopping list in her mind. She mustn't forget to add bread to the list; she fancied a nice cheese and olive sourdough that night. The deed was done within a few minutes, and Jeff rolled over, feeling content and relieved he had managed to go the whole course that morning without going limp. Siobhan was grateful it was only a couple of minutes; sometimes he kept trying for what seemed like hours. "Was that alright for you, darling?" Jeff asked her.

"Lovely, darling," she lied, as she got up and headed to the bathroom. "I'll pick up some shopping later, and we can have dinner at home tonight," she shouted, while brushing her teeth at the same time.

"Great," Jeff continued, "I'll get us some coffee." He put on his slippers and made his way downstairs to the kitchen, whistling happily.

When he got to the kitchen, Jeff heard Siobhan's phone vibrate on the windowsill and glanced over. A message flashed up. It was from Jordan, the harbour boy. *'Lying here, thinking of you and what I would love to do to you right now. Can't wait to see you again and run my tongue all over your body. I can taste...'* Jeff pressed delete angrily and put the phone back on the windowsill. He would have to do something about that boy, he thought.

Chapter 43

Flicking through the dresses in her wardrobe, Blair's head was all over the place. Her mother showing up like that had ruined her life for the second time. Blair had emphatically refused to have any contact with her, but she was astounded that her dad and brother had fallen under her mother's spell so quickly, had they forgotten what she did to them? She forced herself to block the woman out of her head for long enough to concentrate on choosing an outfit for that evening. Blair had been invited to the opening of a trendy new sky-bar in Soho called Sexy Miami, and she had persuaded Riley to go with her. They hadn't seen each other in a while, and she wanted to catch up and tell her about her mother's return.

There was a knock at the front door. Assuming it was the postman, Blair tightened the belt on her satin dressing gown and wrapped her wet hair in a towel. She made her way downstairs and opened the door. The blood drained from her face. Her mother was standing on the doorstep. It was as if Blair was looking into a mirror; the resemblance was so strong. "What do you want?" Blair said flatly.

"Can we talk?" the woman replied, just as coldly. Surprised at her tone of voice, Blair moved to one side, so she could step inside.

Blair led the way into the kitchen and beckoned for her to sit down. Her mother pulled out a chair and put her bag down on the floor beside her. She sat with her hands in her lap and waited for Blair to sit down. Blair would have preferred to have remained standing to make her feel as if she was in control, but her legs were starting to shake, so she reluctantly sat down "I'm sorry to call unannounced Blair, but can't we please put our differences aside and start again?" she asked, hopefully.

Blair glared at her, her heart now thumping wildly. "Are you out of your mind?" Blair continued, "Do you actually know what you did to us. You walked out on us. I'm surprised Dad didn't die of a broken heart; he was so upset. You abandoned your children. What kind of mother would do that? Well, I'll tell you, shall I? A selfish, self-centred, evil, bitch, that's who."

"Blair, please. Let me explain," the woman pleaded. "I was young, and I wanted more; I won't deny it. I thought you would all be better off without me because I could never give you what you wanted," she said.

Blair shook her head and said with a wry laugh, "You mean *love*! You couldn't give us, or rather *me*, love. Now, I don't know why you've come back or what you are up to. But, know this, I am making it my business to find out. Now, get the fuck out of my flat Carrie."

Blair's mother quietly picked up her bag, got up and straightened her skirt and then walked out without looking back.

Riley was trying to get dressed while spoon feeding Calpol into one crying daughter's mouth and looking for the other daughter's favourite Barbie doll. "Daniel!" Riley shouted. She was getting hot and flustered, and soon, her freshly applied make-up would be running down her face if her husband didn't come upstairs and help her. Riley sighed and scooped Patsy up in her arms to comfort her.

Eventually, she calmed down, so Riley laid her down on her bed while she carried on getting dressed. She quickly pulled up her leather trousers and teamed them with a front-zipped, white shirt, which she left unzipped to the top of her cleavage. She ran her fingers through her sleek brown hair, which she had straightened earlier that afternoon, before the chaos had descended when the girls came home from school.

Luckily, it was Friday, so she didn't have to worry about getting their uniforms sorted for school the next day or insisting they go to bed early. Daniel was staying at home with them tonight, so she would leave everything to him. He wasn't a very hands-on dad, mainly because he was a bit clueless about looking after four-year-old girls, but he loved spending time with them and even let them brush his hair and put make-up on him, which they had great fun doing and found hilarious.

Riley handed her daughters to her husband, kissed him quickly on the lips and rushed out to her car with a pair of zebra print court shoes and a black Chanel clutch bag in her hands.

"Wow, you scrub up well, Riley Fairgate," Blair laughed as Riley pulled up in the driveway.

"I try my best," Riley said. It was so good to see her best friend, and Blair was really looking forward to the night. "This is like old times; us hitting the town," Riley told her.

"Sure is! This sky-bar is supposed to be amazing. I just hope I stay sober enough to remember the evening, so I can write the review in the morning," said Blair.

"Well, I won't be drinking, obviously, so I can remind you. Come on, get in, let's go," Riley said, excitedly as Blair opened the passenger door and got inside Riley's sporty white Mercedes.

The new bar was spectacular! It was spread across two floors with a 360-degree panoramic view of Soho and was a magnet for celebrities as it was the new 'in-place' to be. The music was relaxing and subdued, but it was still early, and Blair guessed it would liven up later. She had wanted to come early, so they could have a chat and something to eat before it got too busy.

Blair and Riley sat on one of the dark green leather sofas beside the window. "What a view!" said Riley. "I love the decor too," she added, admiring the natural earthy colours all around them.

"That is reclaimed timber cladding from an old Irish barn," interrupted a man who had overheard her. He had walked up behind them and was holding two menus in his hand.

Riley smiled and took the menus from him.

Blair opened her notepad and took down some notes: *green and cream leather sofas, subtle spotlights, simple designs, pale bleached oak with strong statement colours dotted around. Reclaimed timber cladding from an old Irish bar.*

"You must be Blair Matthews from *Today* magazine," the man said, as he watched her writing. "I'm Robert, the manager." He held out his hand to shake Blair's.

"Pleased to meet you, Robert. Yes, I agree with my friend, what an amazing bar you've got here," she said, subtly looking him up and down, appreciating what she saw. She smiled sexily at him. He must have been about five or six years younger than her, but he was good-looking in a preppy/university graduate sort of way. He was well spoken and friendly, just the sort of guy she liked. He was wearing a wedding ring, but that didn't matter to Blair. She was looking forward to chatting with him again after a few cocktails. "I'm glad you like it, ladies. The designer will be here tonight also, as it is our opening night, so you can send your compliments his way."

Blair was getting more excited by the minute. Maybe he was hot, and she could flirt with him too!

Riley's mouth was watering as she gazed at the menu. Blair's mouth was watering as she watched Robert flitting between tables, chatting to the other guests. His black trousers accentuated his firm, round bum perfectly, and his black designer shirt was undone at the collar, giving him a relaxed but smart look. He returned a few minutes later to take their food order. Blair had already had two cocktails, and one of the bartenders made Riley a delicious mocktail, which she loved.

Giving up alcohol had been hard for Riley, as she found it difficult to find a soft drink she enjoyed. There was only so much coke and orange juice you could drink, but this drink was refreshing and not too fruity. "Could we have two Wagyu burgers, please, with sweet potato fries?" Riley said, pointing at the dishes on the menus. "And maybe Tiramisu after?" she added.

"Ah, our designer is here," Robert said, waving at a tall, fair-haired man wearing ripped jeans and a leather jacket.

As Riley and Blair looked over at him, they both recognised the deep-set green eyes, chiselled cheekbones and strong jawline. "It's Ricky Berg!" both women said in unison.

Ricky walked over, unperturbed and casually said, "Hi, ladies," as if it were the most natural thing in the world to see Blair and Riley again. Blair was speechless.

"So you're a designer now?" asked Riley, politely, hoping he wouldn't notice her voice quivering.

"Yes! I made quite a bit of money from the art gallery, so I started up a design business," he said, sitting down on the chair in front of them.

Riley remembered him telling her about his gallery when they bumped into each other all those years ago at Charlie Chan's nightclub. That night, his mid-length hair was scooped up in a man bun, but tonight, he wore it loose. Riley couldn't help thinking how sexy it looked and how much it suited him. He had always had a cool aura about him, but now, her childhood sweetheart had matured into a confident, successful man with an edgy kind of presence about him, which Riley found attractive.

Ricky spent quite a while chatting with them both, and Blair noticed the chemistry between him and Riley. She suddenly felt like the odd one out again, just like at school. Blair thought about the time he had given her the portrait he had drawn in art class. He was even better looking now, and so laid back and personable. Yet again, Riley gets the prize, she thought. It was obvious Ricky still had feelings for her. She could see Riley was trying hard to pretend she didn't care about him, but Blair knew her friend well. It would be interesting to see where they go from here, thought Blair.

After a few too many cocktails, Blair started flirting with Robert, to the point where she was becoming embarrassing. Riley felt helpless and didn't quite know what to do. "Look, I think we should head home now, babe," Riley said quietly.

"What? No. Robert and I are going to have some fun later, aren't we Robbie," Blair said, slurring her words. She winked at him, suggestively and Robert laughed, politely. He would normally have refused to serve a customer who seemed inebriated, but she was reviewing the bar, so he couldn't really throw her out. Blair's eyes were glazed and her speech was slurred. Riley needed to get her out of there for the sake of her career.

"No, we need to leave now, Blair," Riley insisted. She helped Blair to her feet and guided her towards the lift. "Thank you so much, Robert," Riley said, looking behind her. Ricky suddenly appeared.

"Let me help you," he said. Riley looked at him gratefully. Blair was all over the place and Ricky took hold of her other arm to steady her. When they finally got her safely in the car, Blair leant against the window and fell straight to sleep. Riley laughed. "Well, she's out for the count," she said.

"It was lovely to see you tonight, Riley," Ricky said, reaching for her hand.

Riley didn't pull away. She remembered being young and carefree, smoking behind the bike shed and snogging in the park. She loved that period of her life; when her dad was still alive. Ricky bent down and kissed her gently on the lips, and she closed her eyes and let him. She savoured every moment and felt fifteen years old again.

Blair shifted her body to get more comfortable in the front seat, and then she saw them. She was shocked but not shocked enough to sober up, and she fell back asleep as soon as her eyes closed.

Chapter 44

Riley looked out of the full-length window as she gently blew on the mug of steaming hot coffee she was holding in both hands. She took a sip as she watched Daniel swimming in their outdoor pool. She watched as his perfect body glided effortlessly back and forth as he swam continuous lengths. His face emerged every time his strong arms came out to stroke the water.

Riley's mind wondered back to the night before when she had, stupidly, let Ricky kiss her. Worse than that, she had enjoyed the kiss. Guilt now consumed her. How could she have let that happen? She couldn't even blame alcohol as she had been drinking non-alcoholic cocktails all evening. She had just wanted to be reminded of what it had been like to be young and carefree and Ricky Berg's girlfriend again before it had all gone horribly wrong.

She had been fifteen and naive. The total shock of finding out she was pregnant had sent her into a whirlwind of confusion. Riley had managed to keep the secret from her family all these years, but it was a secret that bore a hole in her life and one she would always regret.

Ricky had cruelly abandoned her after the abortion, and Riley hated him for it, but seeing him again had made her realise that he was young and naive too, and it was his way of dealing with the situation at the time. She actually felt sorry for him as she realised after speaking to him that he regretted it too, and it also haunted him. Her heart had shattered into a thousand pieces that day at the clinic. Kissing Ricky yesterday was just her way of retrieving a tiny shard of her broken heart. The kiss wasn't about love or lust; it was about two young kids rescuing each other.

There was only one man for Riley, she was certain of that. She put her mug down and started to walk towards the door that led out to the pool but stopped when she heard the newsreader on the TV. "The body was washed up on Brighton Beach in the early hours of this morning and was discovered by a local dog walker. As yet, the body has not been officially identified. The area has been cordoned off..." the female newsreader said, delivering the tragic news to the nation. Riley shuddered and turned the TV off.

Daniel stopped swimming when he saw his wife walking towards him. She was completely naked and gazing at him longingly. Her tantalising, never-ending long legs strode towards the edge of the pool exciting every sense in his body as he knew that soon they would be wrapped tightly around him. He held his hand out to her, inviting her into the warm water, and she gracefully dived in and swam underwater until she reached him. She ran her hands up the inside of his legs as she came up for breath.

He swiftly turned her around, so he was behind her and slid his swimming shorts down. Daniel pressed himself up against her, and Riley grabbed on to the bars at the side of the pool as her body moved in perfect rhythm with her husband's; all thoughts of Ricky and the kiss were obliterated from her mind.

Siobhan watched the news on the built-in TV in her bathroom as she relaxed in the bath. The story being relayed by the attractive blonde-haired newsreader disturbed Siobhan. How tragic, she thought; a person had drowned during the night. She wondered if it had been suicide or maybe they had been drunk and depressed, and it was an accident or a cry for help that had gone unheard. That poor lad would be someone's son, someone's best friend, someone's boyfriend or someone's brother.

His family and friends would soon have their whole day and life ruined when the news was delivered to them by a sympathetic looking police officer telling them how sorry he was for their loss and then, the next heartbreaking stage would be to have to go and identify the body. Siobhan got up, stepped out and wrapped a warm, fluffy white towel around her. All of a sudden, her luxuriously scented bath didn't seem so appealing.

The air was stifling, and Blair wished she was anywhere else in the world apart from standing up, clinging onto the rail, while being squashed between two backpacks on a hot train racing through the underground tunnels of the Victoria Line. She had somehow managed to drag herself out of bed to go into the office that morning to sit through a meeting and listen to Selena's monotonous voice. She would also have to type up the review for the Sexy Miami Sky Bar; all while suffering from one of the worst hangovers she had ever had, partly due to the seriously strong cocktails she was downing all night. Images from her night out with Riley were coming back like paparazzi camera flashes in her head. She was cringing with each flare. She remembered flirting shamelessly with Robert, The Manager (she had actually forgotten his name and had to look it up on the website before the train arrived).

Then she remembered Ricky sitting with them but couldn't remember him turning up at the bar. The feelings she had had for him when they were teenagers came flooding back when she saw her roguishly handsome, schoolgirl crush walk towards their table. Suddenly, another image flooded her head like a tsunami. Oh my god! Riley and Ricky kissed while she was in the car.

Blair had passed out after that, so she didn't know what else they had got up to. She couldn't wait to get home and call Riley. Then she thought about Daniel; handsome, loving, sexy Daniel. The thought of him made Blair suddenly feel angry. Riley had Daniel so why did she cheat with Ricky. Did she really need two men?

Daniel buttoned up his shirt while scrutinising his appearance in the mirror. His looks had changed over the last couple of years, he looked more like a dad now as a splattering of grey hair was starting to appear around the sides of his face, and he had a few more lines around his eyes and on his forehead. Riley told him he looked 'mature'.

As long as his wife still found him desirable, that was all that mattered. He was incredibly lucky to have the most amazing wife, two beautiful daughters, a loving family and a thriving business. He hadn't had any more nightmares in a while and hadn't needed to reach for his secret stash of coke to escape from reality recently either. He smiled as he listened to Riley singing in the shower; she had to be the worst singer he had ever heard, but she was the sexiest, worst singer he had ever heard so that made up for it.

Giving himself a final check in the mirror and feeling satisfied with the result, Daniel picked up his watch and glanced out of the window. He was about to turn away but noticed that there was someone standing in the garden peering up at him. Daniel went cold. A bearded, bald headed man in a long black coat was leaning up against the apple tree, casually smoking a cigarette as if it was the most natural thing in the world. Daniel turned and bolted down the stairs and out into the garden, but by the time he got there, the man had disappeared into the woods behind the house.

Daniel searched the area for a short time and then made his way back to the house. He started to panic when he saw the name *Dooley* suddenly flash up on his phone. He thought that was all over. Daniel had paid all the money that was demanded. What the hell did he want now? The message read: *The underpass by the canal, Bridge Street. 11:30 pm.* Daniel replied: *Fuck you* and waited for the reply. The next message read: *Shall I tell Riley what kind of man you really are?* Daniel had an overwhelming feeling of nausea and the desperate need to throw up.

Jeff Deakin was on the golf course and just about to tee off when his phone pinged. He put the golf club down and retrieved the phone which was tucked into his golf buggy. The message read: *Job done!*

Pottering around in the garden was one of Siobhan's favourite hobbies. Wednesdays and Sundays were her days off. She liked to give her hands a rest on those days as she was beginning to get arthritis in the joints of her fingers, but if she noticed a rogue weed poking out from one of her flower beds, she couldn't rest until she had pulled it out. Dark clouds started to gather, threatening rain, so Siobhan straightened the chairs on the patio and put the chintz cushions away in the garden box before picking up her cup of nettle tea and heading into the house. She closed the patio doors after her Siamese cat, Bruno, followed her inside, and then she decided to have a look in the fridge to see what she could muster up for supper that night.

"What shall Mummy cook tonight, Bruno?" Siobhan said, while the cat sat watching her and purring contently. The radio was on low so Siobhan turned it up. She caught the end of one of her favourite Carpenter's songs just before the late afternoon news came on; Moira Stewart was filling in this afternoon. Oscar Pistorius had just been charged with the murder of his model girlfriend. "Wow!" Siobhan said out loud as she took out some chicken pieces and a red pepper.

Bruno's blue eyes lit up at the sight of the chicken, and he jumped onto the worktop beside her. She was thinking of cooking a curry tonight; Jeff would love that after a day of golf. He would have had a late lunch in the club house, but he liked to eat supper with his wife on her evening off.

Siobhan picked up the china cup and took another sip of her herbal tea and stroked Bruno gently. Moira went on to the next news item; the shock discovery of a dead body on Brighton Beach that morning. '*The identity of the man has now been released; 30 year old Jordan Bartholomew...*' Siobhan froze.

Daniel waited apprehensively by the canal. A homeless man, wrapped in an oversized anorak and wearing fingerless woollen gloves, was watching him suspiciously from his padded sleeping bag. Two teenagers whizzed past on their bicycles. "Don't do it mate!" one of them shouted to Daniel, pretending they thought he was going to jump in the canal, and then they both laughed as they sped away.

He walked down to the water's edge and looked at his reflection, he hated himself right now. What had he resorted to? It's not as if Darren Dooley could even prove anything; they had been kids, and it was Daniel's word against his, but it was just the thought of reliving the whole tragedy again, knowing that, ultimately, it had been his fault that his brother had died, and he didn't want Riley finding out.

That day at the reservoir, Daniel had been trying to impress the older boys and James was acting like a baby so when he started pulling Daniel's jumper and crying because he wanted to go home, Daniel had pushed him away, embarrassed that he was causing a fuss. James lost his footing and tumbled into the water. Daniel had been too scared to jump into the water to save his brother and the last image he had was of James crying out to him, begging him to help him. The brothers looked into each other's eyes, and then James disappeared under the water and never resurfaced alive.

Darren finally turned the corner at almost midnight; a sinister-looking figure walking out of the darkness into the light from the nearby street lamp. Daniel watched as the man slowly walked towards him. The two men were soon face to face, eyeballing each other, and Daniel looked at him, scathingly. Darren just smirked, knowing he had Daniel over a barrel.

Was Daniel completely stupid? He was loaded and his dad was a big shot; they could easily have got the police or a lawyer or even a hitman involved who would have seen Darren and his brother off years ago, but Daniel was a wimp and was playing the game according to the Dooley brother's rules. As long as he kept on playing, Darren would keep on making up new rules.

"What do you want?" Daniel asked, bluntly.

"Nothing! It's what I can do for you Danny boy," Darren said matter-of-factly; in a broad cockney accent.

Daniel laughed, and then continued, "Are you fucking kidding me?"

"Nope!" Darren said, straight-faced.

"Is this some sort of joke?" Daniel asked, starting to back away.

"Again, *no!*" Darren said, starting to get irritated. "I want us to go into business together," he said, lighting up a cigarette.

"Doing what?" Daniel asked and laughed loudly while shaking his head.

"I've got the blow and contacts, and you've got the transport," Darren told him.

"My planes? No way!" Daniel said emphatically.

"Just go away and think about it," Darren told him.

"I'm not a fucking drug dealer you moron," Daniel shouted. He had really had enough by now and started to walk away.

"There's big, big money to be made here. I know you like a bit of sugar yourself," Darren called out as Daniel turned the corner and disappeared from sight.

Chapter 45

Siobhan stared at the oak coffin as it was carefully lifted, ready to make its final descent. The funeral service had been traumatic for her, but what made it even worse was not being able to really show her feelings. As far as everyone was concerned, Jordan had just been an acquaintance and helped out on the boat so to break down in tears would have been wholly inappropriate. She had to plaster a false smile across her pale face while she tried to hold back the tears as she paid her respects to his family. As well as being devastated, the family were still in shock and couldn't comprehend how such a strong, capable swimmer could have drowned that night. Siobhan was also dumbfounded.

"It just doesn't add up," she told Jeff.

"Well, you never know what goes on behind closed doors, love. May be he was depressed. Are you ready to go home now?" Jeff said quickly, taking hold of Siobhan's elbow and guiding her across the muddy, uneven ground.

Siobhan's stilettos were sinking into the mud as she walked, and she was grateful for the help. Watching the coffin, topped with beautiful white roses, being lowered into the cold ground had been harrowing for her. What a waste of a beautiful young man.

"May be we could grab some lunch on the way home. I don't really want to go to the wake," she added.

The last thing she could cope with is having to make small talk with strangers about Jordan. She hadn't known him for long, but in the short time she had, they had brought each other so much joy. Siobhan would miss him. Jeff was relieved at her suggestion. It was bad enough having to attend the little toe-rag's funeral; he didn't want to have to pretend he liked him for a minute longer than he had to. He had done the right thing getting rid of him. It was his own fault; he shouldn't have messed around with his wife!

Chapter 46

There was an awkward silence around the dining table as Blair, Carrie and Malcolm waited for Brett to come through the door; they had heard his car pull up, and Blair sighed with relief. She couldn't believe she had agreed to this ridiculous meeting, but her brother thought it would be a good idea, and she hadn't wanted to argue with him. Carrie straightened the front of her skirt a couple of times as if she was trying to smooth away some imaginary creases. Blair remembered her doing that when she had come to see her the other day and thought maybe it was a nervous habit. It was unnerving how similar they both looked; they even had the same pointed chin and dimpled cheeks.

Once Brett had greeted everyone and sat down, Malcolm cleared his throat as if he was going to make an important announcement. He focussed his attention on Blair and began, "Listen love, I know it was a huge shock for you when your mother turned up."

"Carrie!" Blair corrected him. As far as she was concerned, she had lost the right to be called her 'mother' when she walked out on her.

"Yes, yes," Malcolm agreed, nervously. Blair noticed he had gel in his hair and had moulded a small tufty bit of hair to stick up at the front. That must have been Carrie's idea, she thought. "The point is; she is here now and is here to stay."

Blair listened patiently, feeling sorry for her dad, he desperately wanted to believe his wife wouldn't run off again, but Blair wasn't so sure. "I'm not asking you to forgive me Blair, but I'm asking for you to give me a second chance," Carrie said, looking at her daughter with misty eyes. Blair was pleased she hadn't asked to be forgiven. "I thought I could make us all some dinner," Carrie added, brightly.

"Yes. Thanks, Mum that would be lovely," Brett said, looking over at his sister, expectantly. Blair shrugged. Carrie took that as a green light to quickly get up and start preparing dinner for them all.

After a couple of glasses of the New Zealand Sauvignon Blanc that Brett had brought as a peace offering; knowing it was his sister's favourite wine, Blair began to relax and was slowly growing accustomed to the fact that her mother was back and wasn't going to be going anywhere soon, so she may as well just accept it for now. The dinner turned out to be delicious. In fact, it was the best meal Blair had eaten in a long time. The steak was perfectly cooked with a nice spicy peppercorn sauce on the side accompanied by creamy mash potatoes and buttery vegetables. Carrie had even made an apple pie earlier that day in the hope that her daughter would come round to the idea of her being there and agree to stay for dinner.

The conversation flowed nicely with Brett talking about his wife and children, Blair talked about work and Malcolm just sat back, absorbing the family atmosphere that surrounded him. For the first time in years, he felt truly content. It transpired that Carrie and the bar man she had run off with, split up after a couple of months. She had ended up singing on a cruise ship and travelling around the world. She now realised that she had made a huge mistake and been totally selfish and after finally getting all her wanderlust out of her system, she now wanted to lay down some roots and get to know her family again. Blair hoped and prayed that that was true; for her dad's sake.

Brett offered to drive Blair home as she had been drinking, and she gladly agreed. She kissed her dad goodbye and as she turned to say goodbye to Carrie, she threw her arms around Blair and squeezed her tightly. The gesture took Blair completely by surprise, and she stood rooted to the spot, unable to move. Her arms hung limply by her side as her mother started to sob. "I'm so, so sorry Blair. I never meant to hurt you," she cried.

Blair didn't know what to say or how to react to this outpouring of emotion, so she just patted her mother awkwardly on the back which seemed to calm her down and eventually she released Blair from her grip. Blair smiled and said, "Well, bye then and thanks very much for the dinner, it was really nice." She hurried out of the door and got into the passenger seat next to Brett. She noticed he was trying not to laugh. "And what's the matter with you?" she asked.

"Nothing," he said and then burst out laughing.

Blair knew he was enjoying how awkward she had felt, and she playfully punched him. "Just take me home!" she said, rolling her eyes.

"Can I get you another drink?" Riley asked Daniel's friend. She picked up the bowl of nuts and crisps from the glass table at the side of her and offered it to him.

He shook his head, politely. "You know Daniel told me how beautiful you are; you really are incredible," the man told her, as he slowly looked her up and down. Riley suddenly felt self-conscious in her short, strapless summer dress. She laughed at the comment to hide her embarrassment. Thankfully, Daniel arrived just then.

"Oh, honey, hi," Riley said, getting up to give her husband a kiss.

Daniel stopped and stared at the man.

"Hello, Daniel," he said, brazenly.

Riley was confused. This man said he was an old school friend of Daniel's, but her husband didn't look very pleased to see him.

"I've just been having a nice little chat with your lovely wife here," he said.

Daniel tried to look calm, but his mind was racing. What the hell had he been telling her? "This is a surprise," Daniel said, trying to keep his hands steady while he poured himself a whisky.

"Darren tells me you both went to school together," Riley interjected, knowing that her husband wasn't happy to see whoever this man was. You can't live with someone as long as she and Daniel had and not be in tune with each other. She also knew Daniel's face never lied; he couldn't disguise his true feelings if he tried.

"What can I do for you Darren," Daniel said, slowly spitting the words out like venom. "I just wondered if you had thought anymore about our little business venture?" he asked.

Riley turned to the man and said, "Oh, I thought you said you hadn't seen each other in years!"

Darren quickly, corrected himself. "Yes, that's right, but we spoke on the phone, didn't we Danny boy?"

As Riley examined him more closely, she realised he looked quite boorish. His face was gaunt and ashen, and he had dark circles around his eyes making him look even more menacing. He definitely didn't look like the sort of friend Daniel would have.

"I'll give it some thought," Daniel said, standing up. "It's very late, shall I show you out?"

Darren grinned. "Okay mate, I look forward to hearing from you very soon. Nice to meet you, Riley," he said and then reached out and took Riley's hand and kissed it gently.

She smiled between gritted teeth; *this man was seriously creepy*, she concluded.

Daniel opened the front door and followed Darren outside. He grabbed his arm and whispered, "Don't ever come to my house again."

Darren stared at him; his smile disappeared quickly.

"I need this one more favour done, and then your debt is paid," he told him.

Daniel was so enraged. He could hardly speak.

"Call me tomorrow, and I'll let you know the details," Darren said, lighting up a cigarette and walking away, coolly.

Riley waited for Daniel to come back inside. "What the hell was that all about?" she asked him.

"He's just some idiot that keeps badgering me about getting him a job," Daniel lied.

"He looks like he's just escaped from prison," Riley said.

"Well, he has just come out of prison, that's why he's looking for a job," Daniel lied.

"You're not thinking about employing him, are you?" she asked.

"No, of course not."

"What did he do to end up in prison?" Riley asked, curiously.

"Blackmail," Daniel told her.

Chapter 47

Daniel had carried out all the usual checks around the plane and was dressed in his pilot's uniform wondering how the hell he had got himself into this situation. Darren pulled up beside the plane. "You can't park there. Go over to the yard and park up against the fence," Daniel said, agitated.

"Chill man!" Darren said, nodding towards the woman and child with him.

Daniel couldn't believe his eyes; he had brought his family with him on a drug-run. "Are you out of your mind?" asked Daniel.

Darren didn't answer. He turned the car around and drove to where he had been instructed to go.

Daniel waited apprehensively in the plane and watched Darren climb on board with the small, timid looking woman and a young girl. The woman was carrying a beach bag with swimming costumes, towels and sun lotion in it and the little girl had a pink tote bag with a sparkly unicorn across the front, with a bucket and spade, a bottle of fruit squash and a sun hat inside it. The story was: this was a man who had just come into some money and was taking his wife and daughter for a day out to Le Touquet in France. When they get there they would spend some time at the beach and have some lunch in a nice restaurant and then return to the UK with a consignment of cocaine worth £1.2 million which would be concealed in four fuel containers.

Diana Fairgate flicked through the pages of Harper's Bazaar as she waited for her event planner to arrive. It was her 75th birthday in three months, and she was exhausted just thinking about all the arrangements that needed to be made. Her husband, Gordon, poked his head round the door to let her know he was back with the groceries. "Did you get it all?" she asked.

"I think so," he said, looking exasperatedly at the huge shopping list she had given him.

"Look who's here," Diana announced excitedly.

Their eldest son, Joe had turned up. Joe and his father had a strained relationship; Gordon found it hard to connect with Joe as they didn't seem to have anything in common. He also didn't approve of his son's lackadaisical attitude towards work. Joe was an aspiring artist, which, as far as Gordon was concerned, meant he basically just painted a few pictures then went to the pub.

Gordon had drawn the line a few years ago and stopped giving him an allowance; he had reached fifty, and it was about time he earned his own money. Diana couldn't see what all the fuss was about. "What is the problem Gordon? We have plenty of money and our son is happy and enjoying life. Why should he have to go out and do a job he hates? He is a talented artist, he just needs a break," she had told her husband.

Gordon had tried to give him the break he needed. He had bought him an art studio, got him an interview at Saatchi and Saatchi and even sent him to New York to mingle with the elite art agencies there, but his son didn't seem to have any get-up-and-go and failed miserably at every opportunity.

"Hello, Dad," Joe said. Gordon tried to hide his dismay at his son's choice of clothes. The faded Led Zeppelin T-shirt revealing an array of tattoos on both arms and ripped jeans made him look like an overgrown teenager. Joe hated exercise but loved beer so; as a result, he was overweight with a beer belly which hung over his jeans. Gordon thought how completely different he and Daniel were. Thank god he had one son he could be proud of. He mumbled a quick 'hello' and then went to the kitchen to unload the shopping.

Diana showed Joe the pictures in the magazine of the possible themes for her party. "Angelica, the event organiser will be here soon. Will you stay? I'd love to have your input," she asked him.

"Of course, Mum; I'd love to," Joe said.

"Mum, I want to bring Jerry to the party," he told her.

Diana frowned. "Well, you know I don't mind darling, but I'm not sure how your father will react," she said, touching his hand gently.

"It's about time he knew, Mum. I'm 52," Joe argued.

"Yes, darling, I agree, but do we have to do it at my birthday party?" she asked, helplessly.

"I'm sorry, Mum, but if Jerry isn't invited, then I'm not coming," Joe said, defiantly.

"Okay, invite Jerry," she said, defeated. She didn't want to argue today; she had too much to organise.

Chapter 48

The family returned to the plane later that day where Daniel was instructed to wait for them. Darren watched as the Border Control Officers spoke to Daniel. His wife's eyes grew wide, and she gripped his hand in a panic. "Don't worry! He's a professional. He's used to this; he'll know what to say," Darren told her.

The little girl ran up to Daniel, her cheeks were rosy and her hair was still damp from the sea. "Look what I've got!" she exclaimed.

Daniel smiled and bent down to look at the assortment of shells in her bucket. The Border Control Officers smiled and had a peep into the bucket too. They had finished their checks and were satisfied. Daniel nodded gratefully at them as they walked away. He had met the men many times before on his previous trips, so they were familiar with each other.

Everyone remained silent during the journey back to the UK. The little girl had fallen asleep after her exhausting day but looked happy. Daniel felt an unexpected buzz as he flew them all home. They had picked up seven kilos of cocaine, just like that, and got away with it. He couldn't believe how easy it had been.

Daniel carefully landed the plane by a secluded barn in a field near Faversham in Kent where Darren quickly hopped out and waited for Daniel to retrieve the containers. He took them to the back of the barn while Daniel waited and watched. Shortly afterwards, Darren returned with a bag of cash. He threw Daniel a white package and a wad of notes. "For you!" he said, smugly.

Chapter 49

Selena called Blair into her office. "Take a seat, Blair," she said.

Blair noticed that Selena looked different. She had changed her image to a more androgynous look. "Your hair is nice," Blair said as she sat down.

Selena had replaced her long dark curls with a bright red bob and her pencil skirt and blouse with a sharp, sophisticated trouser suit. "Thank you," she said, not looking up from the papers in front of her. "We've been given a huge budget this year for our *Today* magazine awards ceremony as we are going to have some A-list celebrities attending. I'm snowed under at the moment, could you organise it?" Selena asked.

Blair wanted to jump out of her seat and run round the room shouting 'yippee' at the top of her voice; she absolutely loved organising events, and there would be a nice bonus in it for her too. "Sure, no problem. Shall we arrange a time, so you can brief me?"

Selena finally looked up and replied, "No. It's your baby. You have full control. Oh, just a couple of things: Nicole Scherzinger will need a big dressing room, and you can hire a designer if you like too; it'll be easier for you."

Blair's face lit up. "Okay, and thanks for the opportunity Selena," she said, gratefully.

"Well, you are the managing editor. So go manage!" Selena said, reaching out and taking Blair's hand. She held it lightly and gently rubbed her thumb across Blair's fingers and then gave it a little squeeze. Blair blushed. She had a strange feeling of déjà vu.

As Blair sat back down at her desk, dazed from what had just happened, an idea sprung to mind. She picked her bag up and fumbled around amongst the lipsticks and other paraphernalia she hoarded in there until she found a dog-eared business card that had been squashed in a side pocket. She pulled it out and straightened the edges, so she could read the number and then dialled it.

After a few seconds, she cleared her throat and said, "Hi, Ricky, its Blair Matthews."

A gleaming Racing Green coloured Aston Martin Vanquish was parked at the White Horse pub and as Blair drove into the car park her heart skipped a beat. Daniel was there. She knew he sometimes popped in there on a Monday evening when Riley was usually out at a race. She looked in the rear-view mirror and adjusted her, already perfect hair, and checked that her lipstick was still on, and then she picked up her bag and got out of the car. She was so glad she had decided on wearing her black Victoria Beckham dress with the zip up the back as she knew it accentuated her curves and her black court shoes made her petite legs look much longer.

Daniel was sitting at the bar talking to the barmaid when Blair walked in, and they were both laughing. She could tell the waitress was flirting with him and was obviously flattered that Daniel was paying her so much attention. Blair walked up behind him. "Hi, Daniel, fancy seeing you here," she said.

The barmaid gave her a scathing look which Blair pretended she didn't notice.

"Oh, hi, Blair, how are you?" Daniel asked, pulling out a stool from under the bar for her.

"I'm very well, thank you," she said, bending down and giving him a kiss on the cheek, leaving her lips there for an extra couple of seconds, knowing that the barmaid was watching and would be silently seething. Blair turned to her and said pleasantly, "Could I have a drink please?"

The woman nodded and forced a smile.

Time flew by as Daniel and Blair chatted. She told him all about her mum and the awards ceremony she was organising. Daniel talked about Riley and the girls. Blair was conscious that she was starting to feel a bit tipsy as she was coming to the end of her gin and tonic. She would have to leave her car in the car park and get a taxi home, she decided, as there was no way she wanted to leave anytime soon; she was enjoying Daniel's company and knew he was enjoying being with her.

She caught him glancing down at her legs a couple of times, which sent thrills through her whole body. He had the most incredible eyes and smile she had ever seen on a man, and she was completely intoxicated by him. If he hadn't been Riley's husband she would definitely have made a play for him. Images of the two of them with their hands all over each other, ripping each other's clothes off were flashing through her mind. He also smelt unbelievable which was sending her into frenzy.

Daniel's phone started ringing inside his jacket pocket. "Hi, darling. okay, see you soon," he said. All images of her and Daniel together vanished as Blair's thoughts were slammed back to reality like a meteor crashing to earth. "Riley is home now," he said, happily.

Blake felt like a child whose balloon had been prematurely burst. Fuck Riley, she thought. She had drunk too much to be able to drive home but had planned to have a couple more, so she could carry on talking to Daniel, and now, Riley had ruined things, like she always did. *If only Daniel knew his darling, beloved wife had been snogging her childhood sweetheart a few weeks ago*, Blair thought. She picked up her phone to call a cab.

"Can I give you a lift home?" Daniel asked her. Blair's spirits were quickly lifted again.

"If you're sure? I don't want to put you out," she said.

"No trouble at all," he replied, getting off the stool and picking up his jacket. The barmaid stared disapprovingly at Blair again. As Blair walked out of the pub behind Daniel, she turned around and smiled sweetly at her. She felt like the cat who'd got the cream!

Gordon pulled back the heavy duck-egg coloured bedspread draped over their super king sized bed and moaned at having to remove all the cushions his wife had insisted on having on the bed. Diana was in the ensuite bathroom slathering La Mer's night balm over her face. He got into the bed and quickly scanned the messages on his phone. *'Hello, stranger! How the devil are you? It's been too long! Call me x'.* He smiled to himself.

Diana got into the bed next to her husband and reached for her glass of water and the vitamin pills beside it. "So, are all the arrangements for your party finalised now?" Gordon asked her, quickly putting his phone away in the drawer beside him.

"Yes, pretty much," she said.

"Is Joe coming? I thought I heard him telling Adolpho that he may not be able to make it," Gordon said in vexation.

Diana rolled her eyes. She didn't want to get into another argument about their son at this time of night. "Well, it's up to him," she said, lowering her pillow.

"I just don't understand him," Gordon said.

"You never have!" she said, indignantly.

"What's that supposed to mean?" Gordon asked, offended.

"Well, you've always favoured Daniel over the other two; which, to be honest, is rather strange as he's not even your son," Diana told him.

"How can you say that? We have always treated Daniel as our own," he said, looking at her in disbelief.

She sighed. "Yes, of course, we did and still do, and I love him as much as the others. But, that's the point! I love him 'as much' as the others, not 'more than'," she said turning onto her side and pulling the duvet over her shoulder.

"You would think he would want to go to his mother's 75th birthday party though," Gordon continued. "I just don't understand that boy at all. He's never had a proper girlfriend or a decent job; just been taking advantage of our goodwill all these years."

Diana snored gently, oblivious to his ranting. Gordon shook his head in annoyance and reached up and turned off the lamp.

Chapter 50

The guests were starting to arrive, and Blair had a kaleidoscope of butterflies in her stomach. She had been over every single detail with a fine tooth comb and been through the itinerary and checklist over and over again. She wished Ricky would hurry up and arrive, so they could do a final check together. He had chosen the venue, which was a recently closed-down theatre. The proprietors had been grateful for the offer from *Today* magazine to hire the venue for their awards ceremony.

Blair looked at her watch; there was twenty minutes left before the doors opened. The meet-and-greet entertainers were all dressed up as circus characters which were attracting a lot of interest, especially the two men on stilts and everyone was laughing and enjoying themselves outside beside the huge outdoor heaters. The complimentary glasses of champagne were going down a treat too. There were a few celebrity look-alikes that were on hand to escort people to their tables.

Selena waved to Blair from the other side of the red carpet and then gave her the thumbs up. Blair exhaled a sigh of relief; her boss was happy so that was a good sign. She also looked incredibly beautiful this evening, and Blair felt a slight tingling feeling in the pit of her stomach making her feel embarrassed and confused.

A black limo pulled up and Ricky jumped out and held the door open for a pretty dark-haired girl who was giggling about something he had just said to her. Blair assumed that was Ricky's girlfriend. She tucked her short black, spiky hair behind her ears and took his hand as she got out of the car. She looked out of place in her leather jeans and Nirvana T-shirt, but her and Ricky weren't guests; he was the designer and created the whole look for the evening, which Blair was over the moon about, as he had done an amazing job so, as far as she was concerned, they could have both turned up in their pyjamas, and she wouldn't have cared.

"Hi, Ricky," Blair called out running up to him with her clipboard in her hand.

"Hi, Blair. You look great," he told her.

Blair was wearing a sleeveless, red Vivienne Westwood dress with an asymmetrical hemline and was the first person to be papped by photographers, which she was thrilled about. "This is my girlfriend, Emma," he said.

"Hi there," said his girlfriend holding out her hand to shake Blair's.

"Oh, you're Australian," Blair said.

"I was out there designing the interior for a new hotel and ended up bringing Emma back with me," said Ricky.

"Wow, that sounds amazing," she said, enthusiastically.

At that moment, a taxi pulled up beside them, and Riley stepped out. Her thick dark hair was styled in big waves which framed her heart-shaped face, and she wore a deep red lipstick making her lips look sensuous and full. Ricky's eyes roamed up and down the length of her long black, off-the-shoulder dress with a thigh-high split up the side, revealing a toned leg as she walked along the red carpet towards them. Yet again, Blair had been upstaged in front of Ricky, and she was peeved.

Riley was surprised to see Ricky but relieved that he had a date with him. The Brad Pitt look-alike held out his arm for Blair. His job was to escort Blair into the venue first, and then everyone else would follow down the red carpet, stopping for photos and interviews on the way. "Ricky, I wanted to quickly go through everything again with you before it starts," Blair said, starting to panic.

"Don't worry, Blair, everything is in order. I've checked with my guys inside, and they are happy with everything. Just relax and enjoy the evening," he reassured her.

Blair nodded and smiled and then took Brad Pitt's arm and walked down the red carpet. As they walked up the staircase, the indoor fireworks simulator machines fired up and spark fountains were released from giant vases of flowers making it look as if fireworks were streaming out of the flowers. The effects drew gasps from the guests as they followed Blair up the stairs.

Blair couldn't have been happier with the inside of the venue. It was stunning. The walls were covered in deep purple drapes, and there was a circular stage at the front with silver stars sparkling from the purple background behind it. Silver chains and huge chandeliers hung from the ceiling, lighting up the room and ice sculptures were dotted around beside buckets holding bottles of chilled champagne which were guarded by waiters wearing silver blazers.

"This is fantastic Blair. Congratulations," Riley said, excitedly, as she watched a burlesque dancer doing acrobatics around a suspended mirror ball hanging down from the ceiling above them.

Blair led Riley to their table near the stage. They would be sitting with Ricky and his girlfriend, Selena and her partner, Tamsin, and Nicole Scherzinger and her guest. The singer would also be performing at the opening of the show. The tables were laid out with canapés and enhanced with pin spot lights which shone beams of focussed lights on each table so guests could see each other properly if they wanted to chat even when the lights went out.

Once the award ceremony was underway, Blair finally started to relax and knocked back a couple of glasses of champagne. Everything was going according to plan. There was just one more plan she had, that she hoped would work out! Riley moved closer to Blair, so they could chat during the interval, but Blair turned to Emma. "Would you like to come to the ladies room to freshen up," Blair asked her. Emma looked a little surprised but nodded and got up from her seat. Blair turned to Riley, "Be back in a minute, darling," she said, leaving Riley and Ricky alone together at the table.

Blair was re applying her lipstick when Emma came out of the toilet cubicle. "So how long have you and Ricky been together?" Blair asked, not wasting any time wading in with the questions.

"About two years," Emma said, as she washed her hands.

"Oh! He didn't mention you when we saw him at the Sky Bar," Blair said.

"Oh really? Yes, he said he had bumped into you both. You were all friends at school, right?" Emma said.

"Well, a little bit more than friends," whispered Blair, knowing she was about to open up a can of worms. Emma looked surprised but not too bothered. "Did you know he and Riley were childhood sweethearts?"

Emma was starting to feel uncomfortable. "Er yeah, he mentioned they had been together when they were younger," she said, turning to make her way to the door.

"They almost had a baby together," Blair added before Emma could escape.

"Oh, I didn't know that," Emma said, edging herself away from Blair.

"Between you and me, I think they've still got the hots for each other. Can't you see the connection between them?" Blair asked. She knew the alcohol was contributing to her runaway-mouth, but she didn't care.

"Blair, why are you telling me all this?" Emma asked, suspiciously.

Blair blushed. Had she just overstepped the mark? "Sorry, I've had too much to drink. Just ignore me," she said, trying to laugh it off.

"I think we better go back now," said Emma, holding the door open for Blair.

The ceremony had already started again by the time Blair and Emma got back to their seats. Ricky turned to give his girlfriend a kiss, but she turned her head away. Blair noticed the snub out of the corner of her eye and smiled to herself. Her plan seemed to be working. "You okay?" she whispered to Riley.

"Yes, I'm having a great time," Riley whispered back.

Blair started to pour some white wine into a glass for Riley.

"No. Not for me, Blair," Riley said, reminding her.

"Oh, just have one!" Blair said. "I promise I won't tell Daniel."

Riley laughed. "No, I better not," she said, looking longingly at the cold bottle of Chablis in front of her.

"If you want some, have some! I'll look after you. I Promise!" Blair told her as she poured herself another glass. "Where did Nicole go?" asked Blair, just noticing that the singer had disappeared.

"Oh, she left a while ago. She said she had enjoyed herself though," Riley said. It didn't take her long to finish her first glass of wine which Blair swiftly topped up. It was like giving nectar to a bee. Unfortunately, it only took one glass for Riley to remember how good it made her feel, and it didn't take long for her to finish the whole bottle. Emma had decided to go home. She made the excuse of being tired and having to go to work early the next day. Blair had already plied Ricky with enough whisky to convince him to stay, so he wasn't really bothered that his girlfriend had left.

The ceremony had finished, but the after-party was just getting started. The DJ started playing some Ibiza classics and the dance floor was swamped instantly. "Let's go and dance," Blair said, pulling Riley and Ricky up from their seats.

"Oh god, no, Blair, I'm a shocking dancer; you know that," objected Riley as she was being dragged up to the dance floor. Ricky was following behind; it took all his strength to keep upright after all the whisky he had consumed.

The three of them began making some bizarre shapes on the dance floor which had them in hysterics. Blair fell over, causing more hysteria. "Look guys, I think I better go before I make a complete fool of myself," Blair said, slurring her words.

"Okay, we'll come too," Riley said, trying to focus her eyes on her friend.

"No, no! You two stay here and enjoy yourselves. There are lots of taxis outside; I'll be fine," Blair insisted. Riley couldn't think straight and wasn't sure if it was a good idea to stay, but Ricky had assured her that he would make sure she got home safely. It had been ages since she had been out and really enjoyed herself, so she agreed. Blair kissed them both goodbye and staggered to the cloakroom to retrieve her coat.

The cold air hit Blair in the face as she stepped outside, and she breathed it in, gratefully. Riley and Ricky were together and something was bound to happen between them, then Daniel would accidentally find out and that would be the end of their marriage, leaving the door wide open for her.

"Taxi!" she called out raising her arm in the air.

Chapter 51

The house was deathly quiet when Riley stirred. She opened one eye to check where she was as her head was fuzzy. She was relieved to see that she was wrapped up in her duvet in her own bed. She tried hard to recall the events of the previous night, but everything was too blurry, and she had that old familiar feeling of doom in the pit of her stomach. This is why she had given up drinking, she reminded herself.

As she rolled over on to her back, she winced as the throbbing in her head moved with her. Ricky's face flashed into her mind. She started to remember that he had been sitting beside her, and they were talking, but then everything after that was just a blank. She then thought about Daniel, and she sat up quickly. "Ouch!" she exclaimed, holding her head in her hands.

"Daniel!" Riley called out. There wasn't any answer. It must be Saturday, she thought; the girls have tennis lessons on Saturday mornings so Daniel must have taken them. She lay back down, thankful to have some time to herself, so she could try and remember what had happened.

Blair was still in bed. She was watching TV and sipping a cappuccino while scrolling through all the congratulatory emails on her laptop. She adored lazy Saturday mornings when she could take her time getting up. She liked to do her housework and shopping and then get a takeaway and watch a good box set in the evenings. The awards ceremony had made it into the tabloids online.

The celebrities who had attended had all enjoyed themselves so much they had been busy posting theirphotos on Instagram and Facebook this morning. Blair had enjoyed herself even though she had been a nervous wreck the whole week. She was pleased to see her old boss, Caroline as well, who reminded her during their brief conversation at the bar, of the night they spent together. Caroline had hoped they might re-enact the experience later on that evening, but Blair made it clear that as far as she was concerned, it had been a one-off.

Caroline was unperturbed and made a beeline for a well-known actress at the bar who had just won an award for Best Actress in a Continuing Drama.

Ricky heard his phone ringing in the distance and dragged himself off the sofa where he'd fallen asleep. He rubbed his eyes and ran his fingers through his tangled fair hair, pushing it off his face. He walked round the room following the sound of the ringtone until he spotted it poking out from beneath his jeans on the floor. "Hello," he mumbled into the phone.

"Hi, Ricky. It's Blair," she announced cheerily.

Ricky grimaced as the volume was turned up high on the phone, and Blair sounded much too chirpy for the morning after the night before. "Haven't you got a hangover from hell too?" he asked, needing to sit back down.

"Nope. I'm as fresh as a daisy," laughed Blair. "I just wanted to say a massive thank you for all your hard work yesterday. Everything was incredible, and we're in all the newspapers today. Hopefully, you'll be flooded with work as a result of this project," she said.

"Oh great. That's good to know," he said, trying to muster up the strength to sound enthusiastic and grateful.

"So what happened with you and Riley last night?" Blair asked, cheekily.

Ricky frowned. "What do you mean?" he asked.

"Well, where did you both go after I left," she said.

"We left shortly after you did," he said, innocently.

"I got us a taxi, dropped Riley at home and then headed back to my flat."

Disappointment washed over Blair. She was convinced that if she just got the two of them together something explosive would happen between them. All that wasted effort! That was the only reason she had hired Ricky in the first place. Luckily, he did a great job with the venue, so she didn't regret it. "Oh, I'm glad because she is married, after all," Blair said, insincerely.

Later that afternoon, Riley's phone vibrated on the table beside her; she had switched it on to silent as they were all watching a family movie together. The girls were sprawled on the floor in front of the screen eating popcorn, and Daniel was snoring gently beside her. Riley picked up the phone and her body tensed as she read the message: *'Had such a great time. Can't stop thinking about you. I have to see you again'*.

After Blair had left, she and Ricky carried on chatting for a while; Riley couldn't remember what they had been talking about. Then it hit her like a ton of bricks! She started to remember her and Ricky sneaking out of the auditorium, while the party was in full swing, and creeping along the corridor to one of the disused dressing rooms, giggling like teenagers. They sneaked inside and locked the door behind them. She remembered seeing lots of theatre props and some Victorian costumes on a clothes rail at the back of the room, and she and Ricky began clumsily tearing each other's clothes off.

Riley's head started spinning again, but this time, she felt sick and horrified at what she had done. Yet again, she had been in a compromising position with Ricky, and it wasn't what she had wanted, but like an idiot, she had too much to drink and couldn't resist him. She didn't even know why she had drunk at all. Oh yes, now she remembered! Blair had encouraged her. But why would she do that? She was supposed to be her friend. Riley looked back at her phone and deleted the message quickly.

Chapter 52

Daniel was chatting to the Border Patrol Officers. The 'jobs' had all gone according to plan so far and had become a nice little money earner. The buzz Daniel got each time was almost as good as sex. The only downer was having to take orders from that sleaze bag, Darren, but Daniel had played the game and did as he was told. For now!

"Wait!" one of the officers demanded as Darren and his family tried to board the plane. "Open the bag," the man's strong French accent frightened the little girl holding Darren's hand, and she began to cry. He took her backpack away, and she became even more hysterical.

Daniel moved in and scooped her up in his arms. "Come on, darling, let's go and wait over here," he said, as the Gendarmerie turned up. The woman beside Daniel visibly shook with terror and Darren's face drained of all colour. He looked over at Daniel.

"You set me up!" he said in disbelief. Daniel had convinced him to carry a small stash in the backpack for one of the officers.

"If I go down, you go down," Darren shouted. Daniel smiled smugly. He hadn't given the police any information about the illegal laboratory in the Netherlands; he would leave that to Darren. Daniel knew eventually Darren would squeal, but the patrol officers knew Daniel well, and he had given them a generous cut of the profits, so they were happy. In time, Daniel would resume duties again at a different location but without the middle man, and everything would be on his terms this time.

Chapter 53

The rain was lashing down on the window of the cafe as Riley looked out on to the row of cars parked along the uneven pavement; the heaving droplets bouncing off the car bonnets were mesmerising. Everything looked bleak and grey, which was apt, as that is exactly how she felt. She hadn't been able to eat properly for weeks and every time Daniel made love to her, she kept seeing Ricky's face and the guilt was slowly eating her up.

She saw Ricky running down the street and watched as he came in and stood in the doorway dripping wet, his long hair was tied back and his denim jacket was pasted on his body. He looked around and spotted Riley sitting beside the window. "Hi," he said, walking up to her. He bent down to kiss her on the cheek. "Sorry, I'm soaking," he said, out of breath.

Riley beckoned the waitress over and ordered a double expresso and Ricky ordered a flat white coffee and a sandwich.

"You ignored all my messages," he said, confused.

She had seemed more than keen at the awards ceremony and told him that she had always loved him and never got over him, so he couldn't understand her change of heart and why she had been so cold towards him since. "Look, Ricky, you have to understand, I love my husband. He is my life. What happened between us was a mistake. I was drunk," she said, feeling her eyes slowly starting to well up.

Ricky's heart sank; he had hoped she had had a change of heart. "Look Riley, I get it. I completely understand. I won't contact you again but just know that I'll always love you, and I am always here for you," he told her.

Riley looked at him, and suddenly, they were fifteen again. A part of her had wanted him to fight for her even though she knew she would never leave Daniel. "I'll always love you too Ricky. You were my first love, and you'll always be special to me," she said with tears flowing down her cheeks.

Chapter 54

Daniel had been worried about his wife. Riley seemed to be distracted about something she didn't want to share with him. The nightmares had also returned, and he was becoming overwhelmed again. He was relying on cocaine and throwing himself into work as a distraction, but his back had started playing up again too, making him even more miserable and cantankerous.

His PA arranged for him to have another treatment with Siobhan so that evening he drove to the country club after work. He was looking forward to seeing her again. Her soothing voice and firm massage might just be what he needed.

Siobhan showed Daniel to the treatment room, but instead of leaving him to get undressed, she stayed and watched him strip off. Her eyes scanned his tanned, strong body and his familiar smell made her body tremble slightly. She walked over and gently placed her hands on him without saying a word. As the warm oil was firmly rubbed onto his skin, Daniel felt himself slowly start to relax for the first time in a long time. As her fingers roamed their way down to his waist, he felt himself becoming aroused.

To his surprise, Siobhan slowly moved her hand underneath the towel. She then leant over and kissed him gently on the neck. Daniel groaned and turned over. The chemistry between them overpowered them both, and soon, Siobhan was undressed. Daniel felt the towel slip down and replaced with Siobhan straddling him. The sex was quick but intense, as Daniel was thrusting deep inside her, Siobhan softly moaned with pleasure. As they both got dressed in silence afterwards, they somehow knew this was the beginning of something.

Blair was surprised to see the hanging baskets outside her dad's house in such a sorry state. The red flowers had died and turned a murky shade of brown and the dried leaves hung down the side of the baskets, limply. Why hadn't her mother attended to them? *That was very unlike her*, thought Blair. Blair didn't knock on the door but retrieved the key from her bag and let herself in.

The house was quiet and didn't smell of air freshener anymore, a stale smell lingered in the air instead. "Dad! Mum!" called out Blair. She walked into the kitchen and was startled to see her dad sitting at the kitchen table staring into space. A dreadful feeling of deja vu washed over her. "Oh my god! She's gone again, hasn't she?" she said.

Chapter 55

"Come in," Siobhan told Daniel, surprised that he had turned up at her house, unexpectedly.

Luckily, Jeff would be out until late playing golf, but Siobhan was slightly annoyed that Daniel had arrived unannounced. "How's Jeff," Daniel asked, feeling slightly guilty. Jeff had become a friend of Daniel's since he had started hiring his planes for clients, and Daniel reciprocated by taking his clients to Jeff's country club. What had happened between him and Siobhan a few weeks ago wasn't something he had planned.

Cheating on his wife wasn't something he had ever envisaged happening either, but sometimes in life, things just happen that you can't control. There was an unspoken understanding he and Siobhan had; neither wanted to give up their partners, but the chemistry between them was too strong to give up too. Daniel saw something in Siobhan that was special. May be, she might just be the demon slayer who could save him and put him back together again, so he could finally be the man he wanted to be.

Siobhan showed Daniel into the drawing room. "Can I get you a drink?" Daniel shook his head, and she noticed how agitated he was as he fiddled with his tie.

"Tell me what's bothering you," she said, suddenly concerned.

The words blurted out like a fountain. "I killed him!" he said.

"Killed whom?" she asked, calmly.

Daniel couldn't get the rest of the words out. He put his head in his hands and sobbed.

Chapter 56

"Hi, darling," Daniel said.

"What's up? You look dreadful. What's wrong?" Riley asked, surprised to see her husband at the kennels.

"Can we go somewhere and talk?" he asked her.

"Of course," Riley replied, feeling slightly apprehensive.

Daniel drove them both to a spot, off the beaten track, where they had both loved to go before they had children. "We haven't been here for years," Riley said, excitedly.

Daniel knew it was one of his wife's favourite places. "And that's not all," he said, getting out of the car. He walked round to the back of the car and got out a picnic basket.

"Oh, Daniel!" Riley exclaimed.

He took her hand and led her down to the river, where he laid out a blanket on the grass.

"What is this all about?" she asked, curiously.

"I wanted to share something with you," he said. Siobhan had encouraged him to talk to Riley about his nightmares and what had happened to his brother. She assured him that Riley would understand.

Daniel poured his wife a glass of champagne and watched her take a sip and then lie back on the blanket with her long legs stretched out in front of her, her beautiful smile and the way the light reflected on her deep brown eyes making them sparkle, warmed his heart. He loved this woman more than life itself.

Riley listened intently as Daniel told her his story, then she put down her glass and wrapped her arms tightly around him. Daniel's whole body shook with relief, and he sobbed in her arms. It was as if finally, he had been released from confinement, where he had been trapped for years. "It's okay," she said gently. "It wasn't your fault darling. You were 10 years old. It was an accident," she pulled away, holding on to his shoulders.

"You were a child. You had no idea he would fall into the water, and you're not a strong swimmer; you could never have saved him. I think subconsciously you were scared of falling into the water too, that's why your brain kicked in and told you there was nothing you could have done. Forgive yourself and move forward. You have two little girls now who need their dad. It's like you've been on another planet lately, and we want you back," she said, and then she pulled him close to her and kissed him tenderly.

Daniel was disappointed with himself for ever doubting Riley. He didn't think she would be able to accept what he had done to his brother or even understand it, but he had underestimated her. She was *his* strong, practical, unformidable Riley. He knew it from the moment he first met her.

Chapter 57

The waiter brought Blair's gin and tonic over to her table. "Will you be dining with us this evening," he asked her.

"Maybe," Blair replied, curtly, not looking forward to another evening on her own.

"Hi, Blair," said a friendly voice from behind her. Blair swung round and was pleasantly surprised to see Daniel standing there.

"You look like you could do with a drink," Blair said, trying to attract the waiter's attention so that he would come over.

Daniel sat down opposite her. "Spent the afternoon with the girls," he said.

"I can tell from your hair," laughed Blair, looking at his perfectly combed, perfectly flat hair.

"Yes, they thought I needed a make-over," he said as showed her two fingernails which had been painted in pillar-box red nail varnish.

"Just two nails?" Blair asked.

"They got bored and went off to watch TV after that," said Daniel, rolling his eyes.

Blair was pleased Daniel had turned up at the pub. He had managed to shake her out of her bad mood. She looked over at the waiter and held up her glass, indicating that she wanted a refill. Daniel noticed three empty glasses in front of her. "Are you okay, Blair?" he asked.

"Why? Am I starting to sound pissed?" she asked, not really caring if she was or not.

"No, no," Daniel lied.

"Actually, Daniel, no I'm not fucking okay," Blair said, slurring her words. Daniel looked surprised but didn't say anything.

She went on to tell him about her mum leaving again. "My dad is a wreck, and my brother is heartbroken again!" she said, a bit too loudly causing the table of people next to them to look over.

"And how about you? How do you feel?" Daniel asked, feeling sorry for Blair. He knew full well what it was like to feel crushed but unable to admit it to anyone.

"Oh, I'm okay. I'm just annoyed with myself; I should have expected it from her, but I honestly didn't see it coming. I thought she had changed, but I suppose, a leopard doesn't change its spots," she said. Blair took a gulp of her fresh gin, delivered by the waitress this time, as the young waiter was too scared to serve her.

Daniel decided to change the subject quickly before Blair got kicked out for being drunk and disorderly. "Why don't you give Riley a call; she was saying the other day that she hasn't heard from you in a while?" Blair wanted to scream. Fucking Riley again! Why did every conversation have to revert back to Riley? Couldn't she just have her *'five minutes'* for once without having to think about Miss perfect-in-every-way Riley. "Yes, what a great idea, Daniel," Blair said, overenthusiastically.

Daniel was taken aback by her tone but put it down to the alcohol. "Did lovely Riley tell you about the awards ceremony I invited her to?" Blair asked. A little voice deep inside her was whispering *'don't say it!'* But a louder voice in her alcohol- infused brain was saying, *'go on, tell him. He has a right to know!'*

Daniel wondered why Blair was bringing that up. "Yes, she said she had a great time," he said, looking confused.

"Oh, I bet she did!" Blair laughed.

"What are you trying to say, Blair?" Daniel said, starting to feel angry but also not really wanting to hear what she was going to come out with.

"Did she tell you Ricky Berg was there?" she asked.

"No," he said, trying not to sound shocked. He knew all about his wife and Ricky and the abortion when she was 15 years old.

"Well, he was the designer and organiser I hired for the ceremony and guess what? Your perfect wife and her childhood sweetheart ending up shagging in the broom cupboard after I went home," Blair said, feeling smug. She knew it hadn't been a broom cupboard, but she couldn't remember where Riley said it had been when she had confided in her. Daniel tried to stay calm and composed.

"Okay, I think you've had enough to drink now Blair. Can I give you a lift home," he asked, getting up and lifting her out of her seat by her elbow, as all the diners in the pub stared at them with bated breath.

Blair had just pulled out the pin that was going to detonate the grenade; now she was going to have to sit back and watch it explode, and there would be no going back.

Chapter 58

The sun was just beginning to rise outside the huge glass windows when Riley walked into the house. She rubbed her eyes as she walked into the kitchen. She flopped down on the leather sofa beside one of the windows and looked outside. The countryside was beginning to wake up. She watched a flock of perfectly synchronised geese noisily fly past.

The swimming pool was glistening and looked inviting; she looked forward to a nice swim later. She hadn't noticed Daniel beside the coffee machine. He stared at her. She looked beautiful as the early morning hue of the sun shone like an orangey red halo around her, lighting up her chocolate brown eyes and accentuating the coppery flecks in her hair. His Riley! His beautiful Riley! Or was she?

Riley gasped as she saw him. "Oh bloody hell, Daniel; you gave me a fright!" she exclaimed.

"Where have you been?" he asked, taking his cup from the machine and walking towards the fridge. "Little Blaze was poorly last night, so I stayed with him. I left you loads of messages, but you didn't reply," she said, too exhausted to get into a conversation with him.

"I ran out of battery," Daniel lied. He had seen the messages, but after the bombshell Blair dropped, he didn't know whether to believe her or not.

"Listen, babe, I'm shattered. I'm going up to get an hour's sleep before I have to get the girls to school," Riley told him. She gave him a hug on her way out of the kitchen.

Daniel grabbed hold of her hand and pulled her back. Riley gasped in surprise. He pulled her towards him and kissed her hard on the lips. Riley let him kiss her for a few seconds and then pulled away. "I'm sorry, babe, I'm too tired," she said, wearily.

He didn't listen to her and held her gently by the back of the hair, so she couldn't move away and then ran his other hand over her breast and down to her the back of her jeans. He pushed himself up against her, but Riley pushed him away. "Daniel!" she said angrily. "What the hell are you doing?" Daniel backed off, then picked up his coffee and walked out of the room. Riley leant against the worktop, stunned. What the hell had just happened? Her husband had never acted that way with her before.

Blair looked at her phone as she sat outside the Turkish coffee shop in the busy high street. The traffic going past didn't help with the horrendous hangover she had, but she needed to get some air. There were five missed calls and a text message from Riley which she hadn't read. The handsome olive-skinned waiter brought out a Turkish coffee and a Baklava. "Thank you," Blair said as she admired his dark curly hair.

She took off her Gucci sunglasses, so she could read the message on her phone. *'Hi, darling, hope you're okay. Daniel is acting very strange. I need to speak to you x'* Blair typed back... *'Sorry, Riley, really busy at the moment. Will call you tonight. I'm sure everything is fine, don't worry'*.

She would have to come up with a good excuse for not calling Riley that night as she had promised. She couldn't cope with having to speak to her at the moment, and she still wasn't over her mother's betrayal, even though she was trying hard to push it out of her mind. All she wanted to do was keep a low profile and throw herself into her work.

The lawn outside the house, at the front of the estate, was covered in a plethora of bouquets and elaborate flower displays of every description. The celebrity party organiser, Chico Lopez, who had won the contract for Diana Fairgate's extravagant party from a short list of six other designers, had arranged for the flowers to be flown in directly from Holland and had hired a team of award-winning florists to create the vision he had devised for the party. He wanted spectacular constructions of floral ceilings, hand-tied centre pieces and wreaths threaded with all kinds of colourful flowers, from moody blue delphiniums to vibrant vandas.

He ran around the garden like a headless chicken, flapping his hands around and squawking orders at everyone. As money was no object and Chico had an open budget, he had gone completely overboard and found himself in a floral haven and was beyond excited. Carmelita shook her head in a mixture of astonishment and despair. "You are having wreaths at a birthday party? Wreaths are for dead people!" she wailed, throwing her hands up in the air and marching off in a huff.

"No, no, no. You wait and see. I am creating a theatrical masterpiece. Look at the colours, the textures, the shapes and the glorious smells!" he declared, half running and half skipping after her, desperately trying to defend himself. Diana was happy to leave Chico to his own devices; he had organised many exclusive events, and she loved his designs. It also gave her more time to concentrate on her hair and beauty regime and choose a spectacular dress from a selection that the stylist had brought over.

"Hello, love," Gordon said.

"Hello, darling. Did you see all the wonderful flowers outside?" his wife asked.

"I couldn't really miss them; they have taken up the whole garden," he said.

"I'm a bit worried about Daniel," Diana said, holding up one of the dresses in front of her that she could be potentially wearing to her party.

"Why is that?" asked Gordon, hanging up his jacket.

"He seemed a bit preoccupied when I spoke to him," she said, putting the dress down carefully on the bed.

"Oh, I shouldn't worry, he's probably got a lot on his mind at the moment, what with the new plans for the aerodrome and everything," Gordon said, reassuring his wife.

"Hmmm. I do hope that wife of his isn't giving him trouble," she said, haughtily.

"Riley? No, of course not. Oh, and by the way, I like the red dress best," he added.

Riley lit the candles and put an Enya CD on. She was expecting Daniel home any minute and wanted the room to look perfect. The steaks were cooking on the hob and the wine was chilling in the fridge. His behaviour that morning had concerned her, but she put it down to stress at work, and now, she knew about his brother, she understood his moods better. She wanted them to have a nice romantic evening together. She had even put on a sexy skin-tight black dress and heels.

Daniel put his phone on silent, ignoring Riley's calls. He parked his car far enough away, so he wouldn't be seen but close enough, so he could get a good look. It was easy to find the flat as Ricky Berg used his home address as his business address on his website. Daniel wanted to see *the competition* for himself. He had been raging inside since the conversation with Blair.

A tall, good-looking, fair-haired man came round the corner and headed towards the flat. Daniel knew instinctively that it was him. He sat on the steps and lit a cigarette. Before Daniel knew what he was doing, he got out of the car and started walking towards the man. As he got closer, he saw he was scruffily dressed but in a cool, trendy sort of way.

Ricky Berg looked younger than his years which made Daniel feel old. Did Riley think he was starting to look old? He swam nearly every day. May be he should start going to the gym? As Daniel got closer, he tried to look inconspicuous and put his head down. Ricky glanced at Daniel as he walked past. "Excuse me mate, could I get a light?" Daniel asked, pulling out a cigarette packet from his pocket.

"Sure," Ricky answered flicking his lighter towards Daniel. Daniel saw his face clearly in the flame as he bent down to light the cigarette. For a split second, their eyes met, and it was almost like they both had a moment of epiphany.

"Thanks," Daniel said and walked away.

Riley poured herself a glass of wine and served up the over-done steak and semi-burnt chips. She flicked off her shoes and took her dinner on a tray into the lounge where she sat and ate it on her lap watching The Sopranos.

Chapter 59

Chico was struggling to carry a huge '75' sign across the lawn towards the giant marquee which had been erected the night before. The Fairgate estate was buzzing with scores of frantic bodies running around with drapes for backdrops, carrying chandeliers carefully and generally rushing about making sure they had paid attention to every little detail. The party was going to be featured in Country Life magazine and would be a big deal for all the designers and organisers involved. "A bit of help here would be appreciated!" Chico shouted out to anyone who would listen as he balanced the enormous numerals on his tiny head.

Diana pulled the heavy velvet drapes open and looked out of her bedroom window. She made a few commendatory sounds as she saw the herculean effort that everyone was putting in for her. Of course, she thoroughly deserved it. It wasn't every day a woman turned 75 years old and looked as fabulous as she did. Today, she would be pampered and praised, and she would lap it up graciously.

Alphonso was racing around in his buggy checking the grounds and making sure that the lanterns that were lined up along the long driveway leading up to the house were all in working order. Carmelita shouted at her husband for driving too fast. "You stupid man, slow down," she yelled out from the doorway as she threw down her mop angrily. Diana's daughter Kate had arrived early to oversee everything. Carmelita always made her giggle. "He's fine Carmelita; don't worry." Carmelita shook her head and mumbled something inaudible in Spanish as she picked up her mop and dunked it into the bucket.

Kate was stunned by how incredible everything looked. The swimming pool was filled with glittery pink balloons which sparkled in the sunlight. The inside of the marquee was a trove of grandeur in a multitude of different shades of pink. A huge white ceiling canopy was centralised above the mirrored dance floor and scattered along the rest of the ceiling were beaded chandeliers and hanging flower balls. The walls of the marquee were graced with double layered pink backdrops and padded panels giving it a feeling of elegant opulence. The walkway which Diana would enter the marquee from, looked magical as it was lined with Sakura blossom trees.

"Everything okay, Katie?" Chico asked, apprehensively.

"Everything is perfect, Chico. I actually feel quite emotional at how beautiful it all looks. Mum will love it. Thank you so much," she said, touching Chico gently on the shoulder.

He was so small that she towered over him. Chico dramatically burst into tears and sighed with relief. "Oh, thank you so much, darling. You know how much I love your mamma. I hope she will be ecstatic today."

"I'm sure she will, Chico," Kate said. She plucked one of the velvety white roses from one of the displays and held it up to her nose as she walked away. Chico watched her, completely horrified. He suddenly felt faint but quickly pulled himself together and rushed over to rearrange the cluster of roses she had disturbed.

The inside of the house was just as manic as the outside as the hairdresser, make-up lady, stylist and Diana's Zen coach all tried to avoid colliding with each other as they poked and prodded and sprayed calming fragrances around her. The caterers were setting up in a specially adapted kitchen outside and catering vans were coming and going. Gordon had taken the dogs out for a nice long walk to try and avoid the chaos. He also managed to fit in a nice chat with Madeleine. Talking to Madeleine was always therapeutic for him; she had a calming manner which he loved. He could also listen to her sexy French accent for hours. "I must go now darling, thank you for the chat," he told her.

"Of course, Mon Cheri," she said and blew him a kiss down the phone.

Riley was putting in her earrings when Daniel walked into the room and held out his sleeve in front of her, indicating he needed help putting in his cufflink. Riley glared at him. She didn't want to start a row. It was stressful enough having to go to Diana's bloody party without having a barny with her husband too. She helped him with his sleeve and turned back to the mirror to finish off getting ready. Patsy ran into the room. "How do I look?" she asked, in her best grown-up voice as she twirled around showing off her new dress.

Riley turned to look at her daughter and smiled proudly. "You look adorable baby," she said.

Patsy screwed her face up. "I'm not a baby!" she exclaimed.

"No, but you'll always be my baby," Riley said, grabbing hold of her and tickling her while she screamed with laughter and fell about on the floor.

"Don't do that!" Daniel shouted angrily.

"You'll mess up your dress." Patsy ran off, hurt by her dad's outburst.

"What the hell is wrong with you?" Riley whispered, trying not to let the girls hear.

"Why should anything be wrong, Riley?" he scoffed.

"You have been rude to me all week. Do you want to enlighten me as to what exactly it is I have done," Riley said, furiously.

A car tooted outside. "The taxi is here. Come on, or we'll be late," Daniel said, avoiding the question.

Jeff zipped up the back of Siobhan's dress and kissed her gently on the neck. "You look stunning!" he told her.

"Why thank you kind sir," she said with a smile.

"Are you ready?" he asked her.

"Yes. Let's go," Siobhan replied as she picked up her silver Dior clutch bag. Siobhan wasn't a huge fan of Diana, but she liked Gordon a lot. He and her husband played golf together and got on well, so they were going to the party because he had personally invited them both. She looked in on the cat sitter just before she left. "I've left you a nice bottle of wine in the fridge Ashley. Thanks for looking after him," Siobhan said as she looked at her beloved pet snuggled up happily in the girl's lap.

"Thanks, Mrs Deakin. Have a lovely time," said the girl.

Chapter 60

Smartly dressed valets were on hand to escort the party guests to the house. Cars were to be left in the car park on arrival and the guests were then driven in buggies along the lengthy driveway lit up by lanterns, which led to the house. Gordon asked Alphonso to be in charge of personally escorting the family to the house; mainly because his driving was so bad, and he didn't want him to scare the guests, but Alphonso took it as an honour to be asked to drive the family himself. He decided it must be because Mr Fairgate thought he was the safest driver.

The party was in full swing when Daniel and Riley arrived. They could hear the music and laughter coming from the rear of the house. Rose and Patsy loved the buggy ride and didn't want to get off, so Alphonso asked if he could take them for an extra ride and promised he would drive slowly, so Riley agreed. It would give her a chance to try and find out what was bugging Daniel. Daniel marched off in front of her before she had a chance to say anything. She tried to catch up with him but couldn't run in her gold Jimmy Choo's so gave up and let him storm off.

As she entered the marquee, Riley saw that Daniel had already made his way to the bar and ordered himself a drink. Just then, the music stopped abruptly and everyone turned to face the exclusive entrance at the back of the marquee set up especially so that Diana could make her grand appearance. The band began to play 'Isn't She Lovely' by Stevie Wonder as Diana emerged. There wasn't enough room for her and Gordon to both come down the walkway together so Diana walked down on her own holding a bouquet of white roses and Gordon followed behind, happy to let his wife be the centre of attention.

Photographers subtly clicked away behind the guests, trying not to be too much of a distraction. Diana flashed her most charming smile for the cameras, ignoring the guests who were clapping beside her in her honour. She would make it up to them later when she had time to mingle. Riley looked at her mother-in-law in bemusement. This was one occasion where she would definitely need a drink!

"What can I get you?" the barman asked Riley.

"Vodka tonic please," she replied. She didn't give a damn if Daniel or her mother-in-law frowned upon her choice of drink. If she was expected to get through the evening, she would definitely need alcohol. A hand touched her shoulder making her jump.

"Oh, Siobhan! You gave me a fright!" Riley said, hugging her friend. She was relieved to see a friendly face at last.

"How's it going?" Siobhan asked, looking at the vodka.

"I need it Von," Riley said, wearily.

Siobhan never judged; that was the great thing about her and why Riley loved her so much. "Come and sit down, we need a catch up," Siobhan told her, leading her to their designated seats at the table.

Luckily, they were seated on the same table, but Riley's name card was next to Jeff's, so Siobhan swapped them round so that Riley would be seated next to her. Riley giggled. "I feel better already," she told Siobhan.

A hush fell over the room as Joe Fairgate walked in, hand in hand with his boyfriend, Jerry. Gordon's jaw dropped. Diana's eyes opened wide in surprise at the devilishly handsome man who had walked in with her son and lit up the room. Riley was excited to see her brother-in-law had, at long last, revealed his true identity and brought this fabulous looking man to the party.

With his rock star attire, caramel coloured skin and long dreadlock hair he reminded her of Lenny Kravitz. She was the first to walk up to them and give them both a hug. Jerry smiled, revealing a set of perfectly straight, brilliant white teeth. He liked Riley straight away and had a feeling they would hit it off.

The band wrapped up their session and the lead singer thanked everyone and assured them they would be back soon. The guests made their way to their designated seats and tables for dinner. By the time the desserts were served, Riley had managed to polish off a whole bottle of Chardonnay, and she was finally relaxed and happy. Joe and Jerry had also had quite a bit to drink and the three of them were roaring with laughter over something trivial and only hilarious to them. Riley excused herself and wondered off to find her daughters while Daniel watched, silently seething.

"Are you okay, Daniel?" Siobhan asked, as she moved round the table to sit beside him.

"Hi, Von. Yes, I'm good thanks," he said, smiling at her. He squeezed her knee playfully under the table. Siobhan ignored the gesture and carried on talking.

"Is there something wrong between you and Riley?" she asked.

"I really don't think that's any of your business, Siobhan," he said, defensively.

"Jeez, aren't you prickly this evening?" Siobhan said, sitting back in her chair. She coolly took another sip of wine and brushed his hand away from her knee. Daniel got up and walked away; he didn't need a lecture from Siobhan tonight.

Gordon took Diana to one side. "Did you know about Joe?" he asked her.

"Oh, for god's sake, Gordon! Did you really not have any idea that your son was gay?" Diana said, irritated that he had pulled her away from a gossipy chat with her friends. Gordon looked at her, miffed.

"Did you?" he asked. Diana rolled her eyes at her husband.

"Yes, of course! I suppose though, I have the additional advantage of having a good relationship with all my children," she told him, bluntly.

"What's that supposed to mean?" Gordon asked, defensively.

"When you said he was bringing Jerry, I thought you meant Jerry as in Jerry Hall. You know; as in, a woman!" he said.

"When was the last time you actually had a proper, one-to-one conversation with him?" Diana asked.

Gordon couldn't actually remember. He and his eldest son didn't have much in common, and he had always found it difficult to build a rapport with Joe about anything.

Diana added in a whisper, "Did you never think it was strange that he used to always insist on wearing a pink baseball hat when he was younger and preferred to play with the girls because he got on with them better?"

Chapter 61

Daniel found his wife perched on a bar stool, knocking back a tequila shot while the good-looking young barman laughed and chatted to her, glimpsing down at her long legs every now and then. "Don't you think you've had enough?" Daniel asked.

Riley glared at him and looked back at the barman. "Excuse my very rude husband," she continued in a slurred voice, "he's got the hump about something." Riley started to giggle which irritated Daniel even more, so he grabbed her wrist and dragged her off the stool.

"Come with me," he said, angrily.

"Hey!" the barman called out. Daniel turned round to him, his face red with rage.

"What did you say?" he asked.

The barman moved round to the front of the bar and squared up to Daniel. "That is no way to treat a lady," he told him.

Before he could say anything else, Daniel punched him squarely in the face. Voices were heard gasping all around them. The barman threw his hands up to his face to stop the blood pouring down from his nose while his colleagues rushed round looking for ice and towels. Patsy and Rose looked at their father in horror as they ran into the marquee and witnessed the whole incident. Rose burst into tears and ran back into the house while Patsy clung on to her mum.

Riley stared at her husband in disbelief and shock. Daniel walked away and headed back to the house while Riley ran after him with Patsy following behind, clinging onto the back of her dress. She saw Kate and called her over. "Kate, take Patsy, please."

Kate nodded quickly and picked her niece up. "Come on, darling, let's go get you a nice drink," she said.

Riley ran into the house to find Daniel. She saw him go into the study and followed him in, slamming the door behind them both.

"Right, do you want to tell me what the hell is going on?" she shouted.

He swung round, so they were both face to face. "You, two-timing bitch!" he spat the words out at her as he looked into her eyes.

Riley was speechless as it slowly dawned on her. After what seemed like an eternity, she managed to whisper, "You know!"

"How could you do it?" he whispered.

Tears of shame poured out of Riley. She didn't want to lose the man standing in front of her; the man she loved most in the whole world. "I didn't want it to happen; I promise! I love you so much Daniel. You are my everything," she said, shaking.

"It's over!" he told her.

Riley started to panic. "What do you mean?" she cried.

"I mean it's over Riley. You and me; we are finished!" he said angrily.

She didn't know what to say or do next. Her whole world had just crumbled. She knew there was no point trying to reason with him; one thing she knew about her husband was that once he had made up his mind, there was no way to change it. She suddenly felt hot and claustrophobic; she had to get out of there quickly.

Riley rushed back to the marquee to retrieve her bag from the bar. Patsy saw her and cried out to her mother. "It's okay baby; we're going home now. Where's Rose?" Riley asked, wiping away the smudged mascara from under her eyes.

"She's upstairs asleep in Mum and Dad's room," Kate told her, handing her a tissue from her bag.

"Thanks, Kate. Can you look after Rose, I need to get out of here," Riley said, finding it hard to breathe.

"Are you okay?" her sister-in-law asked her, confused and concerned.

"I think I'm having a panic attack; I need to go," Riley said, carrying Patsy up into her arms.

"Hang on. How are you getting home?" Kate called out as Riley ran out of the door.

Riley placed Patsy into the passenger side of the buggy and then drove them both to the car park. "Hold on tight baby," Riley told her daughter, as she tried to get her breath. Being in the fresh air was making her feel slightly better.

When they got to the car park, Daniel was already there, waiting for a taxi. Riley saw him and quickly grappled around in her bag for the car keys. She needed to get away fast, as she didn't want another scene with her husband. Daniel ran over to her. "Hey, what are you doing?" he shouted out to her.

Riley managed to unlock the doors and fumbled with the seat belt of the car seat as she tried to strap Patsy in. Once she had clipped her in, she ran round to the driver's side and leapt in, but as she started up the engine, Daniel jumped in beside her. "What the hell are you doing? You are way over the limit," he bellowed at her.

The wheels on the car spun as Riley accelerated out of the car park, hysterically shouting, "Leave me alone, Daniel."

"Just stop the car now, Riley! I haven't had as much to drink as you; let me drive," he wailed. The next thing she knew, Daniel was leaning over her, grabbing the steering wheel as Patsy was screaming and crying in the back of the car.

Chapter 62
Two Weeks Later

The crunching sound of metal grating on metal, a pair of terrified eyes looking inside the car from the jagged windscreen, a little shoeless leg sticking up from behind the head rest and a man lying beside a tree; then a long time of complete darkness and deafening silence. That is the image that swirled around Riley's head and forced her deep brown eyes to spring open. She didn't know where she was, but she felt strangely calm. All she could hear was her own breathing. She felt the comforting rhythm of her chest moving up and down, but she couldn't feel the rest of her body.

Was she dead? A face hovered above her. It was a face she knew so well. Her heart started racing, and she was consumed with a sense of relief. She tried to talk, but her lips wouldn't move. In her mind, she was saying, *Daddy. Have you come to get me?*

The familiar smile on his big round face made Riley want to burst with joy. He was, smiling at her lovingly, then slowly his face began to fade, and Riley held her breath. *No! No! No! Don't go,* she was pleading in her mind, hoping he could see it in her eyes, as the sounds refused to come out of her mouth. It was a similar experience to the one she had when her dad died, and she saw him at the end of her bed.

"It's not time, Riley," he told her, shaking his head.

"Please!" she screamed with all her might, but she still couldn't move.

"Riley," a voice said. "Riley!" Her dad was gone but in his place appeared a woman she had never seen before.

Riley became afraid and tried to move her arms, but they felt like they were tied up. "Help!" she screamed, but only a tiny whimper trickled out.

"It's okay. Don't try to talk. You're in the hospital," said a woman in a blue and white uniform.

Patsy was sitting upright in her bed, laughing at SpongeBob SquarePants on the TV in her room. Her body still hurt and her leg was heavy in the plaster cast that held it firmly in place, but Aunty Blair said she was being a very brave girl. She had just got her appetite back and started to eat again and was happily demolishing a bowl of ice cream. "Can I get you some more?" asked Blair, who had been sat beside her day and night since the accident.

"Yes, please, Aunty Blair," said Patsy. Blair kissed the little girl on her forehead and went to get some more ice cream from the kitchen.

Daniel was walking up and down the stairs of the hospital balancing carefully on each step with the help of his crutches. "That was good, Daniel," said the physiotherapist.

"You've come on really well. I'm happy to let the doctors discharge you," he said, ticking a box on a sheet of paper on his clipboard.

"Thanks, Ben," Daniel said, happily. He was looking forward to going home to be with Rose but worried about leaving Patsy; thank goodness Blair had been there to help out. Daniel didn't know how he would have coped without her. Eden was going to fly back from New Zealand, where she had been working, but there was a delay at the passport office, so she hadn't been able to get there after the accident, but Blair had insisted on taking time off work to help him.

Daniel was worried about Riley; she hadn't regained consciousness yet and had suffered a severe head injury as she hadn't been wearing her seatbelt. He felt guilty for causing the row that night that led to the accident and would do anything to turn back time, if only he could. If anything happened to Riley, he would never forgive himself. He remembered the car spinning then turning over after hitting a tree, and he had been thrown through the window onto the grass.

Patsy was at the back of the car, trapped in her car seat and screaming. The lady police officer at the scene held her hand and calmed her down while she was cut free. Riley had been falling in and out of consciousness but had been breathalysed before falling into a coma. Daniel had managed to crawl over to her, even though he had been in excruciating pain before he too, fell unconscious.

Gordon's driver had arrived at the hospital to collect Alphonso. He had been dressed and ready to go home since first thing that morning, even though the doctors said he would need to wait for his medication to come up from the pharmacy. The impact of the car hitting him had damaged his pelvis and femur causing a problem with his hip. He had been operated on as soon as he had been brought in by the ambulance and was recovering well. It would take him a while to be able to drive again or do anything strenuous, so he would need to rest at home for a few weeks.

Carmelita carried his bag for him and held his arm tightly, guiding him carefully to the lift. They saw Daniel coming down the stairs. Carmelita looked down at the ground and avoided eye contact with him; she was still furious and deeply upset that Riley had been driving while over the limit and running Alphonso over, as well as nearly killing herself, her husband and her little daughter. The lift doors opened and the couple stepped inside.

Alphonso acknowledged Daniel with a nod but didn't say anything. He couldn't remember much about that night and hadn't seen the car coming towards him until it was too late. He hadn't known that Daniel and his family were in the car; it all happened so fast. "Mr Fairgate?" a doctor called out. "Your wife has regained consciousness."

Daniel breathed a sigh of relief and made his way along the corridor towards her room.

When Daniel got to Riley's room, Blair was already there holding her hand. Riley wasn't able to sit up as yet and had tubes coming out all over her body. He hobbled over to her and cautiously held the tips of her fingers which were sticking out from under her cast. They were freezing cold, and Riley didn't seem to be able to feel his touch. She wasn't able to turn her head around but moved her eyes towards him. As their eyes met, they both began to cry.

Blair took that as her cue to leave the room. "I'll go and check on Patsy," she said.

Riley opened her mouth, and the words came out as a whisper. "I'm so sorry." She closed her eyes as the guilt became too overwhelming.

"Shhh," Daniel whispered back, stroking her hair. "I need you to just get better now, darling," he told her.

Riley turned her head away. She would never forgive herself. She had nearly killed them. How could she ever live with herself?

Chapter 63
One Month Later

Riley sombrely walked across the car park and carefully negotiated the low position of the car seat as she got into Daniel's car. He followed behind with her bags and was going to help her in, but she had managed by herself. The apprehension she felt was stifling, but she put on a brave face; she didn't want to cause Daniel any more stress. It was a terrifying feeling leaving the safety of her hospital room and being thrust back into reality. Not only would she have to become acclimatised to life again but would also have to face up to the impact of what she had done.

While in hospital, she could just live in a little bubble of doctors' visits, caring nurses and physio sessions. Now, she was vulnerable and felt like she was blindly feeling her way into unknown territory. She still hadn't completely recovered physically and neither had her daughter. She dreaded to think about the emotional damage she had caused everyone too. She was also probably facing a criminal charge as she had been breathalysed and found to be four times over the limit.

And then there was poor Alphonso. Riley would normally have had a full blown panic attack, but she was dosed up with strong medication to prevent her having a complete meltdown.

Daniel pulled into the drive and Rose burst out of the front door and ran towards the car. Riley gasped and slammed her foot down on the floor, where the brake would have been if she were in the driver's seat. Daniel automatically put his hand across her body to protect her, as the memories flooded back into his head too. They both sighed with relief as they realised the car was stationary in the driveway.

Daniel put his head in his hands rubbed his face a couple of times as if he was waking himself up from a terrible nightmare. "Being in the car is just something we'll have to get used to," he reassured his wife. Riley nodded but didn't say anything and then opened the door and bent down to hug her daughter tightly.

Patsy was sitting on the sofa with Dudley curled up, snoring in her lap. "Mummy," she called out to Riley.

Riley burst into tears when she saw her little girl. "You've lost weight baby. Have you not been eating properly?"

Blair, who was also in the room, walked over to Riley and said, "Of course, she has. She had a McDonalds yesterday, didn't you, honey, as a special treat?"

Riley remembered what a terrible cook Blair was. "Thanks for looking after them all, Blair," she said, gratefully.

"Oh, it's been no problem at all, darling," Blair said.

"But I'm here now," came a voice from the kitchen. Eden came into the lounge, wiping her hands on a tea towel she was carrying. "I am here to look after all of you for as long as you need me," she told her sister.

Riley burst into tears again. "I'm so glad to see you Eden," she said, throwing her arms around her sister. "I've made a fish pie and lots of fresh vegetables to go with it," Eden added.

Blair's cheeks burned. What about her? She had been there for weeks, in and out of hospital, cooking and cleaning, and now, Eden shows up and steals her thunder.

Daniel caught a glimpse of Blair's hurt expression and flashed her an apologetic smile. "Thanks so much for all your help, Blair. I really couldn't have managed without you," he said, walking over to her and planting a quick kiss on her cheek.

Blair felt her heart leap. As long as Daniel was happy, that was all that mattered. "You need to get some rest Daniel; you look tired," Blair said gently, rubbing his arm.

Riley let go of her sister and turned towards her friend; not noticing the way Blair was gazing at her husband. "Sorry, Blair, I sound so ungrateful. I can't thank you enough." she said, feeling yet another pang of guilt wash over her. Could she get anything right these days? Blair forced her lips into a smile, but her eyes told a very different story.

Chapter 64

A single drop of hot sweet tea landed on the cream shaggy rug as the tea cup shook in Riley's trembling hand. Sitting on her padded dressing table stool, she stared as the drop disappeared into the long, thick yarn, then she moved her feet slowly, back and forth, so she could feel the warmth and texture of each layer between her toes. It's amazing how much we take for granted, she thought to herself.

Picking up the pink lip liner, she carefully outlined her already perfect lips. She then put the angled square tip of her new Charlotte Tilbury lipstick, which her sister had bought her, onto her top lip and applied it smoothly around her mouth and then rubbed both top and bottom lip together. Eden had insisted she use the matt nude-pink shade, as it was subtle, flattering and classy, apparently.

"Are you ready, babe?" Daniel asked, as he poked his head round the bedroom door.

Riley took her blazer off the wooden hanger and put it on cautiously so as not to mess up her sleek, straightened hair. She picked up her handbag and looked around the room, taking in every single detail. She then followed Daniel down the stairs. At the bottom of the stairs was a case packed with all her 'essentials'.

Daniel stared at it for a few seconds and then tried to compose himself so that his wife couldn't see the terror in his eyes. He took a deep breath and picked the case up and walked outside with it. Riley didn't take her eyes off it as he placed it into the car boot, diligently, as if it was a wired-up explosive. They both knew that if that case was unpacked later that day, it would mean that Riley would also be unpacking the trauma of the past few weeks, alone in a prison cell.

The car journey seemed never-ending. Riley couldn't stop the dark thoughts from pouncing as her brain went into overdrive. Sadness floated between her and Daniel. She desperately wanted to reach out and touch him, but she kept her hands firmly in her lap; knowing that if she made any kind of contact with him, they would both fall to pieces.

Daniel kept his eyes fixed on the road in front of him, glancing in the rear-view mirror every now and then, with the words of the last song he had heard that morning on the radio, swirling round and round in his head. He had to just focus on the song and not think about anything else while he drove. He couldn't afford to think about what might be, or he would crumble, and he needed to be strong for Riley.

"Do you think we should go?" Gordon asked his wife.

Diana looked at him blankly. "Are you mad?" she asked, as if her husband had just asked her if they should go to the moon.

"Well, I'm just thinking about Daniel; maybe he could do with our support," he added.

Gordon didn't dare say he would like to go to support Riley as well, as he knew the response he would be fired with would be abusive.

"Joe and Jerry will be there for him," Diana said curtly, as she carried on arranging the blush pink peonies in the Waterford crystal vase on the table in front of her.

Gordon shook his head and walked away; there was no reasoning with his wife at times. He thought of Madeleine and the answer she would have given him. He was sure it would be the complete opposite of Diana's.

"Have you forgotten what she did to Alphonso?" Diana called out after him. Gordon stopped in his tracks and was going to answer her but thought better of it and carried on walking. Alphonso suffered a stroke after the accident. The doctors didn't know if it was the accident that had brought on the stroke or if it would have happened regardless, but in Diana's eyes, it was all Riley's fault.

The jury slowly filed back into the court room. It had been a long day, but the deliberation didn't take long, and they had come to a unanimous decision. Siobhan, Jeff, Daniel, Joe, Jerry, Eden and Blair sat in the front row of the gallery, while the Mulligan family took up the next four rows behind them. The Judge came into the room, and Riley stood up in the dock. She absentmindedly wiped the palms of her sweaty hands on her skirt. She nervously glanced at the prison officer seated beside her.

Lots of words were being spoken, but her brain had switched off. It was only when she heard the words, "...causing serious injury by dangerous driving. I am sentencing you to 30 months in prison," that her legs gave way, and she fell to the floor while shocked screams coming from her aunts could be heard echoing around the court room.

Chapter 65
2015
One Year Later

A small group of mourners were gathered around the burial site watching the pallbearers lowering the straps holding the coffin, gently into the grave. A small, muffled weeping sound could be heard from Carmelita, as she held her white, lace handkerchief to her mouth. Gordon put a comforting arm around her shoulders.

Diana lifted her large, Jackie Onassis style, sunglasses up slightly and dabbed her eyes. Padre Roberto was taking forever to wrap up the funeral and Diana desperately needed a gin and tonic. She was shivering from the cold, even though her Armani coat was made from double-cashmere Casentino wool, but she had been standing out there for nearly an hour; even a woolly mammoth would have died of hypothermia by now.

As soon as the Padre stopped to take a breath, Diana stepped forward. "Thank you so much, Padre. That was so beautiful; I'm sure our dear Alphonso will be looking down and smiling. Please could I invite you to come back to the house for refreshments?" she asked.

The man looked at her with his mouth still open in mid-sentence. "Yes, yes. Thank you," he stuttered as he closed his bible.

"Great! Follow me everyone," Diana said, clapping her hands as if she were talking to a group of children on a school outing.

Gordon obediently followed behind.

Daniel caught up with Carmelita and put his arms around her. "Are you okay?" he asked, quietly.

She looked up at him; her eyes red and swollen from crying and said, "I will never be okay Daniel. Never!"

Daniel knew Carmelita held him responsible, as Riley was his wife. He had apologised so many times and insisted on paying for the funeral and flying Padre Roberto over from Vitoria in Spain. He was a childhood friend of Alphonso's, as well as being the parish priest in the couple's family home town. Carmelita walked quickly ahead of Daniel; she didn't want to engage in a conversation with him. Blair saw the crestfallen look on his face and was quickly by his side, holding his hand. "It's okay darling; she'll come round eventually," she said.

Daniel made his excuses and left the wake early, as he knew he wasn't really welcome. "I'll drop you off at home to be with the girls. I've just got a bit of business to do, and then I'll be home for dinner," Daniel told Blair.

"Of course," she said, getting into the car. Blair didn't try to speak to Daniel on the drive home; she knew he needed time to process the day, he had been fond of Alphonso and his death had hit him hard.

"Thanks for coming with me today," he said. Blair smiled sweetly.

"You don't have to thank me, my love. I'm always here for you and the girls," she said, reaching over and squeezing his knee gently.

Siobhan was lighting her white sage incense sticks when she heard a knock at the door. She put the bamboo sticks down and checked her hair quickly in the hallway mirror before answering it. She was surprised to see Daniel on the doorstep. "Can I come in," he asked.

Siobhan looked concerned; Daniel never arrived at her house unannounced. "Sure. What's up?" she asked him.

"It was Alphonso's funeral today," he said, taking his tie off and undoing the top button of his shirt. Daniel knew Jeff was away, and even though he would not usually see Siobhan without prior arrangement, he really needed to see her today. She was the only person who could ease the burden that weighed heavily on his mind. "I'm sorry to just turn up," he apologised.

"No problem. Was it awful?" she asked pouring him a brandy.

"Carmelita hates me," he said with a sigh.

"Well, it wasn't you who was driving Daniel; you shouldn't feel guilty. There was nothing you could've done and anyway, it wasn't the crash that killed him. He might have got the stroke anyway, and he just never recovered from it. It is very sad, but it is not your fault!" she said, sitting down beside him.

The familiar smell of her perfume reminded Daniel of the last time they were together, and he turned to face her and pulled her towards him. He kissed her hard on the lips, and she lifted her arms up and ran her fingers through his thick, silver-flecked brown hair. Daniel usually kept his hair short and neat these days, but Siobhan loved this longer look on him; it made him look even sexier, if that was at all possible.

After a few seconds, she pulled his head down towards her neck, where he kissed her slowly from her chin down towards the top of her breast. Siobhan undid her blouse, and Daniel moved his head further down. He undid her bra strap as she shuffled herself further down the sofa and hurriedly undid the button and zip of his trousers. She wanted him so badly that she didn't even bother to take her clothes off. She moved her knickers to one side and guided him into her. Weeks of built up tension and stress came hurtling to the surface as Daniel fucked her hard and groaned loudly.

"Fuck!" Siobhan cried out in ecstasy as a warm sensation spread throughout her body. Daniel stayed on top of her for a while, while he caught his breath, and then lifted himself off slowly and sighed as they both lay in each other's arms in a tangle of clothes. Daniel felt a huge surge of relief, and Siobhan felt relaxed and happier than she had in a long time. Sex with Daniel was always amazing.

Eden sat across the table from Riley. "You look pale and skinny," Eden told her sister.

"I look exactly the same as I did last week," Riley replied. "I saw my probation officer yesterday."

"And what did she say?" asked Eden.

"That things are looking promising," said Riley. She knew the news would please her sister, but she didn't want to talk about it any further and jinx it, so she changed the subject. "How are my babies?" Riley asked.

"Fine!" Eden said, bluntly.

Riley rolled her eyes. "She must be doing a good job then," Riley added.

"She's a conniving, manipulative bitch, Riley," Eden said, angrily.

"I know, Eden, but she's looking after them and that is the main thing."

"I could look after them better!" insisted Eden.

"Yes, but you wouldn't want to shag Daniel, would you?" asked Riley.

"Yuk! No!" said Eden, pulling a face.

"Well then!" Riley said, lifting her hands up in defeat. Riley had been horrified when she first heard that Blair and Daniel had become an item, and she had moved in with him. Talk about jumping in someone's grave before they were even cold! So, that had been Blair's plan all along! To tell Daniel about that night with Ricky, knowing full well Daniel would never forgive her, leaving the door wide open for Blair to pounce and steal her husband away. Riley hated Blair with a vengeance, and it took every bit of strength of character to turn the other cheek and think about her daughters' welfare. She knew Blair would be a good stand-in mother so, for now, that was a good thing.

Blair was reading the instructions on the back of the macaroni cheese ready meal. Patsy had told her that she loved macaroni cheese after having it at her friend Sophie's house so Blair had got up early and gone to the supermarket and bought them all macaroni cheese for dinner before getting ready to go to the funeral. She picked up some meatballs to go with it for her and Daniel. It wasn't the home-made stuff that Riley cooked, but it was from Marks & Spencer so probably tasted just as good anyway.

Blair knew Riley was a good cook, and she couldn't compete with her, but in every other way, she would be the perfect wife and mother, and she was always careful not to drink any alcohol, whatsoever, in front of the girls. Their mother had failed miserably in that department, but Blair would be a shining example of what a mother should be like. It was also a way of sticking two fingers up at her own shambolic mother.

Daniel and the girls meant more to her than her career or anything else in the world. Riley, clearly, didn't deserve them, or she would have been a better wife and mother and not taken them all for granted. As far as Blair was concerned, as soon as she could convince Daniel to divorce Riley, her and Daniel would fight for custody, and they would all live happily ever after.

Chapter 66

Siobhan was scrolling down the sheets of skincare products with her finger, checking the shelves in front of her, making sure that everything on the list was on display, when she felt a pair of hands around her waist which caused her to jump and drop the list she was holding. "Sorry, darling; I didn't mean to scare you," Jeff said, bending down to retrieve the papers.

Siobhan laughed and pretended to slap him round the face. "What do you want?" she asked, playfully.

"To take you to lunch," Jeff said.

"I can't today I'm afraid; I've got Diana Fairgate coming in for a De Luxe Facial," Siobhan said, in her poshest voice.

"Besides, I think I ate something dodgy the other day because I haven't felt great since," she said.

"What do you mean?" Jeff asked, looking worried.

"Nothing to worry about I'm sure, but I seem to have lost my appetite," she said.

"Okay, well if you don't start feeling better tomorrow, perhaps make an appointment to see the doctor."

"Yes, I will. Don't worry. Now, go and leave me in peace," Siobhan said, pushing him towards the door.

The skip outside the house was nearly full. Blair dragged the heavy duty garden sack along the hallway. Blair was purging the house of all traces of Riley. She had bagged up all her clothes and dumped them on Eden's doorstep for her to deal with. Daniel had given her permission to redecorate the house, so she had booked holiday leave she was owed from work and got an interior designer in to help.

Riley's taste was rustic and traditional with lots of wood and worn-looking sofas and armchairs. The kitchen had no particular design features but was a mishmash of odd cutlery, mugs with the children's photos on and lots of clutter everywhere. The house was going to be transformed into an on-trend, timeless but refined home; the house of Blair's dreams.

Daniel stood outside watching the furniture Riley had chosen been chucked away, heartlessly, into the skip along with all their happy memories too. Daniel was trying hard to hold back the tears. He knew this was the right thing to do. Riley would never be able to come back and resume the life she had left behind. She hadn't even let Daniel go and visit her in prison.

Blair had been a huge support to him though. She had waded in without a second thought to help him with the girls; he couldn't be more grateful to her. They had also grown close over the past year. Daniel had missed Riley so much, but Blair was filling the gap she had left. He would never love Blair the way he loved Riley, but she was certainly helping to take the pain away.

Blair shook her head in disgust as she picked up the thick, grey, moth-eaten blanket and headed out to the skip. Dudley trotted after her, voicing his objection with a disgruntled whine. "Sorry, boy, but this has to go! You've got a nice new blanket in your new dog bed," she told him. "Hello, darling," she said as she spotted Daniel.

"Dudley has never slept in a dog bed in his life. He's always slept on his special chair," Daniel said, looking sympathetically at his dog who was looking up at him doe-eyed.

"It'll be a new experience for him then won't it?" Blair said as she lovingly wrapped her arms around Daniel's waist.

Daniel was glad the girls weren't there to see their mother's things being tossed away. He had insisted on sorting through Riley's personal belongings himself so that Blair could give them to Eden; it would have been disrespectful to Riley to let Blair do it, even though they had been best friends. The whole idea of Blair moving in still didn't sit comfortably with Daniel, but he just wanted an easy life, and if it made Blair happy, then it was fine with him.

"Blair is moving in with you?" Siobhan asked Daniel on the phone.

Daniel sighed. He knew she would find out, but he didn't anticipate it would happen this quickly. "News travels fast!" he answered.

"Your mother told me," Siobhan said, frostily.

"I bet she couldn't wait to spread the gossip," he said.

"Well, you know what she's like and how much she hates, Riley," Siobhan continued.

"It's understandable I suppose after what happened to Alphonso," Daniel said.

"Oh for fuck's sake, Daniel. Riley is still your wife. Have you even told her?"

"She probably knows by now," he said, feeling guilty. He knew he should have been the one to tell her, but Blair had told Eden when she dropped Riley's belongings over to her.

"She's what?" Riley had screamed.

"Keep the noise down," grunted one of the prison guards.

"That bitch has taken over your house and your family!" Eden hissed, angrily.

Riley closed her eyes and counted to ten in her head. "Okay. It's fine. It's just a house. She will never be their mother," she said.

"How can you be so calm?" Eden asked her. Riley knew if she got angry the panic attacks would start again.

"Because, Eden, what the hell am I supposed to do about it? I can't actually go round there and confront her, can I. So what do you want me to do? Let it stew in my head 24/7 while I'm locked up in here? Do you know what that could do to me?"

Eden felt sorry for burdening her sister with that news. She was right; what could she do, apart from worry about it. "I'm sorry, Riley. I'm just so angry. But don't you worry. Those girls won't forget their mother no matter who is living in that house; I won't let them. That house is half yours remember," Eden had said, gripping Riley's hand tightly across the table.

The sterling Silver Bomber plane cufflink shone as it lay on the glass coffee table. Jeff had been staring at it for fifteen minutes. He had found it poking out from the side of the sofa. He knew exactly who it belonged to. He and Siobhan had bought the cufflinks for Daniel a few years ago for his 40th birthday. He remembered the day well.

They had been invited to travel with Daniel and Riley to St Topez in one of Daniel's planes. The two couples had spent a fabulous weekend together in the sun-drenched resort drinking champagne on a luxury yacht and going for romantic walks in the old town below the citadel. Jeff remembered thinking how stunningly beautiful Riley was, but he would never have made a move on her as he loved his wife and took his marriage vows seriously, but here he was sitting in the dark, in total shock from the realisation that his wife was at it again but this time with the husband of one of her best friends.

Chapter 67

Riley took off her apron and walked out of the kitchen, wiping the perspiration from her forehead. She had served up the lunches with her roommate, Sue, and helped clear up afterwards, but her mind had been wandering all day, and she had accidentally burnt her hand on a tray of curry as she was serving it up to the inmates. She desperately wanted to speak to her girls, but Blair had taken charge at home and didn't accept any of Riley's calls, so she had resorted to writing to them instead. She looked forward to their handmade cards and drawings and cried each time she saw their handwriting on the envelopes.

She picked up the phone and dialled Daniel's number. "Daniel, it's me," Riley said. Her heart was thumping. It was the first time she had spoken to her husband since she had been incarcerated.

There was a silent pause, and then a voice replied, tentatively, "Hello, Riley." Daniel was caught off guard, and the sound of his wife's voice had overwhelmed him.

"Daniel," Riley whispered again, closing her eyes. She wanted to tell him she loved him and missed him.

Daniel felt tears spring to his eyes, which he let fall down his cheeks as he thought of her standing there with her huge brown eyes and cute turned up nose. He could hear her breathing. In that precious moment, they felt like two lost souls calling out to each other.

"Hurry up!" came a voice from behind Riley.

Suddenly, conscious of the queue starting to form behind her, Riley quickly cleared her throat. "Can I speak to the girls tomorrow?" she asked.

Daniel wiped his hand across his wet face. "Erm actually, Blair doesn't think it's a good idea," he said.

Riley felt the flame being ignited in her belly at the mention of Blair's name. "Well, I don't actually give a fuck what Blair thinks. They're my children, Daniel," she said, indignantly.

"Actually, they are *our* children Riley, and they are in my care at the moment, so they are my responsibility," he said, hating himself for causing her so much pain. He knew how much it would mean to her to speak to Patsy and Rose.

"So you make the decision then Daniel. Why are you letting her dictate? What has happened to you? Are you a man or a mouse?" she said, angrily.

Daniel knew she was right, but he couldn't face a row with Blair. Since Riley had been in prison, he felt like a broken man, struggling to cope without her. Blair had helped put the pieces back together and the girls loved her. May be she was right anyway; speaking to Riley might upset the children too much.

Riley knew she was getting nowhere with Daniel, so she hung up on him and walked back to her cell. She felt defeated, deflated and completely exhausted. "Riley, the probation officer wants to see you," the warden called out, as she walked past her.

Siobhan splashed cold water on her face in an attempt to liven herself up. She had been putting in a lot more hours at the spa as the run up to Christmas was always busy, and she hated turning clients away. "You are working too much, darling," Jeff said, as he brushed his teeth at the sink beside hers.

She dried her face and hugged him. "I know, but you know I love it," she said.

"We haven't spent much time together," Jeff said, trying not to sound like a whining child. "How about dinner tonight? You pick the restaurant," he said.

"Okay," Siobhan replied, trying to sound enthusiastic. She had lost her appetite recently and wasn't sure why. It was probably something to do with the menopause, she thought, and she made a mental note to call the herbalist when she got into work.

Jeff had noticed she had lost a bit of weight and wondered if she had done it on purpose to be more alluring for Daniel. The thought of the two of them together had been eating away at him. His imagination had been running riot since he had discovered the cufflink. When he was in the bathroom, he imagined them having sex in the shower. If he went into the kitchen, he envisaged Siobhan lying across the table, half naked with Daniel on top of her. He was driving himself mad, and he decided he wouldn't put up with it any longer.

"Darling, are you okay?" Siobhan asked, as she watched him staring at the sink as it was filling up with water from the running tap.

"Oh. Yes. Yes, I'm fine," he said, closing the tap and placing the electric toothbrush on the side. "You book the restaurant and text me," Jeff told her. He kissed her lightly on the cheek and walked out of the bathroom. As he walked into the bedroom to get dressed, his phone buzzed and vibrated on the crumpled silk sheet on the bed. He picked it up quickly and typed in the password code and a message flashed up; *job done!* He smiled to himself and began to whistle happily as he slipped on his favourite, crisp white shirt.

Chapter 68

Selena burst through the door of the conference room. "Sorry, all. Bloody traffic again," she said, agitated.

Blair noticed she was starting to look older. The Botox clearly wasn't working, and her grey roots were stubbornly glistening through her russet tinted locks. It must be the stress of the job, she thought. It served her right; that's what happens when you sleep your way to the top. Blair knew all along that the position should have gone to her years ago, not Selena. She had the talent and the stoicism to run that magazine with her eyes shut.

Finally, Selena slumped down in the chair at the head of the table and spread her folders out in front of her. "Why was the traffic so bad today?" Blair asked Selena, knowing full well that rush hour traffic would be over by now.

"Oh, there was a nasty accident on the A414 and the road was closed in both directions," she continued, "The carcass of a car was upside down across one of the lanes. It looked like it had been in some sort of explosion or something. I heard on the news it had been an Aston Martin."

Blair looked up from the magazine copy in front of her. "What colour?" she asked.

"Racing green, I think they said," Selena replied.

Blair leapt up from her chair and ran out of the room. Her hands were trembling as she sent the papers on her desk flying in all directions as she looked for her phone. She spotted it under her glasses case and desperately searched for Daniel's number. To her relief, he picked up straight away. "Hi there," he said, cheerfully.

Blair leant over her desk and sighed with relief.

"Blair? Are you there?" he asked.

"Yes. Sorry, love. I just heard there was a car accident and for one horrible minute I thought you were involved," she said, still shaking. "It must have been another green Aston Martin then," she said. Daniel froze!

"Where was it?" he asked.

"On the 414," Blair answered.

"What's wrong?" It was Daniel's turn to tremble as he answered. "Joe borrowed my car!"

Jeff raced into the country club car park and pulled into his parking space. Today was going to be a good day; he could feel it in his bones. As he got out of the car, he was surprised to see Siobhan walking towards him. "Everything okay? Did you book the restaurant?" he asked.

"Diana Fairgate has just rushed home. She got a call saying her son had been involved in a horrific accident," said Siobhan.

"Is Daniel okay?" asked Jeff.

"No, it was his brother, Joe. Apparently, he had borrowed Daniel's car. I think he might be dead," she said.

Jeff stood on the tarmac, rooted to the spot.

"I've got to go, Jeff; I've got a client waiting," Siobhan said and hurried off.

Jeff took his phone out of his pocket and quickly typed, *What the hell happened? You got the wrong man you idiot!*

Chapter 69

Diana sat holding her eldest son's hand with tears of relief rolling down her cheeks. By some miracle, Joe had escaped the car explosion with minor injuries. One of the windows had blown out just as the fire started, and he managed to drag himself out of it and across the grass verge which led into a field, just before the eruption.

Jerry burst through the door of the hospital. Worry was etched across his handsome, caramel coloured face, and he looked to Diana for reassurance.

"It's okay, he is going to be fine," she said wearily, getting up to hug the helpless looking man in front of her.

"Thank god!" he said. "How did this happen?" he asked.

"No one knows yet. It might be some electrical fault, but the police are investigating," Diana told him.

Daniel was the next to enter the room. Joe tried to open his eyes; one was too swollen and bruised, and he grimaced with pain. Jerry immediately bent down and hugged him gently. "I'm so sorry, Joe," Daniel said. "I just don't understand what could have happened."

"Well, maybe someone doesn't like you very much, Dan," Joe joked. A lightbulb went off in Daniel's head. Could this be something to do with Darren Dooley? After the whole drugs fiasco, Darren had revealed his source to the police and shortly afterwards ended up at the bottom of a canal.

Riley's hands shook as she dialled the number on the phone. Eden picked up almost straight away. "Well?" she shouted down the phone.

Riley burst into tears. "I've been granted parole," she sobbed. "I'm coming home, sis."

Chapter 70
2016

Terence Patrick Mulligan. Founder of Mulligan's Racing Kennels. Champion Trainer of the Year, 1981. GBGB Greyhound of the Year Award Winner 2012—GWA Services to Greyhound Racing.

Riley ran her fingers along the words on the brass plaque on the wall outside the office door. She smiled and whispered, "I'm back, Dad!"

Prison life had left a nasty taste in her mouth that she would never be able to forget, but her core values and principles would always remain the same. She was still Riley Mulligan at heart.

The staff turned to look at the woman who opened the door and walked in. After a few seconds of stunned silence, applause broke out and everyone leapt out of their seats to hug Riley. "Hey, boss! So great to see you," cried Shirley, as she squeezed her tightly.

"You too, Aunty Shirl. But seriously, I can't breathe," said Riley, as she was being squeezed to death.

The woman laughed and undid her grip on her niece. "You look so thin, darling. We need to feed you up," she told her.

Riley rolled her eyes at her and walked over to greet her workmates and catch up with events that had happened at work and in their lives. She then made her way out into the yard and felt her heart start to pound in her chest. This was the moment she had been waiting for, for so long. As she approached the kennels, the excited barking started; it was the most beautiful noise in the world. Before she got to the dogs, she went to check on the kennel assistants who were preparing breakfast for the dogs. The pups would have already had theirs by now and would be out in the paddock. Riley quietly walked up behind one of the kennel assistants, Tessa, and whispered, "Boo!"

"Oh my god, Riley!" she screamed and burst into tears. After a few minutes of tears and hugs, and finally, laughter, Tessa asked, "Does this mean you're back?"

"Of course, I'm back! Did you think I could really stay away?"

"Let's go see the dogs," she said, leading the way to the kennels.

Riley thought her heart was going to burst when she saw him. He was sitting on his bed, lined with straw; his shiny bright eyes were looking straight at her. She could see his brindle coat glistening in the morning rays of sunshine that were seeping into his kennel. She was worried he might have forgotten her, but as she got closer, his tail started wagging furiously and his teeth started chattering; a common trait that greyhounds have when they get excited. Then the loud, familiar barking erupted. Riley opened the kennel door and collapsed onto the bed while her beloved Blazing Zippy leapt all over her, frantically licking her tears away.

When he had finally calmed down, Riley stroked him gently, savouring the touch of his soft fur. Blaze always made her feel calm. If only she had turned to him instead of the booze, how different her life would have been.

Most of the dogs were home bred. Mulligan's kennels had always bred and reared pups which had been a dream of Terry Mulligan's since he was a young boy. One particular litter of puppies had a pup that was very poorly and not expected to survive, but Riley knew from the look in his eyes that he was a fighter and with her help he grew stronger and fitter. She took care of him herself; cutting his nails, taking him out in the paddock separately, so he could become more confident, feeding him porridge and bananas; his favourite. She would wrap him up in a warm blanket each evening before she left and looked forward to seeing him each morning. Soon, he became one of a phenomenal team of dogs that Riley built up, and she named him Blazing Zippy.

It felt good sitting at her desk again. Riley opened one of the drawers and took out a purple plastic folder. She opened it and pulled out the old newspaper cutting. 'Sexy Greyhound Trainer, Riley Mulligan, Brings Glamour Back To The Tracks!' Riley had mixed emotions as she read through the article. That article had catapulted her career and brought her attention and recognition, which she welcomed and appreciated. It had also lead to a much deserved promotion for the writer; her best friend, Blair Matthews.

Chapter 71

Diana Fairgate lay on the sun lounger beside the swimming pool. Her short blonde hair was scraped back and held in place with a Liberty print knotted headband. Her pale skin was fully protected by a huge cream parasol, large floppy hat and Chanel sunglasses. She took a sip of her Margarita and grimaced. "Carmelita!" she called out.

"Yes, Mrs Fairgate?" answered the housekeeper through gritted teeth. Carmelita knew Diana was going to moan about her drink. Diana liked to moan about everything, but she paid well, or rather Gordon Fairgate paid well, so Carmelita never complained. She and Adolpho had been given a small, but comfortable house to live in, in the grounds of the sprawling country estate, which suited them both as they didn't have any children or commitments.

"Daniel!" shouted Diana, in surprise, as she saw her son walking through the patio doors out onto the sun-bleached balau wood deck.

"Hi, Mum," he said, bending down to kiss her cheek.

"Sit! Have a drink," she demanded. Daniel took his t-shirt off and lay down on the sun lounger beside her.

"Hello, Daniel," said Carmelita politely. "Would you like your usual?"

"Just a beer, thank you, Carmelita," Daniel told her.

Diana pulled her sunglasses down slightly and looked at her son solicitously. "You look tired, son. Has that woman been giving you trouble again?" Daniel rolled his eyes under his sunglasses, so she couldn't see. He knew she was talking about Riley. His mother had never been fond of Riley; she couldn't understand why a woman would want to work with dogs and be covered in fur and mud all day.

When Riley was put in prison, Diana was completely horrified and couldn't attend any women's lunches or speak to her friends, as she was so ashamed. It was she who had suggested that Blair encourage Daniel to file for divorce straight away and reminded him that he needed to think about his daughters' welfare.

When Daniel introduced her to Blair, Diana couldn't have been happier; now this is what a proper daughter-in-law should be like, she decided. It was okay for Blair to have a career, but her priority should always be Daniel and her granddaughters, and of course, Blair did not disappoint! She assured Diana that she only had Daniel's best interests at heart and would always be there for him.

Chapter 72

"James… James… Swim! Help! Someone Please…" shouted Daniel.

Blair stirred in her sleep. "Daniel?" she said, drowsily and reached over to comfort him.

Daniel's eyes shot open, and he gasped. It took him a few seconds to realise he had been having another nightmare.

"Are you okay, darling?" asked Blair, gently stroking his arm.

Daniel sat up and rubbed the perspiration off his forehead. "Yes. Just a dream. Sorry, go back to sleep," he said. If only he had looked after his brother better, he would still be here today. Daniel thought about his mother, Elizabeth. He could still remember the smell of her skin when she hugged him; she always smelled of Imperial Leather soap. She had never got over his brother's death and one morning Daniel had walked into her bedroom and found her laying in her bed, face down with her hand hanging down the side of the bed. Daniel ran over and touched her hand, but it was cold and stiff. He knew his mother was dead.

Daniel's thoughts raced back to the day it happened; 25 July 1976. The worst day of his life!

Their mother had made them both a packed lunch for the day and waved them off at the front door. "Have a good time and don't be late back for your tea," she shouted as they got on to their bicycles. "And don't forget to look after each other," she yelled, even louder as they pedalled away.

The boys were excited; it was the first day of the school holidays, and they had a whole summer of fun ahead of them. James followed Daniel. He would always happily let Daniel lead when it came to most things such as where they went, who they played with and even what they ate. The brothers were ten years old, but Daniel was older by five minutes and liked to remind his younger brother of this fact constantly. They weren't identical twins; James had fine, fair hair like their mother's, but Daniel's was dark and thick.

"Where are we going, Daniel?" called out James, as he pedalled hard to keep up with his brother.

"To the Welsh Harp," Daniel shouted back. Daniel knew their mother didn't like them going down there as it had strong undercurrents, and she had warned them never to swim in it.

The grass around the reservoir was deceiving as it merged with the water and people had been caught out as they thought they were walking on grass but ended up falling into the water. Daniel knew that a couple of older boys from the local secondary school were going to be down there building a raft, and he wanted to join in. James had cried when the older boys; Darren and Dean insisted that he and Daniel help them. He wasn't happy being there, but Daniel was adamant. James knew their mothers didn't like each other and his mother would have been furious if she found out they had been playing with them. She always described the boys' mother as 'the awful, loud woman from down the road'.

Daniel and James were given the task of finding all the sticks and fallen down branches nearby and bringing them back, so they could make the raft. Darren and Dean sat back on the grass and laughed as they watched the younger boys running up and down, while they smoked the cigarettes Darren had pinched from their mother's handbag.

The rest of the afternoon had always been a blur in Daniel's mind. He had only been able to remember bits and pieces but was unable to fit them together to complete the puzzle. He was taken to see a psychiatrist a few months after the accident, but they were unable to successfully decipher what had taken place. Daniel had pushed the experience into a deep dark place in his head and that is where it was lodged. He had flashbacks of him and James being on the raft and Darren and Dean laughing and messing around.

The next memory he had was of James stumbling backwards and falling into the water. His head bobbed up a couple of times, and then he was gone! Later that evening, police sirens had been going off, his mother was screaming, neighbours ran out of their houses and the press arrived with microphones and cameras. Daniel remembered that part in slow motion, and then the next thing he remembered was being led away by someone who lifted him into his car and drove him somewhere, but he couldn't recall where.

Chapter 73

Daniel pulled his trousers up over his muscular thighs while Siobhan admired him from her bed. He looked even more handsome after sex; his blue eyes became even brighter and the frown he often sported disappeared leaving him looking much calmer and happier. She loved the overgrown stubble on the sides of his face and chin making him look sexy and distinguished. She had never seen a more perfect looking man.

Siobhan sighed and dragged herself out of bed. She had to get back to work for a client who was due soon. She felt Daniel's eyes on her. "You've lost weight Von," he said; as he looked down to fasten his Gucci belt.

Siobhan nodded. "Yes, I've been rushing around recently, back and forth to Galway to visit my mother. She's poorly, and I'm not sure how long she's got left," she said sadly.

"Oh, I'm sorry to hear that," Daniel said walking over to hug her. Siobhan had found that all her clothes were starting to become loose, and she made a mental note to cook lasagne that night for the extra calories.

Riley struggled into the house laden with bags of new home accessories. Her daughters were going to be staying with her at weekends from now on, and she wanted the house to be perfect for them. The house, which once belonged to her dad, had been redecorated when Eden first moved in, but as she worked abroad a lot of the time, the house had slowly fallen into disrepair and looked tired and outdated. Riley had set about painting the walls and buying new furniture. It had given her a new lease of life, and she was ready and looking forward to her new chapter.

She would focus on her daughters and her work from now on, as that was her main priority. She would give anything to have Daniel back in her life, but she knew that was just a dream. Blair had muscled in on her husband, but she certainly wasn't going to have her daughters as well. The divorce papers were safely stored in a drawer in the kitchen, but she was in no hurry to sign them.

She put all the bags down and flicked the switch on the kettle. Riley then picked up her phone and typed out a message to her husband. *'Looking forward to having the girls tomorrow. Remember to bring Dudley too'*. She paused and then added, *'...feel free to stay for breakfast if you like'*.

The traffic had been heavy for the past hour and by the time Daniel reached the traffic lights for the last leg home, they turned red. "Fuck!" he shouted and leant back in his seat. His phone pinged, and he glanced down at the message. It was from Riley. He felt the familiar excited feeling in the pit of his stomach when he saw her name flash up on his phone, and he smiled to himself when he read that she had invited him over for breakfast the next day. The four of them together again; a perfect Saturday morning, thought Daniel as the light turned green, and he sped away.

Blair needed to finish editing an article she had been working on, so she picked Patsy and Rose up from school and took them back to the office with her. They had been sitting patiently on the sofa in her office, but boredom was now setting in. "Can we go home now," moaned Patsy.

Blair looked up from computer. "In a minute, darling. I just need to finish this before tomorrow morning. It's very important," Blair said.

"Why don't you both walk over to the vending machine and get some chocolate. Here, come over and get some money and ask Marilyn at the front desk to help you," she said, feeling frustrated and guilty at the same time. Blair was finding it difficult to cope with working and looking after the girls, but she didn't want Daniel to notice, so she worked hard to juggle everything with a smile on her face as well as keeping an eye on her dad who seemed to be developing dementia.

It was beginning to rain so the florist decided to pack up slightly early that day. As she started carrying the silver buckets into the shop, Jeff pulled up beside her. "Can I grab that bunch of red roses, Jane" he asked, holding out some cash for her.

"Sure," she said, grateful to be selling the last bouquet of roses.

"Keep the change," Jeff called out as he wound the window back up and pulled away.

Siobhan kicked off her shoes and sank into the sofa. She was exhausted and just wanted to sit and watch boring soaps on the TV with her feet up for a couple of hours and let her frazzled mind unwind. She really needed to slow down and take things easy. She heard Jeff's key in the door.

"Hello, darling," he called out, handing her the flowers.

"Thank you; they're beautiful honey," she said.

"Are you okay? You look pale," he told her.

"I'm fine; just a bit tired," she said.

"I'll run you a bath and pour you a glass of wine. You just stay there," he said. Jeff frowned as he walked out of the room. It wasn't like his wife to be so tired; she was usually bouncing with energy. He would have to keep a close eye on her, he decided.

"Alright girls, I'm finished. Let's go home," Blair called out as she gathered her papers and put them into her briefcase. She stopped and looked out of her office, but there was no sign of the two girls. She rushed out and called out to them again. "Marilyn, have you seen Rose and Patsy?" she asked.

"No, Blair, sorry," the receptionist answered.

Panic started to descend, and Blair ran round the open-plan office, calling their names. "Shit!" she whispered under her breath.

"They couldn't have gone far, Blair," Marilyn said, trying to reassure her.

After half an hour of searching, with the help of two security guards, Blair's head started to spin. She would have to phone Daniel!

Marilyn handed Blair a mug of sweet tea and some tissues. Blair shook her head and wiped away the smeared mascara running down her face. "Drink it, it'll make you feel better," Marilyn insisted.

They both then heard something. A muffled sound was coming from the stationery cupboard. Blair jumped up and flung open the cupboard door. The two girls were sitting on a pile of toilet rolls with their hands over their mouths trying to stifle their giggles. Patsy burst out laughing, but Rose looked down at her feet, worried she was going to be in trouble.

Blair felt the anger rise up through her body. "What the hell do you two think you're playing at?" she yelled, just as the lift doors opposite her opened, and Daniel walked out. Both girls burst into tears and ran into their father's arms. Daniel glared at Blair as a look of shock spread across her face.

Daniel and Blair travelled home in silence. The girls had fallen asleep in the back of the car, and Blair was trying hard to swallow back tears. She was sorry for shouting at the girls and even sorrier that Daniel had witnessed the outburst. She had apologised incessantly, but the look of fury still hadn't left his eyes, so she thought it would be better just to keep quiet.

Daniel pulled into the drive and gently woke his daughters up. "Shall I make some hot chocolate?" Blair asked him, sheepishly.

Daniel nodded. He had finally calmed down, but he would have to have a chat with Blair in the morning; he didn't want that happening again.

Chapter 74

"Breakfast in bed," announced Jeff, breezily, as he entered the bedroom with a tray of tea and poached eggs on toast. He had a red rose between his teeth and a dishcloth folded neatly over his arm. Siobhan smiled.

"Very debonair!" she told him. She looked at the food and felt nauseous. "Just leave it on the table," she continued, "I'll eat it in a minute."

"Yes, madam," Jeff said. "Will that be all, m'lady?" he asked.

Siobhan giggled, "Yes, for now, thank you, kind sir." As Jeff walked out of the room, Siobhan sunk down under the covers. She needed a bit more sleep; the exhaustion was getting too much for her these days.

Riley woke up at dawn, bathed in excitement. She had the radio turned up and was dancing around the kitchen while she prepared breakfast. She was grilling sausages and bacon, the eggs were whisked and in a bowl ready to be scrambled, the baked beans were in the microwave and the slices of sourdough were all in a row in the toaster. There were new colouring books, pencils and magazines on the kitchen table for the girls and Dudley's new tartan, fleecy dog bed was beside the fireplace in the lounge waiting for him to snuggle down in it. She was desperately hoping Daniel would stay for breakfast; she knew how much he loved his cooked breakfasts at the weekend.

Loud knocking on the front door made Riley jump, and then a smile spread across her face. She rushed out of the kitchen and saw the figures of the girls and Daniel outside behind the bevelled glass door. As she flung open the door, Rose burst in and grabbed her around the waist. Patsy came in behind her, apprehensively. She hadn't seen her mother since the altercation at the school playground and felt a bit uneasy.

Riley could hardly see through the tears spilling down her face. She crouched down and hugged both girls so hard that they all ended up falling over in a heap on the floor in fits of laughter. The laughter was infectious, and Daniel found himself laughing along with them. Dudley started barking excitedly, leaping around on top of them and joining in the fun. Rose quickly jumped up and grabbed Daniel's hand, pulling him down on top of them too; which caused even more hysteria. *It was just like old times*, thought both Riley and Daniel, and then their eyes met, and neither of them could look away.

As Daniel looked into his wife's deep brown eyes, he felt like she was looking right into the very depths of his soul and as Riley gazed into Daniel's piercing blue eyes she felt as if she was being sucked into an ocean of love and tenderness. They both knew that if their daughters hadn't been there, they would have ripped each other's clothes off then and there and let the emotions bubbling up inside them both explode like a volcanic eruption.

"I'm starving," Rose finally shouted, pushing her sister off her and jumping out of the family scrum.

"Well, that's good because I've got all your favourites," Riley said, pulling herself up off the floor. The family made their way into the kitchen, chatting and laughing as if they had never been apart.

Rose and Patsy were happily talking over each other telling Riley what they had been doing at school. She had missed them so much and had a lot to catch up on. "How about you Daniel? How are things at work?" Riley asked as she put down her knife and fork. She noticed Daniel had eaten like a horse; he even had a second helping, and she felt a wave of satisfaction. She knew Blair would never be able to compete with her where food was concerned. She listened as he talked enthusiastically about what was happening at the flying centre and as she knew most of the staff, he was filling her in about how they all were.

"Thanks for doing this, Riley; it was delicious," he told her as he put the ketchup and butter back into the fridge. He watched her as she stacked the dishwasher. She was wearing her trademark style of vest top and shorts. She had let her naturally wavy hair grow longer, and he loved the way she had scooped it all over to one side so that it fell sexily down over one shoulder, leaving the other shoulder bare. He wanted to walk over and kiss her shoulder. He wanted to feel her arms around his neck and take in her intoxicatingly fresh smell and then lift her up while she wrapped her long legs around his waist.

"I'm glad you enjoyed it. I know how much you enjoy a big breakfast at the weekend," she told him, not daring to look up. She carefully slotted the cutlery into the dishwasher basket, trying to stop her hands from shaking. She could feel his eyes boring into her, and she could hardly breathe.

"Mummy," Patsy called out, breaking the spell between the couple. "Can we go out into the garden?"

Riley kissed her daughter on the top of her head. "Of course," she said and went to unlock the door. Daniel looked at his watch. Blair would be wondering where he was. He hadn't told her he was staying for breakfast.

Riley watched while Daniel walked down the path towards his car. He turned and waved to her before he got in, and she swore to herself that she could see tears in his eyes. He still loved her; she was sure of it.

Blair had a feeling of dread in the pit of her stomach. Daniel had been gone for ages. They had planned on going out in the plane that afternoon as they had the weekend to themselves. She had been looking forward to a nice romantic lunch somewhere and then cuddling up on the sofa to watch a 'grown-up' film in the evening instead of the usual Disney films that she was made to watch.

She didn't hear Daniel come in as she ran the hoover up and down the carpet in nice neat, straight lines. A pair of hands wrapped around her waist and made her scream. She turned round and unexpectedly felt Daniels lips on hers. He began kissing her fiercely and then pulled away. She looked at him, confused. He smiled then leant back towards her and kissed her again.

This time she was hungry for him and kissed him back, passionately, as she ran her hands down his back and made her way to the front of his jeans. She could feel that he was hard, and it turned her on even more. She lifted up her dress and unzipped him. They both fumbled around pulling down knickers and pants and kicking them across the floor, and then Daniel turned her around and entered her from behind and all the sexual tension that had been building up while he was with Riley was released as he shouted out in pleasure and relief.

Blair was a bit surprised and disappointed when Daniel quickly put his clothes back on and told her he had to go and see his father. "I thought we were spending the day together," she said, frowning in confusion. "We were going to fly out somewhere for lunch," she added.

Daniel didn't look up as he was typing out a text. "Oh sorry, babe. I'm actually full up. I don't think I could eat anything more until this evening. Can we do it another time," he said, distractedly.

It then dawned on Blair. He had stayed and spent the morning with Riley and the girls. She didn't know whether to cry or slap him. She needed to get out of the house. "I'm going to see Dad then," she said, nonchalantly, trying to sound as if she wasn't really bothered.

"Okay, let's catch up tonight then. We can have a takeaway or something if you like," Daniel said, looking up briefly. He smiled at her and carried on with his text. Blair stared at him in disbelief, then shook her head and went to get her bag and car keys.

Patsy and Rose were taking their jobs very seriously. They had been given the responsibility of helping to prepare dinner for the greyhounds at the kennels, and their mother had told them that it was important to make sure they all ate healthily so that they would be able to win races. Rose was carefully scooping out the greyhound meal biscuit into their bowls and Patsy was adding a teaspoon of cod liver oil to each. "What is cod liver oil?" asked Patsy.

"It's a special oil to keep their coats nice and glossy," Riley told her.

"What is cod?" Rose asked.

"It's a fish," Riley said. She missed hearing her girls asking her a million questions every day.

"I like fish. I had a fish burger yesterday," Patsy said.

"And then Blair lost us," said Rose. Both girls giggled.

"What do you mean, she lost you?" asked Riley.

Her daughters told her about the trip to the office and how Blair screamed at them. Riley felt the hairs go up on the back of her neck. How dare that bitch shout at her daughters! She would be having words with Daniel about that.

Blair found her father sitting in his chair staring at the television. "Hi, Dad," she said, kissing him gently on the head. He was watching a cookery programme. "Why are you watching this?" she asked him. "Shall I find a channel with a nice film on?"

"No, leave it. Your mother likes this programme. She has just popped to the loo. She'll be back soon," he said. Blair froze.

Surely, she hadn't come back! Blair raced up the stairs, but the bathroom door was open, and no one was upstairs. Blair's face fell. The dementia was getting worse. She was slowly losing her dad, and it was breaking her heart.

"Can I make you a cup of tea, Dad?" she asked him.

"No, it's okay, love; Mum has just made me one," he said, brightly.

"Well, where is it then?" Blair asked him.

"Oh, I must have finished it. She must have taken it into the kitchen."

Blair went into the hallway and phoned her brother. "Hi, Brett. I'm at Dad's. He seems to be getting worse. Could you come over?"

She knew their dad would have to go into a home. At first, they thought he was just forgetful due to his age, but as time went on, he was getting more and more confused. He had forgotten how to use the microwave and oven and had also forgotten how to get home a couple of times when he had been out walking.

Luckily, all the locals knew him and had guided him back. Blair loved her dad with all her heart. He was her rock. He had brought her and Brett up on his own and had done an amazing job.

Neither of them had ever gone without, and he had always been encouraging but never domineering. He had always trusted his children to find their own way in life without him having to lecture them, and they both loved him for it. He had even been there to help look after Riley after her abortion. Blair couldn't bear what was happening to him, and she couldn't even talk to Daniel about it.

She loved Daniel, but he wasn't the most supportive person in the world when it came to emotions. She remembered his sister, Kate, joking at one of their Sunday dinner get-togethers that Daniel suffered from 'empathetic bankruptcy'. It was at times like these that she missed Riley.

Chapter 75

Riley helped the girls pack their bags with a heavy heart. She had had such a great time with her daughters and Dudley, but it had all come to an end too soon. She knew she would be seeing them again next weekend, but how was she supposed to get through a whole seven days without them? "Do we have to go home?" asked Rose, climbing into Riley's lap.

"I'm so sorry, baby, but Daddy wants you back home, but don't worry, you'll both be coming back again next weekend," she said, cuddling her daughter tightly. Patsy sat quietly finishing the picture she had been colouring in. "Are you okay, Pats?" Riley asked, noticing that her other daughter had been a bit distant that afternoon.

Patsy looked up from her book and asked, "Is Blair going to be our new mum?"

Riley was taken aback at the question. "No, of course not. Did someone say that she was going to be?" Riley asked.

"Blair said that one day, she would be our mummy," Rose said.

Riley felt rage simmering inside her. "That will never, ever happen," she said indignantly.

Just then, Riley heard Daniel pull up in the drive, and she went to open the door. To her surprise, she saw Blair sitting in the passenger seat. She kissed Dudley on the nose and handed his lead to Daniel. She wanted to wipe the smug look off Blair's face so without thinking it through, she walked up to the car and opened the passenger side door. Blair was startled.

"So you lost my girls on Friday night? And then you shouted at them! Who the hell do you think you are? You are not, and are never going to be their mother, Blair," Riley said, shaking with anger.

Blair composed herself and said flatly, "You're upsetting the girls, Riley. Calm down. It was a misunderstanding. Daniel and I have sorted it out." Blair reached for the handle and slammed the door shut.

Patsy and Rose looked at Riley helplessly from the back windows. Daniel didn't look at his wife as he got into the car and started the engine. Riley saw one of her neighbours watching her across the street, from the corner of her eye, so she calmly walked away and went back into the house feeling humiliated, yet again.

A couple of hours went by and the silence in the house was almost deafening. Riley's heart ached for her children. She hadn't been able to move off the sofa since they left. She couldn't muster up the enthusiasm to do anything. She felt lost and alone as she pulled the cushion close to her and sobbed into it.

A few hours had passed, and the room was in complete darkness when Riley opened her eyes. She tried to focus but felt disorientated and confused. She then remembered that the girls had left, and she had fallen asleep.

It was only four thirty in the afternoon, but the cold December days had turned into long, dark evenings. She could murder a bottle of wine, she thought, as she rubbed her eyes. She reached for her phone which had fallen onto the floor and saw a couple of unopened messages. One was from her sister. She sat up when she saw that the other message was from a number she didn't recognise. She opened the message and gasped. *'Hey, Riley, long time, no see!'*

Riley got up and turned on the lamps and then went to make herself a cup of tea. Thank goodness there wasn't any alcohol in the house. She had been tempted to go out and buy some but was proud of herself for having some self-restraint and deciding against it. She took her phone into the kitchen with her and typed a message back: *Who is this?* After a few seconds, a reply appeared. *It's Ricky. I was wondering how you are.*

Chapter 76

Riley grabbed her packed dinner from the fridge and the flask of coffee she had made and put it all in her rucksack to take to the track with her. She had been nervous all afternoon at it was going to be the first time she would be running Blaze since the injury to his wrist a couple of months ago. Her and her team were taking three other dogs with them that evening too and a couple of the owners were going to meet them at the track. It would be a long night, and she probably wouldn't get home until gone midnight, but she didn't mind. This was what Riley was born to do, and she loved every minute of it.

At the racetrack, the dogs were taken into the kennel room to get weighed. Riley looked into Blaze's eyes, and she knew he was smiling at her. She was so proud of him and how far he had come from the sick little pup she nursed back to health. He was built from solid muscle and was powerful now. He wagged his tail, excitedly.

"You're going to smash this, boy!" Riley told him. Riley rubbed her hands together to keep warm. It was a bitterly cold night, but all her dogs had warm fleeces on under their racking jackets. Blaze was in his black and white stripped jacket, and Riley couldn't help thinking he was the most handsome dog there. After they were weighed, they were muzzled and rugged up, ready for the races.

Blazing Zippy went happily into trap number 6, while Riley walked behind, so he couldn't see her and be put off. The greyhound behind him was less happy about going in and had to be lifted in by his handler while he yapped in protest.

Riley waited with bated breath until all the dogs were in their traps and ready to go. The bell rang out and the commentator started speaking. After a short time, the mechanical hare whizzed past and the traps opened. There was a sudden burst of action as the dogs flew out in a blur of fur.

Blaze was the first out of the trap, just as Riley had expected. She was pleased with his turn of foot, but she saw the dog from the inside trap nicely building up pace. There was something beautiful about watching these incredible animals glide around the track with their sleek bodies, long limbs and pointed faces.

Riley watched as the dog eventually caught up with Blaze and then streaked past him to the finishing post. It was all over in a matter of minutes. Blaze was completely unaware he hadn't won and bounded over to Riley, jumping up in delight. Riley laughed at him. "Well done, boy!" she said, hugging him tightly and kissing him all over his face.

Riley saw that she still had more work to do with Blaze. They weren't lucky that day, but she would get him back up to speed. She would get him on the treadmill and use laser treatment and massages; whatever it took. They had to prepare, as there was one ambition she had to fulfil before Blaze retired.

Terry Mulligan had been one of the most experienced greyhound racers in the country and won Greyhound Trainer of the Year many times, but Riley wanted the most prestigious award. She had been described as one of the country's leading lights before the accident. She was working her way back up again, and she was coming back with a vengeance. Her and Blaze were going to compete in the Greyhound Derby. And they were going to win!

Chapter 77

An emergency meeting was called at Fairgate Flying Club, and Daniel entered the boardroom with some trepidation. The directors were already seated and looked worried. Daniel's father was discussing something from a file with Annalisa, Daniel's PA. "Ah, Daniel," Gordon said, looking up from the papers.

"Sorry, I'm late," Daniel apologised. "Let's begin," he added.

"I'm afraid it's not good news," said Harry Trent, Daniel's Finance Director, as he nervously straightened his large pink spotted tie which didn't quite reach the end of his rather portly stomach. "The Government Inspector has reviewed the new landowner's housing plan, and we cannot operate a safe working airfield here in Elstree anymore," he said, wiping away the sweat from his forehead with the back of his sleeve. He knew that wasn't the news Daniel wanted to hear and watched helplessly as Daniel put his head in his hands. It was his own fault. He should have kept on top of things.

Daniel knew that the lease on the land was coming to an end, and he should have made a bid for it, but he had let his personal life get in the way. He had been too wrapped up with Riley and Blair and the children and had taken his foot off the gas. He was so used to letting his staff make all the decisions on his behalf these days, which was a good thing as far as Daniel was concerned as he trusted each and every one of them, but Annalisa had warned him about the sale of the land.

Always one step ahead, Daniel's PA and confidante was bright and astute and had a razor-sharp mind. She had urged him to get in quick. It had always been Daniel's intention to eventually buy the land that the flying club operated on, but Housing Hertfordshire had also had the same idea and pipped him to the post. They had proposed to build 600 new homes on the land as it was within easy reach of London.

"What about the petition?" Daniel asked, as a last desperate attempt to save his business.

Annalisa shook her head. She was also Sales and Marketing Director and had looked into every option possible. "We submitted the petition to the Head of Planning at the council, signed by local residents, the pilots, aviation organisations and the members of the club, but we still failed to attract enough signatures, unfortunately," she told him. "We tried to get permission to realign the runway but like Harry said, it's not feasible."

Daniel was not a man who gave up easily. "Okay, so we relocate," he said. "Start looking for new premises. This is not the end of Fairgate Flying Club."

When everyone had left the room, Daniel walked towards Annalisa, who was stacking up all the empty cups. "Thanks for trying," Daniel told her.

"No worries," she told him. Annalisa had worked for Daniel for five years and loved her job.

Daniel watched as she moved around the table. She had inherited her olive skin from her Italian parents and didn't wear much make-up as her skin had a healthy natural glow and even though she was in her forties she didn't have a single wrinkle on her face. Her thick dark eyebrows complimented her hazel eyes and long, straight black hair. Daniel had always found Annalisa attractive, but he had always been in love with Riley, and Annalisa had been married until two years ago, when her husband had passed away from a heart attack.

Of course, Daniel had no idea what to say or how to comfort his PA, so he sent flowers and told her to take as much time off as she needed. He was relieved when she came back to work though as he relied on her and valued her opinions.

"Let me take you out to dinner tonight," he said, "as a thank you for being my rock over the years."

"Oh, Daniel, you don't have to do that," she said, blushing.

"No. I insist," he said.

"Okay then. That would be lovely," she agreed.

"Pick you up at 8:00 pm?" Daniel asked, as he walked out of the room.

Blair had a list of care homes to call. She had decided her dad would have to go into a home eventually and thought it would be a good idea to make a start on the arrangements. She was sitting outside by the pool, wrapped up in a blanket when Daniel arrived home. He was surprised to see her outside. "What are you doing out here?" he asked.

"Hello, darling. Looking at care homes for Dad," she said, deep in thought.

"Any good ones?" Daniel asked, picking up the brochures.

Blair felt a little wave of happiness wash over her at the fact that he was taking an interest. He sat down beside her, and she showed him the ones she liked. After they had shortlisted it down to the best three, Blair sat back in her chair, suddenly feeling tired. "How about a takeaway and an early night?" she suggested.

"Oh sorry, love, I'm out tonight," Daniel answered as he got up from his chair.

Blair frowned. "Where are you going?" she asked.

"Out to dinner with Annalisa," he said matter-of-factly.

"Oh, have you got a business meeting?" she asked.

"No. I'm taking her out to dinner as a 'thank you'," he said.

"A thank you for what?" Blair asked, confused. Daniel looked at her in annoyance.

"What is this? Twenty questions?" he retorted.

"You are taking your secretary out to dinner Daniel. I think I have a right to know why?" Blair said, defensively.

"You're not my wife, Blair!" Daniel said angrily and stormed off into the house.

The words took Blair by surprise and stung deeply. "Yes, it's all that bitch, Riley's fault," she said under her breath. If Riley had just signed the bloody divorce papers, she would be closer to being Mrs Fairgate by now.

Annalisa's daughter, Natalia, looked up from her laptop as Annalisa strolled into the living room in a white figure-worshipping, bodycon dress and thigh-high black suede boots She wolf-whistled at her mother. "Who's the lucky man?" she asked.

Annalisa rolled her eyes. "I'm going to dinner with Daniel," she said. "It's no big deal!" Annalisa added.

Natalia knew better. "He's always fancied you. I can't believe it took him so long to make a move," she said and carried on typing.

Annalisa checked the contents of her bag before zipping it closed and then picked up her long black leather coat. "Don't wait up, darling," she told her daughter. "Be good!" Natalia called out as Annalisa made her way to the front door.

It wasn't the first time Annalisa had been out for a meal with Daniel, but this time, it felt different. It felt like she was going out on a date, and she had butterflies in her tummy. She shook her head, deciding she was just being silly.

Of course, it wasn't a date. Daniel was still married and in a relationship with another woman; surely he wouldn't want any more complications in his life.

Anyway, she was much too professional to date anyone she worked with; that was a recipe for disaster, and she loved her job too much to risk jeopardising it even if it was with the boss. She wasn't looking for a relationship and wasn't even sure if she was even ready for a relationship. Losing her husband, Brad, had been devastating and totally unexpected. Annalisa felt she was in a much better place now and had accepted it, but he had left a huge gap that she wasn't sure any man would be able to fill.

Daniel pulled up in a black Ferrari and reached over to open the door. Annalisa's eyes popped open in astonishment. "Do you like my new present to myself?" he asked her as she walked around admiring the car.

"Seriously?" she asked.

"Absolutely! Do you want to go for a spin?" he asked as his eyes wandered up and down her body. He had never seen her look so incredible and felt like an excited teenager on his first date. Annalisa carefully lowered herself down onto the seat and swung her legs around into the car. It was completely the wrong dress to negotiate getting in and out of a sports car. She wished she had worn her leather jeans instead.

"You look amazing," he told her. Annalisa noticed his voice change and caught him looking at her breasts a couple of times. She felt like a giddy schoolgirl. He smelt divine and looked so incredibly sexy. The car was the icing on the cake. She felt like she had died and gone to heaven.

Annalisa suggested The Beaumont for dinner. It was a classy restaurant with superb food, crisp white table cloths and smooth, classic music playing softly in the background. It was a regular haunt for the rich and famous who wanted a great night but also wanted to be off the radar and away from the attention of photographers or love-struck fans. There was a security system at the gate leading up to the long driveway to the restaurant so only those who had booked were allowed in. Annalisa was a regular guest at the restaurant so the manager knew her and adored her.

"Great choice!" Daniel announced. He knew he could rely on Annalisa to pick the perfect place; that's why he worked with her. She seemed to have the ability to read his mind. They walked across the gravel car park to the restaurant which was lit up with Christmas lights. A huge outdoor Christmas tree was tastefully decorated with silver and gold decorations, and Daniel could see the roaring fire in the fireplace from the window inviting them inside.

"Bella!" Ronaldo called across the reception area.

Annalisa laughed and held out her arms. A tall, smart Italian man strode up to her and hugged her tightly. "Ronnie! It's so good to see you," she said, hugging the manager of the restaurant. She introduced him to Daniel.

Ronaldo said, "I have the best table in the house for you tonight. Would you like to sit by the fire first while you have a drink and look at the menu?" he asked, calling the Sommelier over.

"Yes, thank you," said Annalisa, sitting down in a velvet armchair. Daniel sat opposite her and admired her figure.

"You really do look incredible tonight Anna," he said.

Annalisa flashed him an appreciative smile.

"Eat, drink and be happy!" Ronaldo announced and then blushed. He quickly hurried away, not wanting to intrude on the date. He knew Annalisa well and had been extremely fond of her late husband, but he hated to see her on her own for so long and was pleased to see her out on a date.

"He's a character," Annalisa said.

"He certainly is. How come I've never been here?" Daniel asked.

"It's exclusive and special. Brad and I used to come here for anniversaries and birthdays. We had Natalia's Christening party here too," she said.

"Oh, I'm sorry, Anna, I didn't mean to bring back memories," Daniel said, apologising.

"No, no. They are happy memories. That is why I wanted to come here. I knew you would like it here," she added. Daniel reached across the table and squeezed her hand affectionately. He felt a warm affectionate energy between them.

Riley opened the bathroom window to let the steam out and then wrapped a towel around her head and went into her bedroom. She lay down in the middle of the bed and sighed. Looking up at the ceiling she contemplated what she should do. The message from Ricky had been such a surprise; but a pleasant surprise. She reached for her phone and stared at the message again. She then dialled his number. She heard his voice answer straight away which took her by surprise. "Oh, erm, hi, Ricky" Riley said, feeling strangely embarrassed.

"Riley!" he replied. "How are you?" he asked. The sound of his voice sent shivers down her.

Daniel finished the last remnants of his Beef Wellington and sat back in his seat in satisfaction.

Annalisa smiled and said, "You really enjoyed that didn't you?"

"Blair isn't the best cook in the world," Daniel laughed.

Annalisa looked at him seriously. "What are you going to do about Blair? Will you divorce Riley and marry her?" she asked.

Daniel thought carefully about how he was going to answer the question. He hadn't really thought about his feelings. He just wanted his daughters to be cared for, and Blair had just taken it upon herself to wade in and take charge. He appreciated all her help and, at first, thought they could play happy families, but as time went on, he realised his feelings for Blair weren't deep enough. Riley had come out of prison and had been making an effort to be a good mother, and he saw what an incredible connection the children had with her. He still couldn't forget about the affair with Ricky and wasn't sure he could ever forgive her, but the truth was he still loved her and all those feelings put together scared the life out of him.

Daniel and Annalisa chatted as he drove her home. Conversation between the two of them was always easy and comfortable. "You know, I almost made a move on you this evening. You look so beautiful," Daniel said.

"So why didn't you?" Annalisa asked, curiously.

"Because you would have probably slapped me across the face," Daniel said.

Annalisa burst out laughing. "You know me so well," she said.

"I wouldn't want to ruin things between us, Anna. I really value you and appreciate you; I hope you know that," he said, sincerely.

"I know that, Daniel. I love working for you, and I love my job, but I have a proposition for you," she said, turning in her seat to look at him.

Daniel was intrigued.

"I've heard about a new location and some land for sale which would be perfect for the flying club," she said.

Daniel loved how Annalisa could always keep them afloat in choppy waters. "Tell me more?" he said, curiously.

"I'll tell you all about it tomorrow," she added. "I want to invest. I want us to be equal partners."

Daniel was flabbergasted. He wasn't sure what to say.

"Don't say anything. Think about it, and we'll talk tomorrow," Annalisa told him as she got out of the car. She closed the door behind her and waved and then walked away. Daniel sat in the car trying to absorb what he had just been told. As he turned the ignition and drove home, he warmed to the idea of being partners with Annalisa. By the time he pulled into his driveway, he was excited about the idea. It would be a new year and a new start for him, and he was looking forward to the future.

Chapter 78

The Fairgates were gathered around the dining table in their usual places. Joe was at the furthest end of the table from Gordon with Jerry beside him, and Daniel was sat on the left of his father who has at the head of the table. Rose and patsy sat in-between him and Blair. Diana was on the right hand side of her husband with Kate and her family next to her. It was clear to see the pecking order of the family from the seating arrangement.

Gordon stood up to carve the beef when Carmelita brought it to the table. Diana poured herself another glass of wine. She was in her element with all her family around her, and she chatted excitedly about Christmas. "Of course, I want you all here on Christmas Eve, and I thought we would have a nice dinner and plenty of drinks once we've put all the children to bed. On Christmas day, we can have a lovely breakfast and open the presents, and I thought we would go out for dinner this year if you are all in agreement. You are all welcome to stay as long as you wish," she said, not stopping for breath.

Joe was the first to speak. "I'm afraid we've already made plans for Christmas, Mum," he said. He watched as his mother's jaw dropped open in shock. He knew she would be disappointed, but there was no way he was going to spend more time with his father than was absolutely necessary.

"Joe and I have booked a week in Croatia with some friends," Jerry added, feeling slightly guilty but relieved that Joe had agreed to escape the Fairgate festivities this year.

"Patsy and Rose are going to Riley's for Christmas," Daniel told his mother. Her jaw dropped open even further.

"Really?" she asked.

"Yes, we've agreed. Riley will have them for Christmas, and I'll have them for New Year," he said.

Blair looked as shocked as Diana. "That's the first I've heard of it," she said.

As a surprise for Daniel, Blair had been contemplating booking a weekend in New York for New Year. She had found the perfect hotel and had been planning excursions and looking up restaurants and bars for them to go to. Having the girls would mean they wouldn't be able to go.

Kate looked sheepish as she added, "I'm sorry, Mum; we can't make it either. We'll be in Lapland."

Diana became visibly pale. She raised her eyebrows questioningly. "Are you all trying to tell me that you can't come for Christmas?" she said as her voice quivered with emotion. A feeling of guilt filtered around the table.

"May be we could all get together just before Christmas?" Kate suggested, hopefully.

Diana slowly pushed her chair back from the table. "Excuse me. I just need a minute. Start eating; I don't want the food to get cold," she said in a quivering voice as she walked out of the room.

A short while later Diana returned. The family were laughing and chatting around the table but stopped when she entered the room. She had been shocked at their decisions, but she had pulled herself together. They all had their own lives to lead, and she just had to accept it. "Why don't we all get together the week before Christmas then?" she suggested. Everyone agreed that that was a fabulous idea. They didn't dare upset her again, or there would be hell to pay!

Joe had been watching Daniel and his father all afternoon. They had been discussing the flying club and new premises and Gordon had offered to put some money into the business. Jealousy reared its ugly head again. "It's always about *him* isn't it? Darling, perfect, butter-wouldn't-melt-in-his-mouth, Daniel," Joe said, shaking his head.

"Don't be such a drama queen, Joe!" Gordon retorted, angrily. The comment went down like a lead balloon and a mixture of rage, hurt and insecurity swirled round in Joe's head until he completely lost all control. "It's not like he's even your son!" he yelled.

Daniel felt as if he had been punched in the stomach. Diana burst into tears. Kate looked at her brother, horrified and shook her head in despair.

"Actually, he is!" Gordon roared back.

The room fell silent.

Chapter 79
1965

Elizabeth sat in the corner of the hall at a table beside the window. She had a Babycham and a paper plate with sausage rolls and cheese sandwiches cut neatly into perfect squares in front of her, but she had lost her appetite. The long skirt of her pale blue dress covered the bruises on her shin and the shawl she had thrown over her pale shoulders covered the ones on the back of her arm. A stunning, blonde woman in an emerald green silk dress sat down beside her. "Hello, Elizabeth," she said.

"Hello, Diana, how are you?" Elizabeth asked.

Diana sighed. "Bored!" she added. "I don't know why Gordon made me come to this awful party."

Elizabeth's face turned red in embarrassment. "Actually it is my mum and dad's fiftieth wedding anniversary party," she replied.

Diana didn't know what to say, so just smiled. She excused herself quickly and left the table, whispering something in Gordon's ear before making a hasty exit.

Douglas Fairgate was the life and soul of the party. As usual, he had had too much to drink and was flirting with all the younger women and before long he was up on one of the tables singing and dancing to a Rolling Stones song. Elizabeth's parents were far too polite to ask him to get down and stop ruining their party and the other guests didn't want to upset Douglas as his family were very wealthy and well-known and did a lot for the community.

Gordon approached Elizabeth and sat down beside her. "Are you okay Lizzie?" he asked.

His kindness towards her always brought tears to her eyes. "I'll survive," she said, quietly. "Thank you for asking, though."

When Elizabeth found out Douglas had invited Gordon and Diana to the party she had been mortified. She knew Diana would be horrified as she probably had never been to a party in a village hall before, but Gordon was a lovely, dear man and Elizabeth knew he would come to support her and her family. He, like her, found Douglas to be embarrassing and annoying after a few drinks.

Elizabeth and Douglas had been in the same year at school. She was not pretty like the other girls in the class, but she was fun. Douglas took a shine to her straight away as he had his own insecurities too. He felt inferior to his brother. He wasn't as clever or handsome as his brother, Gordon, and always felt like he walked in his shadow.

It wasn't until after the marriage between Douglas and Elizabeth that he showed his true colours. The drunken rows which lead to beatings would then leave him consumed with guilt. Elizabeth felt trapped. She didn't want to upset her family by telling them the truth about Douglas as they adored him. Gordon suspected something was wrong between them though. He noticed a change in Elizabeth. She went from being a confident, happy woman to introverted and sad.

Gordon had been worried about Elizabeth after seeing her at the party, so he decided to drop by his brother's house unexpectedly one evening. As he approached the house, he heard shouting. The curtains were only half drawn in the front window and as he peered in to see what the fuss was about, he saw his brother shouting at Elizabeth, and then he struck her across the face, sending her reeling backwards into a chest of drawers. She fell to the floor like a rag doll. Gordon ran to the front door and banged hard. Douglas didn't answer so Gordon ran round to the back door and started thumping and calling out, "Open the bloody door, Douglas!" Gordon ended up kicking the door open. He picked Elizabeth up and lifted her on to an armchair while Douglas made his escape.

Elizabeth woke up dazed and began sobbing uncontrollably.

Gordon held her tightly until she had calmed down and then got her a cold, wet flannel to put on her face. "Would you like me to stay with you tonight Lizzie, in case he comes back?" he asked her.

Elizabeth nodded in relief.

"How long has this been going on? I knew there was something wrong at the party last week," Gordon said.

"It's been going on since our wedding," she sobbed.

"Well, it stops now!" Gordon said, angrily. *"He will never hurt you again. I won't let him."*

Chapter 80
2016

"Oh my god!" Diana said. "That night you went to Douglas and Elizabeth's house and didn't come home," she said, looking at him in shock.

Daniel stared at his father, unable to take it all in.

"You had an affair with Daniel's mum?" Kate asked.

"Douglas used to beat her black and blue. She was a good woman. I was comforting her. It was only one time," Gordon explained. He felt crushed and humiliated. He had always intended to tell Daniel one day but never wanted it to come out in such a hurtful, deceitful way. "I'm sorry, Diana," he said, with tears in his eyes. For the second time that evening, Diana was forced to leave the table.

Chapter 81

Not a single sound could be heard across the still, calm water. It was as if the night had been paused and muted. Daniel pulled the collar up on his grey woollen jacket as an eerie chill trickled down his back. The rowing boat looked tiny in the darkness, and he seemed to be too large to fit in it properly. He felt like Alice in Wonderland after she ate the cake.

His arms dangled loosely over the edge as he held on to the oars and his legs were scrunched up, uncomfortably, in front of him. He wondered how he had got there; out into the middle of the lake and what he was doing in this tiny vessel. He usually felt excited and happy after snorting coke, and it was usually an escape from the nightmares, but maybe his body had got too used to it or something, and it had stopped having the desired effect now.

Something underneath the boat caused it to start to vibrate. Daniel looked around, worried. What the hell was going on? He heard a rumbling sound coming from the deep depths of the lake. He looked cautiously over the edge but only saw his own reflection.

Very slowly, the boat started to rotate, like a car on a waltzer at the fairground, and stopped abruptly with a jolt. He was facing the opposite direction. Daniel's breathing quickened as he realised something was about to happen. As much as he tried, he couldn't stop himself looking down into the water. To his horror, something appeared to be looking back at him.

At first, he couldn't make out what it was. It then became clearer. A shape of a face moved upwards, slowly and hovered just below the water. Daniel was paralysed with fright.

After a short pause, something shot out of the water and landed in front of him in the boat. The skeleton of a small child was facing him, and Daniel screamed in terror. His arms shot up to his face to block out the image, but the bony arms of the skeleton wrapped around his waist, tightly. "Get off me,"

Daniel shouted as he flung his arms and legs around kicking and punching in all directions.

The boat was rocking violently, threatening to tip over. He forced himself to open his eyes and the skeleton flew backwards across the boat with its jaw locked open as if it was screaming as well. After a few seconds, it jumped back over the boat into the water. Daniel watched it disappear to wherever it had come from, and he gripped onto the side to stop himself from falling in too.

Blair threw her arms around Daniel and hugged him tightly. He tried to fight her off and ended up elbowing her in the cheek. "Ouch," she cried.

Daniel's eyes shot open, and he realised it had been another nightmare. He hadn't had one in such a long time. "Oh god, I'm so sorry, darling," he apologised as he got up to turn the light on. "Are you okay?" he asked her.

Blair nodded as she rubbed her face. She knew it had been the bombshell that Gordon had dropped at the family dinner that had caused the nightmares to come back. She gently rubbed his back, and he turned and wrapped his arms tenderly around her. They lay back down on top of the duvet in each other's arms, and Daniel dozed back off to sleep as he lay on Blair's warm chest listening to the comforting beating of her heart. It broke her heart watching him have these terrible dreams, but she was glad she was there to comfort him. She would always be there for Daniel; the love of her life.

A neat handwritten list was secured to the fridge door by a magnet with a picture of the New York skyline on it. Daniel frowned as he got a carton of orange juice out. "What's that?" asked Patsy.

"It looks like one of Blair's lists," he told his daughter.

Patsy stood on tiptoes as she struggled to read it. "Christmas shopping," she said.

"Looks like Blair is going Christmas shopping today," Daniel said.

"So it's just me, you and Rose today?" Patsy asked, excitedly.

Daniel was surprised at his daughter's question and then felt guilty. May be he hadn't been spending enough time with them. "Yes, just the three of us. What would you like to do today?"

"Can we go and see, Mummy?" Patsy said, clapping her hands.

"I'm sorry, honey-bun, it's not Mummy's turn to see you this weekend," Daniel said, bending down so that he was face to face with his daughter.

Patsy screwed her nose up. "I miss Mummy," she said, sadly.

"So do I!" shouted Rose as she bounded into the room.

Daniel felt uncomfortable with the way the conversation was starting to go, and he was also worried about Blair walking into the room and hearing them. "How about we go out for breakfast and then may be go and see grandma and grandpa?"

The girls loved the idea and danced around the kitchen happily.

Riley was sitting at the kitchen table with a pile of paperwork in front of her that she had decided to wade through as she wasn't seeing the girls that weekend. Her heart skipped a beat when she saw Daniel's car unexpectedly pulling up in the driveway and Rose and Patsy leaping out of their seats to run to the front door. "Mummy!" they both called out.

Riley rushed to open the door. "What a lovely surprise!" she called out.

Daniel smiled. He loved seeing his wife and children together; it always made him feel proud of the family he had created.

"Hi," Riley called out to him. As usual, the sight of her blew him away. She looked happy and beautiful, and he couldn't help himself. He walked up and hugged her warmly. Riley froze for a second, surprised. She hugged him back, and it felt familiar and comforting.

"Mummy, can you come to Potty Pancakes with us?" asked Patsy, hopefully. Riley opened her mouth to speak but wasn't quite sure what to say.

"We would love you to come," Daniel added.

She looked into his sparkling blue eyes and felt her knees go slightly weak beneath her. "Erm, okay. I'd love to," she said. "Just let me grab my jacket."

"It's for the best, Dad," Blair told her father as she stroked his thin, veiny, liver spotted hand. *When did he get so old?* She wondered. Malcolm sat in his armchair and stared out of the window, oblivious to what was going on around him. Brett carried the last cardboard box down the stairs and placed it in the hallway on top of a pile of boxes. The brother and sister both looked at the boxes, sadly. This was what was left of the Matthews family; four cardboard boxes of memories which the patriarch of their family no longer had any recollection of.

As Blair walked around the house one last time, all she could think about was her mother. For the first time in a very long time, she missed her. "Come on, Dad, let's get you to your new home," Brett said as he helped the old man out of his chair.

Malcolm stood up, obediently. "We were happy here once, weren't we?" he said.

"Yes, Dad, we were very happy here," said Brett.

Malcolm tilted his head, "Happy where?" he asked confused.

Brett laughed, "Never mind, Dad. Come on, let's go."

Blair followed her brother to the car. She shut the front door for the very last time and put the keys through the letter box. "Bye, house," she said, sadly but fondly, as she walked away.

Chapter 82

Riley sat on the old wobbly park bench watching her husband and daughters playing football. The girls shrieked with delight as they chased their dad towards the goal. Daniel expertly flicked the ball into the net and playfully taunted his children, "Daddy scored!" he roared triumphantly.

Rose and Patsy pretended to be really angry and pulled him to the ground.

"Help, help," he shouted. Daniel's T-shirt accidentally slid up his chest during the kerfuffle, and Riley was treated to a glimpse of his golden torso with that cute line of hair he had down the middle of his stomach, which she loved to play with when she used to lay on his chest. How she missed that body! Her eyes slowly ran down his strong muscular thighs, disguised by his pale blue jeans. She gazed at his salt-and-pepper stubble which subtly covered his chin and jawline. He looked even more handsome as he got older.

Riley wanted desperately to be his 'wife' again. She wanted to wake up with him every morning and fall asleep wrapped in his arms each night. She missed him and the girls so much.

Daniel jumped up and dusted the grass from his clothes then ran his fingers through his hair. Riley felt like she was going to explode. Her whole body ached for him. The girls ran off to play on the swings, and Daniel flopped down beside her on the bench.

Without saying a word, he turned towards her and stared into her eyes. It was as if he could see the longing in her eyes. He moved towards her and kissed her gently on the lips. Riley lost all control and reached up and pulled him closer to her. Daniel moved his hands to her hips and then up under her jumper. Riley groaned softly as his lips left her lips and moved down her neck. "Daniel," she whispered. "I want you." He moved his lips to her ear and said, "I want you too."

Daniel stopped at Riley's house before going to drop the girls off at his parents' house for the afternoon. "I'll be back soon," he whispered to Riley and winked at her as she got out of the car.

Riley giggled as she shut the door. The pair of them felt like naughty teenagers about to have sex for the first time. She blew kisses to the girls and rushed inside to freshen up.

"Room service," a voice called out.

Madeleine wrapped her maroon silk dressing gown tightly around her body as she opened the door. She indicated to the waiter to put the tray of food down on the table outside. It was a crisp fresh winter's morning and the sun was shining directly on to the balcony. In the distance, the Eiffel Tower stood proudly overlooking the Capital.

Madeleine always chose the same room in the hotel especially for the exquisite views of Paris. She and her lover had enjoyed champagne and oysters in bed the previous evening and made love all night, and this morning, Madeleine felt exhilarated. Gordon emerged from the bathroom in a white bathrobe. "You smell delicious," Madeleine cooed in her sexy voice as Gordon bent down to kiss her.

"I can't believe I have to leave you so soon my, darling," he said, sadly. He always had the most amazing time with his beautiful mistress, and it broke his heart when the weekend came to an end.

Each time he was reunited with her, Madeleine made his head spin in confusion. He would leave his wife in a heartbeat for her, but the guilt would eventually eat away at him. He knew Diana couldn't survive without him. She always pretended that she was the one who wore the trousers in the marriage, but it was all an act. Diana adored Gordon and her family, and if he ever left her, he knew she would never get over it and his children would despise him.

"Don't be sad, my love," Madeleine said, stroking Gordon's hand.

"But you deserve so much more Maddie," he continued. "I want to have you on my arm and show you off proudly not hide you away in a corner. You are such an incredible woman."

"It's an impossible situation Gordon; we knew that when we first got into this. I want nothing more than to be your wife, but I've always known that was impossible. I am happy to share you if it means we can always have our special weekends," she told him.

"The only thing that keeps me going is seeing you. My marriage is dreary, as you know. You excite me, you always have. You are an extraordinary woman, Madeleine," said Gordon, as he gently kissed her hand.

"Has Diana forgiven you for your revelation about Daniel?" Madeleine asked.

Gordon sighed and said, "She hasn't even mentioned it so, to be honest, I don't know how she feels."

"Oh well, this weekend is about us. We have a couple of hours left before I have to let you go, and I want to make the most of it," Madeleine said as she cheekily ran her bare foot up his leg.

The house was in darkness when Daniel pulled into the drive. The girls had fallen asleep in the back of the car. "Girls. We're home," Daniel said, gently.

Patsy rubbed her eyes and poked Rose. "Wake up," she said.

Rose groaned. "Leave me alone," she said.

"Come on now. No fighting," Daniel told them as he coaxed them both out of the car.

Daniel turned the light on in the kitchen and jumped back in surprise as he saw Blair sitting in the darkness. "What's wrong?" he asked.

She looked up at him, and he noticed that her eyes were red from crying. "It's Dad. He died this morning," she said, bursting into tears.

Daniel knelt down and hugged her. "I'm so sorry, Blair," he said. He felt sorry for Blair; of course, he did. He cared deeply for her, but that afternoon, Daniel had made up his mind. After spending a mind blowing afternoon making love to his wife, he realised he had to be with Riley again; no other woman could ever satisfy him like she did, not even Siobhan, who was an experienced lover and understood him emotionally.

Siobhan had been his guilty pleasure, and he had been hers, but they had never been in love with each other. Daniel had always been good at compartmentalising his life. He had always taken risks and never really worried about the consequences. He never stopped to think about how Riley would feel if she found out about Siobhan or how Blair would feel if she found out he had spent the day with his wife.

As far as he was concerned, what they didn't know couldn't hurt them. Maybe that made him a selfish bastard but; surely, it was a win-win situation for everyone as everyone ultimately got what they wanted. Only this time,

Daniel knew he had to choose, and he chose Riley. "I'll go out and get us some food. Do you fancy Thai?" Daniel asked.

"Yes, that would be lovely. I'll put the girls to bed," Blair said, wiping the tears from her cheeks.

Blair had no idea what had got into the girls that evening. They were being unusually difficult with her. "Rose, please get in to your pyjamas," Blair asked for the third time.

She was starting to lose patience. She didn't need this insolence right now. "No. I don't want to," Rose said, adamantly.

"Okay, Rose. You go to sleep in your clothes then. I don't think your dad will be very pleased when he gets home," Blair said, throwing her hands up in despair.

"I want Mummy!" Rose announced.

Blair felt her cheeks burning. She tried hard to stay calm. "Well, Mummy isn't here, Rose. It isn't her weekend to see you I'm afraid."

Rose screwed up her eyes angrily. "Well, we did see her today. We went to Potty Pancakes, and then she and Daddy were kissing in the park," she said matter-of-factly.

Blair froze. Her ears must have been playing tricks on her. Why would Rose lie and be so cruel? "It's not nice to tell lies, Rose. Why would you say something so hurtful?" Blair asked.

"She's not lying," Patsy said, walking into the bedroom. "We saw them."

Blair sat down on the edge of Patsy's bed to stop herself from collapsing onto the floor.

Riley smiled as she looked down at the message on her phone: '*I love you!*' it said.

'*I love you too!*' she typed back.

Everything was falling back into place again. Daniel had forgiven her for the affair with Ricky and the crash, and soon, they would be one big happy family again.

The takeaway cartons were spread across the table, and Daniel scooped up spoonfuls from each one and filled up his plate. He was famished. He had worked up a good appetite after his afternoon with Riley. He envisaged her naked body writhing around on the bed, and he felt himself becoming aroused again.

Blair picked at the pieces of chicken on her plate. She had completely lost her appetite. She glanced over at Daniel and watched him demolishing his meal. She had just lost her father and found out her boyfriend was cheating on her, and they were supposed to sit there like nothing had happened. She carried on picking at her food even though what she really wanted to do was pick up her plate and smash it across Daniel's head and then scream at the top of her voice and cry like a baby for the two men she had lost today.

Daniel was already asleep when Blair climbed into the bed beside him. She moved in close to him and lay her head against his bare back. She breathed in his smell and kissed him. She then moved her hands across his body and kissed his shoulder. He stirred and moved over on to his back.

Blair stroked the fine hairs on his chest and then moved her head down towards his groin, kissing his stomach on the way. Daniel woke up slowly and felt Blair on top of him. He gently put both hands on her head and stroked her blonde hair as she moved her mouth backwards and forwards. Daniel finally arched his back and groaned with pleasure. Blair rolled on to her back and smiled in satisfaction. "Fuck you, Riley," she said, under her breath.

Chapter 83

The choir sang *Abide with Me* as the pallbearers slowly walked down the aisle towards Malcolm Matthew's coffin. Only a handful of people had turned up to pay their respects, and Blair was silently seething. The most wonderful, gentle, caring man in the world was being laid to rest and only a few pitiful friends actually cared enough to attend. She looked at the two couples in the second row.

The two men had been her father's friends from work and the women beside them were their wives. They all looked genuinely upset, but the oldies from the *Over 70s* club sitting behind them looked like they were on an OAP's day out. They chatted constantly during the service, and Blair even heard one of them say they were looking forward to the buffet.

Brett and his family were sitting beside her and Daniel. Patsy and Rose had refused to come, and Blair was flabbergasted when Daniel sided with them and said they could stay with their mum. "But my dad loved the girls," Blair had protested.

"They're too young to go to a funeral," Daniel insisted.

Riley had sent her a condolence card with a huge long story about how much she loved Malcolm and would be eternally grateful for the kindness he had shown her when they were young. Blair read the card then ripped it into tiny pieces and threw it in the bin.

Something caught Blair's attention at the back of the church. She turned round and was astonished to see a woman dressed in black sitting at one of the pews. She felt herself inwardly explode, and it took all her strength to stop herself running to the back of the church. Daniel squeezed her arm, shaking her out of her trance. "Are you okay?" he whispered. He looked behind and then understood. Carrie Matthews had re-appeared.

As soon as the coffin was safely back in the hearse and on its way to the crematorium, Blair made a beeline for her mother. Her steely grey eyes were filled with rage. "What the hell are you doing here?" Blair hissed.

"Please don't start, Blair. Malcolm was my husband," Carrie said, calmly.

"You're not welcome at the crematorium or at the wake, so don't you dare try and worm your way in. Oh, and by the way, there's no inheritance; just in case that is the reason why you are here," Blair spat the words out.

Carrie opened her mouth in shock. "That's not why I'm here, Blair," she said, tearfully.

It had been a long day at the kennels; Riley needed a hot shower and her bed. As she turned into her drive, she was surprised to see Daniel's Ferrari. She got out of her car and before she could say anything, he cupped his hands around her face, pulled her close and kissed her tenderly. "I can't live without you for one more day, Riley," he told her.

"You don't have to," she replied.

"I'll end things with Blair tomorrow," he said.

Riley nodded. "Stay with me tonight. The girls are with Eden," she said as she took his hand and led him into the house.

Chapter 84

Annalisa had called a meeting in her office. Gordon and Harry Trent were already present and exchanging pleasantries when Daniel walked in. Annalisa looked at her watch. "Sorry, Anna; I got held up," Daniel apologised.

One thing Annalisa detested was bad punctuality. She flicked her long black hair back over her shoulder and shifted her body, so she was sitting upright at her desk; ready for business. It was the first time Daniel had come face to face with Gordon after discovering that he was his biological father. The two men looked at each other and a silent acknowledgement was exchanged between them. It was so obvious to Daniel now that Gordon was his real father; they were practically identical in every way. How could he have not known?

"Right. Well, as you know, I've found a new site for the flying centre. It's in Essex. I've been in touch with The National Air Traffic Service, and they have no objections to the plans. The County Council's Minerals and Waste Team asked for a detailed site waste management plan which we submitted and has been approved. The final decision now rests with the council, but I don't envisage any problems there so, gentlemen, I think within the next few weeks, we will be good to go," Annalisa told them, feeling pleased with herself for, yet again, sorting out the way forward for the flying centre. Her hazel eyes sparkled, and Daniel wanted to hug her.

"That's amazing Anna. Thank you so much," said Daniel.

"Oh, and I found out who bought the land here," Annalisa added, sitting back in her chair.

"The council bought it," Daniel said.

"Jeff Deakin bought it," she corrected him. She knew that nugget of information would hit them like a ton of bricks. "He then sold it on to the council, making a tidy profit." The men fell silent trying to process what they had just been told. Daniel looked at her, puzzled.

"Why?" he asked.

Annalisa shrugged. "Are you sure you don't have some beef with him?" she asked. Annalisa was very intuitive and insightful, she knew either Daniel or Gordon would have had to have done something pretty offensive to warrant Jeff Deakin pulling the rug out from beneath them like that, but Gordon was a very placid, easy-going man and didn't have any enemies that Annalisa knew of, so it must be something to do with Daniel.

"Not that I know of," Daniel said, defensively.

Gordon shook his head. "I thought we were friends," he said, in disbelief.

Blair left another message for Daniel. She had stopped feeling anger towards him for abandoning her after the funeral and was now starting to feel panic building up. Had she pushed him too far? He couldn't split up with her. She couldn't live without him. She had come too far and worked too hard to lose him now. She kept pushing away thoughts of Daniel and Riley together; laughing, kissing, holding hands, ripping each other's clothes off.

Blair slapped herself around the face to try and bring herself to her senses. It was all too much to cope with. Her dad had died, her mother had come back, and now, she was losing Daniel. What had she done to deserve all this? She was a good person. She worked hard. She gave to charity. She looked after Daniel's girls. She looked after Daniel. What more could she do? Why wasn't she good enough?

Daniel stood sheepishly on the doorstep. He hadn't thought things through properly. He should have phoned Siobhan first. They hadn't seen each other for a while. May be she would think he was a nuisance just turning up like that. The door opened and Jeff looked at Daniel in surprise. Daniel was just as surprised to see Jeff at home; his car wasn't in the drive, so he assumed he was out. "Oh hi, Jeff," Daniel said, awkwardly.

"Daniel," Jeff said.

"I was just wondering if I could speak to Siobhan. It's about Riley," Daniel said, thinking quickly for an excuse to be there.

"I'm sorry, Daniel. Siobhan can't see you right now," Jeff answered.

A voice called out from the top of the stairs. "It's okay, darling. Show Daniel in."

Reluctantly, Jeff moved away from the door and beckoned for Daniel to enter.

Daniel stopped suddenly when he saw Siobhan coming down the stairs. He was stupefied. "Siobhan," he gasped.

"Come into the kitchen," Siobhan said, leading him across the hallway. She knew he was shocked at the sight of her. She hadn't seen any friends or family for a couple of months and in that time she had lost quite a lot of weight. She had a scarf tied around her head to disguise the fact that she was completely bald. Daniel was surprised to see how pale and gaunt Siobhan looked. She had lost so much weight she looked like a small child and her voice was just a whisper. Siobhan sat down at the table, and Daniel sat opposite her. "I've got Pancreatic Cancer," she told him.

Daniel gasped. "When?" he asked.

"I've had it for some time. The doctors thought it was diabetes and by the time they found out what it really was, it was too late," she said, numbly.

"What do you mean too late?" Daniel asked.

"I'm dying, Daniel," she said. Siobhan looked into his eyes and felt sad to have had to tell him. She had got used to the idea and almost accepted it, but telling other people and watching their faces crumble killed her every time.

Daniel felt tears spring to his eyes. "I'm so sorry, Von," was all he could manage to say.

Siobhan reached across the table and held his hand. Her grip was so weak he could hardly feel her hand on his.

"Riley…" Daniel began.

"No. Don't tell her please. I'll tell her soon, but I know she'll come storming round here, and I won't be strong enough to compose myself. I'll be a mess if I see her," Siobhan said, fighting back the tears.

Daniel walked around the table and bent down and hugged Siobhan tightly. What was once a strong, fit body felt like a bag of bones in his arms. "Is there anything I can do?" he whispered in his ear.

Siobhan pulled away and touched his cheek tenderly. "Just remember the fun times, and please look after my Riley," she told him.

"I will. I promise," he said.

Daniel watched Siobhan walk away from him for the last time and struggle back upstairs. He wiped his eyes and went to the door. Jeff got there just before him. "I'll see you out," he said flatly.

When both men were outside, Jeff shut the door behind him. "I'm so sorry for what you're going through, Jeff," Daniel said, sympathetically.

"Are you?" Jeff asked. "Or are you just sorry you can't fuck my wife anymore?"

Daniel froze. He felt his throat start to close up. He then realised why Jeff had bought the land, forcing him out of business. "You know?" Daniel said.

Jeff looked at him in disgust and slammed the door in his face.

Daniel got back into his car sheepishly and reversed slowly out of the driveway. Blair looked down at her phone in total shock. Daniel hadn't ended the call after speaking to her just before he arrived at Siobhan's, and she had just heard every word Jeff had said.

Chapter 85

Blair sat naked at the dressing table. She combed her freshly washed hair and then carefully applied the black mascara onto her pale lashes with gentle flicks of the wand. She patted some concealer around her eyes and felt more like herself again. She then reached for the bottle of Chanel and sprayed it across her neck and down her chest. Lastly, she secured the clasp of her diamond bracelet around her wrist. All she had to do now was choose a dress, and she would be ready.

Daniel threw his keys onto the table in the hallway and headed to the bar. He had never wanted a drink so much in his life. As he poured out a brandy, he felt Blair's arms around his waist behind him. He closed his eyes and sipped his drink. The liquid burnt his throat as it trickled down. He necked back the rest of the drink and put the glass down on the bar. Turning to Blair, he said, "We need to talk."

Blair sat on the edge of the armchair, twiddling her earring around, nervously. "What is it?" she asked.

Daniel leant back in the chair opposite her and rubbed his face hard. He was exhausted and could do without the drama that was about to unfold, but he knew it needed to be done, and there was no point putting it off anymore. He looked at her and felt a twinge of guilt. She looked so small and lost; could he really do this to her now, so soon after losing her dad? He then thought about Riley and knew he was ultimately doing the right thing. "I can't do this anymore, Blair," he told her. He wasn't able to look at her face because he knew this was going to destroy her. Daniel waited patiently for Blair to scream or cry or even throw something at him.

Surprisingly, she said, "Okay."

He looked at her in shock.

Blair got up from the chair and walked out of the room.

Daniel followed her upstairs. "Are you alright, Blair?" he asked.

"I'm fine, Daniel," Blair continued, "I take it you will be getting back with Riley."

"I've never really got over her," he explained.

He and Riley had made plans for their future, but he didn't want to rub salt into the wounds.

"Well, I wish you every happiness," Blair said, taking off her jewellery and putting it away neatly in the jewellery box.

"All I ever wanted was for you to be happy, Daniel, and if Riley makes you happy, then good."

Daniel took her hand and pulled her towards him. "Thanks, Blair, that means a lot," he said, gratefully.

Blair smiled her sweetest smile and kissed him gently on the cheek.

"Would you like something to eat?" Daniel asked her.

Blair shook her head. "I'm actually really tired. I'm just going to go to bed. Oh, do you want me to use a different room?" she asked matter-of-factly.

"No, no, of course not. I'll sleep in the spare room. Listen, thank you for being so understanding," Daniel told her.

Blair waited until she heard Daniel's car pull away and then went into the bathroom. She reached for the cabinet door and as she opened it she stopped and looked at herself in the door mirror. Her hair was nice and her make-up was perfect, but still, she wasn't good enough for him. The moment she had dreaded had arrived. She now had to carry out the plan she had devised.

Blair wasn't going to lose Daniel without a fight. She reached up to the top shelf of the cabinet and took out the bottle of painkillers Daniel kept in there for when his back played up. She opened the bottle and tipped half the tablets down the sink. Then she filled the glass beside the sink with water from the tap and went back to the bedroom. She took off her dress and draped it neatly on the little floral chair beside the window and then got under the duvet on the bed.

Blair tipped the rest of the tablets from the bottle into her hand and put them in her mouth. She washed them all down with the glass of water. She typed out a message to Daniel and pressed the 'send' button. Blair slipped further down the bed and let her head sink down into the soft, cool pillow. She would now go to sleep and wait.

Chapter 86

Blair blinked a few times as the bright light in the hospital room hurt her eyes.

"Are you okay?" asked Daniel. Blair turned her head and smiled with relief.

"Daniel," she whispered. The pain in her throat was excruciating, and she started to cough.

"Try not to talk," said Riley, rushing over to lift Blair's head up slightly.

Blair looked at Riley, confused. *What the hell was she doing here?*

"It's okay, I've got her," interrupted a woman who had just walked into the room.

Blair was even more distressed to see her mother walking towards her.

"I'll take over from here, thank you," said Carrie, abruptly.

"Yes, of course. We'll leave you to it," said Daniel.

"We'll come back and see you later, Blair," Riley said, blowing her a kiss as they left.

Blair was confused and angry, but she was in so much pain she couldn't think straight. "I need pain relief," she whispered to her mother.

"Yes, darling, I'll get the nurse," her mother told her, quickly going to find a member of staff.

Blair lay back down on the pillow. She was devastated. The plan had gone horribly wrong. It was supposed to have brought Daniel to his senses and make him realise he couldn't live without her, but all it had done was leave her with severe throat pain and a sore stomach and headache.

Carrie returned shortly after with a nurse who wasn't too pleased at being dragged away from the patient she was attending to. "How can I help?" she asked, sternly.

"She needs painkillers, I just told you," Carrie said, rudely.

"And I told you, Mrs Matthews, your daughter has had all the pain relief she is due and can't have any more for another three hours I'm afraid. The best thing for you to do Blair is to rest and try not to speak," the nurse told her.

"Look, I'm feeling a bit better now. Can I go home?" Blair muttered.

"I'm afraid not, Blair. You need to stay in overnight for observation, and we need to do a psychiatric report on you."

Blair rolled over on to her side in despair.

"Don't cry, darling. I'm here with you now, and I won't be going anywhere," Carry told her, rubbing her back gently.

"I feel awful just leaving her, Daniel," Riley said as she sipped the hot cup of coffee in the cafe opposite the hospital.

"What else could we have done babe? Her mother wanted us to leave," Daniel said, wiping away the ketchup that was running down his chin from the bacon sandwich he was devouring.

"It was a cry for help," said Riley, feeling helpless that there was nothing they could do to help Blair.

"She's in hospital; it's the best place for her," Daniel said.

"Yes, but don't you feel even a bit guilty? I know I do," said Riley.

"Yes, a bit I suppose. I hurt her, and I'm sorry for that, but you're my wife, and I want to be with you. I never even asked Blair to move in with me, she just sort of started helping out with the girls then just assumed she would be moving in," Daniel said, defensively.

Riley stared at her husband across the table. What he was saying sounded so callous and heartless. "Right, we better go and pick up the girls," he said, wiping his hands on his serviette. I'll go up and pay at the counter, you finish your drink.

Diana was at the supermarket examining an avocado, before deciding it was good enough to go into her trolley. As she strolled down the cold meats aisle, she was surprised to see Jeff Deakin heading towards her. He looked slightly bewildered as he searched the shelves for something. "Hello, Jeff, are you looking for anything in particular?" asked Diana.

Jeff looked up, surprised. "Oh hello, Diana," he said. "I'm just getting a few bits in for Siobhan's family. They're coming over from Ireland tomorrow to stay for a while," he said, half-heartedly.

"Is everything alright Jeff? You don't look too well," Diana said. She liked Jeff and was genuinely concerned. Diana's words seemed to hit a nerve and

Jeff felt himself stumble. He grabbed hold of his trolley with one hand for support and put the other hand up to his face, and he began to sob quietly. Diana quickly rushed over to him and reached up and put her arms around his shoulders. "Whatever is it?" she asked.

Jeff cleared his throat; feeling embarrassed and wiped his face with the back of his hand. "I'm so sorry, Diana," he apologised.

"Don't be silly. Don't apologise. I'm just worried about you Jeff. Are you unwell?" she asked.

"It's Siobhan. She's dying," he murmured.

Diana's mouth dropped open. "Look why don't I help you with your shopping, and we can go and have a coffee in the cafe before we leave and have a chat," she said.

"Yes. Thank you. I'd like that," Jeff said, meekly.

Rose and Patsy were flopped on the sofa watching TV when Daniel and Riley turned up to collect them. Diana pulled up in the drive at the same time and wondered what Riley was doing there with Daniel. Daniel walked over and held the door open for her. "Hi, Mum," he said, kissing her on the cheek.

"Hello, Daniel. Hello, Riley," she said flatly. Riley was used to Diana's brusqueness and let it go over her head.

They all walked into the house and the girls sprang up off the sofa and ran to hug their mother. "I bumped into Jeff Deakin at the supermarket," Diana said. Everyone turned round to face her. "Poor man didn't know what he was doing. I don't think he's ever been shopping on his own before," Diana continued.

"Apparently, Siobhan's family are flying over from Ireland tomorrow. They are all frantic. The poor woman is terminally ill and hasn't got long left, apparently."

Riley gasped. Daniel glared at his mother. "What do you mean?" Riley asked, in a panic.

Diana looked at her as if she was a moron. "Did you not hear what I said?" she asked.

"Okay, Mum. Riley is just in shock," Daniel said, angrily. "I think it's time we went. Get your things girls," Daniel told his children. He then gently took hold of Riley's hand and led her out of the house.

Chapter 87

The women stared at each other on the doorstep and the memories of how their lives had become inextricably intertwined flooded back, and they both broke down in tears. Riley caught Siobhan as she seemed to lose her footing and both women ended up on the ground in each other's arms. Siobhan's scarf slipped off revealing small tufts of auburn hair randomly scattered around her head. Riley carefully lifted Siobhan off the floor, then lead her inside where she gently helped her lie down on the sofa. She curled up on the sofa beside her and put her head in Siobhan's lap, just like she used to do when she was a teenager.

Riley could feel the bones of Siobhan's thin legs digging into her cheek. Siobhan gently stroked Riley's hair. If only she could turn back time. She had had such happy times with the Mulligans, and she had adored Terry. If only she had been a bit older and wiser and not so full of wanderlust; she could have had a good life with Terry and the girls.

The two women didn't speak; there was nothing to say. It was a foregone conclusion that Siobhan was going to die, and Riley was going to be devastated so what was the point of talking about it and making themselves even more sad. Just sitting with each other in the silence with their thoughts and memories was all they needed to do.

When Jeff entered the house he saw someone lying on the sofa with Siobhan, in the dark. He immediately turned on the lamp and was relieved to see that the other person was Riley. Both women had fallen asleep. Riley stirred when she heard Jeff come into the room. She lifted her head from Siobhan's lap, but Siobhan didn't move. She was still and cold. Riley jumped up and Jeff fell to his knees beside Siobhan. He felt her pulse and gasped. She had gone!

Chapter 88
Christmas Eve

Outside the Fairgate family house, a woman gazed in through the window. She wrapped her big heavy coat tighter around her small frame and watched as they all played happy families inside. The children were excitedly shouting and running around and the adults were drinking and eating and talking about their lives. She was once part of that family for a short time and had never been happier.

Now, she had nothing. Her dreams for the future had been tossed away without a care by the man who was supposed to have loved her. Blair watched as Daniel took Riley's face in his hands and kissed her tenderly. She then turned around and walked back to her car. This wasn't going to be their happy ever after; she would make sure of it!

Riley sat on the step outside. For the first time in ages, she craved a drink. It was being in that house again with the Fairgates; it brought back all the memories of the crash. She looked at the pathway she had run down, dragging Patsy with her. She remembered all the shouting and screaming as Daniel had tried to pull her out of the car, then the terrifying thud of a body being hurled onto the windscreen in front of them.

The next recollection she had was waking up in hospital. Riley shuddered. Her heart started to pound and her breathing began to quicken. She felt herself becoming detached, and she gripped the step with both hands to steady herself from the dizziness that was making her sway from side to side.

"Riley, are you okay?" said Jerry, rushing down the steps. He got to the bottom step and put his arms around her shoulders. Riley leant against him; grateful for the support. He hugged her tightly, and she felt her body start to relax. Soon, she had calmed down. Jerry rubbed her arm gently. "What happened?" he asked, concerned.

"I'm sorry, Jerry. I haven't had a panic attack like that for a long time. It's just being here again and remembering the accident," she told him.

Jerry looked at her sympathetically. "I get it! It must be hard," he said.

Riley thought how out of place Jerry looked. He was a cool, talented musician from New Orleans; he should be with like-minded people in a blues bar in Bourbon Street listening to jazz not being forced to converse with the over-privileged, over-indulged Fairgate family. Riley was fond of Joe, but his sense of entitlement was off the Richter scale. As if he was reading her thoughts, Jerry said, "I feel like we are both the outsiders of the family. Am I right?"

Riley nodded. "Diana detests me. She thinks I'm common!" she said, and they both started giggling. Soon, the giggling turned into laughter and before they knew it they were in hysterics.

"It's so good to laugh. I've haven't laughed like that in ages," Jerry said, trying to catch his breath.

"What are you two doing out here," Daniel said, rubbing his shoulders as the night air hit him. "It's freezing, come inside." Riley and Jerry got up and followed Daniel inside.

Chapter 89

Carmelita had joined the family for Christmas dinner. She had dressed up in her favourite dress which Adolpho had bought for her on their honeymoon in Catalonia. Her tiny frame had not changed over the years and the dress fitted her perfectly. It was knee-length and heavily decorated with designs of brightly coloured flowers woven into the fabric and had ribbons around the waist and lace around the hemline. "You look beautiful Carmelita," Diana said, approvingly.

Carmelita blushed. She wasn't used to receiving such compliments from her employer. "Yes, you really do Carmelita," Riley reiterated.

Carmelita's smile vanished, and she looked down at the mash potatoes in front of her. "Who would like mash?" Carmelita asked. Riley looked away, embarrassed. Carmelita was never going to forgive her, and she didn't really blame her. Daniel squeezed Riley's knee under the table and smiled lovingly at her. He didn't want his wife to have to pay for her mistake for the rest of her life. After all, she hadn't killed Adolpho, even though Adolpho's family blamed her for his death.

Blair sat at the little kitchen table in the apartment she was renting. It was small but beautifully furnished and overlooked the river. She had spent a few days in a health retreat and felt calmer and stronger. Her mother held the end of a cheap gaudy cracker out in front of her. Blair stared at her in disbelief. Did she actually want her to pull a cracker?

"Come on, Blair," Carrie urged her daughter.

Blair rolled her eyes and pulled the cracker. A mini screwdriver fell out and rolled across the table. "Who thinks up this tat?" Blair asked, in disgust.

"It's just tradition, darling," Carrie said. She was trying her best to make the day nice for them both, but Blair was making it impossibly difficult. Not in her wildest dreams had Blair envisaged spending Christmas day alone with her mother. She had to admit though, the dinner smelt unbelievably good.

"Thank you for going to all this trouble," was all that Blair could muster up to say to her mother. She still hadn't forgiven her for running out on them a second time, but she didn't have the energy to keep up the stubbornness. If her mother wanted to look after her now then she would let her; after all, no one else wanted to.

"I know this isn't the Christmas day you had planned Blair, but I'm afraid this is as good as it gets for both of us, so we might as well make the most of it," her mother told her.

Blair nodded in agreement. She planned to stuff herself silly with all the amazing food her mother had cooked and then sit and watch *The Holiday*. She would cry along with Kate Winslet while eating Quality Street chocolates. Her mother coming back into her life had actually happened at the right time. She had managed to rescue her daughter and nurse her back to health.

Blair didn't kid herself and believe her mother would stay permanently, but she was here now, and Blair didn't have anyone else. Daniel hadn't bothered to contact her since the overdose drama, but then what did she expect? She had always known he was emotionally unavailable and couldn't cope with women with 'issues' but she still loved him and wanted him back.

One by one, all the members of the family began to leave the Fairgate house and return back to their own homes. Diana sat back in her favourite armchair with a large gin and tonic in her hand and sighed. Gordon bent down and kissed her on the head. "You did a wonderful job darling. What a wonderful weekend," he told her.

She smiled, appreciatively. "Family! Isn't that what life is all about?" she asked, feeling totally satisfied with herself.

"Of course!" Gordon replied.

Gordon went outside for some air and sat down on the bench by his favourite majestic old oak tree at the bottom of the garden. He took out his phone and dialled Madeleine's number. "Ah, my darling, how are you? Have you had a good day?" he asked his lover.

"Mon Cheri," Madeleine purred down the phone. "I have had a wonderful day. Thank you. When will I see you again?" she asked.

"I can fly out the day after tomorrow, my love," Gordon told her, excitedly.

"Perfect! I can't wait," Madeleine replied.

What Gordon hadn't noticed was someone else had also come to the bottom of the garden for some air and to be alone with her thoughts. Carmelita watched in total disbelief as Gordon got up from the bench and walked back towards the house.

Chapter 90
January 2017

Blair watched with a smile on her face as Daniel drove away. Her little plan had worked. Daniel felt sick to his stomach. Why the hell had he just done that? What was wrong with him? He had only gone over to Blair's flat because she had called him, hysterically crying and frightened for her life. She had told him she had a weird stalker who had been following her, and she was worried he was outside as she had heard strange noises.

Daniel had gone round and checked thoroughly, but there were no signs of anyone hanging around. The next thing he knew, she was pulling him down on to the sofa and reaching for the zip on his jeans. He wasn't thinking about his wife when he pulled up Blair's jumper and stroked her small pert breasts. Before he knew it, she had climbed on top of him. He grabbed Blair's hips and fucked her hard.

Blair screamed with pleasure as her whole body shuddered in ecstasy. Daniel slipped out from underneath her and tried to catch his breath. Blair kissed his warm stomach, breathing in his familiar smell. She was on cloud nine. As far as she was concerned, this proved to her that Daniel could not possibly be still in love with his wife!

Chapter 91

Riley walked past The Lighthouse Grill restaurant at the bottom of the newly built, Herts Wharf building, and nervously got into the lift and pressed the button for the top floor of the apartment block. When she reached the correct floor, the doors opened, and Riley saw Blair waiting for her. She looked as immaculate as ever in a navy woollen dress and knee high boots. Her blonde hair had been cut into a mid-length bob, which made her look elegant and sophisticated.

Riley hadn't known what to expect when Blair had contacted her out of the blue. She walked through the open doors and felt underdressed in her tight jeans, cowboy boots and long cable-knit chunky cardigan. Blair smiled at her and opened out her arms. With a sigh of relief, Riley laughed and hugged Blair tightly.

"Have a look at this view," Blair said, excitedly, holding Riley's hand and guiding her towards the roof terrace.

Riley was astounded at the views across the Hertfordshire countryside as well as the river and local restaurants and shops. "It's lovely, Blair," Riley told her.

Blair then led Riley into the apartment and showed her around the exposed brick-style rooms with modern contemporary fixtures and fittings. She was describing everything enthusiastically, and it made Riley smile. "This is so 'you', Blair," Riley told her friend. "You've always had such a great eye for design and fashion."

Blair wanted to show Riley that even though losing Daniel had nearly destroyed her, she was over it and stronger than ever. "I'm only renting for now, but if I'm happy here, I might buy the apartment," Blair told her.

"I'm so glad you got in touch, Blair," said Riley.

Blair smiled. "Life is too short, Riley, and we did say all those years ago when we were fifteen that we would never let a guy ever come between us," she said.

"Yes, I remember. Let's put everything behind us and start again," Riley said, relieved.

Blair bent over and hugged her friend. "I'd like that. How about some champagne to celebrate?" she asked.

"Oh, no thank you," Riley told her.

"But don't let me stop you having a glass of fizz," she added. Blair went to the kitchen and came back with a glass of champagne for herself and a Garden Watermelon Sour cocktail for Riley.

The two women chatted about family and work and found they were able to piece together their friendship again, with unexpected ease. All their past problems were now water under the bridge as far as they were both concerned. "You know I never meant to steal Daniel away from you," Blair said. She had had a couple of glasses of champagne and felt herself opening up to Riley. They were both sat opposite each other with their legs curled up in the snug armchairs.

"I know, Blair. I'm grateful you looked after them all for me. I don't blame you for falling in love with Daniel; what's not to love?" said Riley.

Blair felt her cheeks starting to burn. She could feel Riley pitying her, and that is not what she intended to happen that afternoon. "Well, I realise now, Riley, that it wasn't love. I was infatuated with him. He's a charming man but…" Blair's voice trailed off.

"But what?" asked Riley.

"No, don't listen to me, I've had too much to drink," Blair said.

Riley laughed. "You've only had two glasses, Blair," she said.

"Actually I had a couple of glasses of wine before you got here for Dutch courage," Blair said, blushing.

Riley was intrigued and wanted to know what Blair was about to reveal. "Go on, tell me," Riley insisted.

Blair hesitated.

"No, I really don't want to cause trouble, Riley," she said, pouring herself another drink.

Riley's heart began to thump in her chest. What did Blair know? "You won't be causing trouble. You can't leave me hanging like that," Riley said, trying to make a joke out of it but actually started to feel a bit sick. Riley noticed that Blair started to sound a bit tipsy.

"I'm telling you this because you're my friend, Riley. Daniel was having an affair with Siobhan," Blair said, looking directly into Riley's eyes for a reaction.

Riley burst out laughing, and then realising Blair wasn't joking, her whole body went cold. She shook her head and said, "You must be mistaken, Blair."

"I heard them, Riley. Just before Siobhan died, Daniel went to her house. He didn't realise he hadn't ended our phone call on his phone, so I heard the whole conversation. That is why Jeff bought the land to try and force Daniel out of business. He must have found out somehow. They had been having an affair for years even before I came along."

Riley jumped up. "No, that's not true. Why would you say such a thing?" she shouted.

Blair put her hands up to her mouth and felt tears spring guiltily to her eyes. "I'm sorry, Riley, I shouldn't have said anything," she apologised.

"I think I should go," Riley said, picking up her handbag. "Thanks for the drink," she added. She felt numb with shock, and she needed to get away from Blair.

Riley sat in her car feeling completely traumatised. A million thoughts were racing through her head. Why would Blair lie? Is that why she had asked Riley over that afternoon to humiliate her? Was it even true? Daniel did used to have massages with Siobhan. What if one thing had led to another? Surely, Siobhan wouldn't have betrayed her? Her mind vacillated between doubt and disbelief.

Riley remembered that Siobhan had always been a free spirit and did as she pleased. But, Daniel? Would he really cheat on her with one of her best friends? Riley's head started spinning, and she found it hard to breathe. She opened her car door and dragged herself out of the car. She ran towards the bridge over the river and as she clung onto the rail, she leant over and threw up.

The gushing sound of the water below being pushed downstream by the strong current was so loud; it was making her head hurt. She took some deep, long breaths, and slowly, her breathing became less erratic and calmer. She decided she wasn't going to confront Daniel with this information just yet. She needed to think about what she was going to do. She took her phone out of her pocket and saw ten missed calls from Blair. She couldn't talk to Blair until she figured things out first.

Riley pulled up in the car park of Jeff's country club. She decided she would get to the bottom of the allegation by confronting Jeff before approaching Daniel, but once she got there, she wasn't sure whether she could go through with it. Riley saw Jeff's car parked in his space. "You can do this, Riley," she said to herself.

"Can I help you?" asked the receptionist, as Riley approached the front desk.

"Yes, I'd like to see Jeff Deakin, please. Could you tell him it's Riley Fairgate?" Riley said, politely.

By the end of the meeting with Jeff, Riley would know if her husband was a liar. If he wasn't, then her best friend was a liar. It would be a lose/lose situation whatever the outcome was.

The woman phoned through to Jeff's office. "I've got Riley Fairgate in reception Mr Deakin," she said. She hung up and smiled at Riley. "He will be down shortly. Please take a seat."

Riley sat down but kept thinking about Siobhan. She remembered the many times she had seen Siobhan floating around the club, smiling and chatting away to everyone she walked past. Her Irish charm made everyone fall in love with her. Had that included Daniel too?

The country club reception was light and airy and fresh looking with lots of potted plants dotted around. It wasn't long before Jeff appeared. Riley watched as the tall, smart looking man with very long legs flung the double doors open and strode down the corridor towards her. Jeff was dressed in his usual uniform of brown tweed jacket, shirt and beige trousers. "Good to see you, Riley," Jeff said, embracing her warmly.

"You too, Jeff," said Riley. She loved Jeff, so this wasn't going to be an easy conversation. Riley noticed that Jeff seemed to have aged a lot since Siobhan died. He looked a bit lost and forlorn and had deep lines along his forehead and under his eyes. He also had an empty look that Riley recognised. It was the same look her beloved dad had when her mum passed away.

"So what brings you here, Riley?" Jeff asked, as he beckoned for her to follow him into one of the meeting rooms nearby.

"This is a bit painful for me, Jeff, and I'm sorry to have to ask this, but I've just been given some news that has frankly knocked the wind out of my sails."

They both sat down in the large black swivel chairs next to each other at the long table in the small room. Riley took a deep breath and told Jeff what Blair had said. His face fell, but he didn't look surprised. He looked out of the tiny window in front of him, so he didn't have to look into Riley's eyes. "I'm afraid it is true, Riley," he said. His face was expressionless, so Riley couldn't tell how he was feeling. She couldn't speak for a few seconds.

"I can't believe it," she whispered.

"He wasn't the first," Jeff said, matter-of-factly.

"There were others?" Riley asked, shocked.

"She wanted an open marriage. I'm afraid I couldn't fulfil her needs," Jeff said, sadly.

Riley felt deeply sorry for him. Jeff was a good man, and he had been devoted to Siobhan. Then she thought about Daniel and her blood started to boil. "Is that why you bought the land from under him?" she asked.

"I'm ashamed to admit it, Riley; but yes. I was angry, not only about what he did with my wife but also what he did to you too," Jeff said, sadly.

Riley sat in her car in the car park mulling over what she had just found out. The adrenaline was raging through her body. How dare he do that to her!

Daniel's car was parked in the drive when Riley got home. Damn! She was hoping she could have downed a quick drink before he got home from work, but he had got back early. She had planned to stay calm and confront him sensibly, but her good intentions flew out the window when she pulled up and saw his car. She had fiery Mulligan blood coursing through her veins; staying calm was something they found difficult to do.

Riley stormed into the house and slammed the door shut.

Daniel came rushing out into the hallway. "Hi, darling," he said, looking worried.

"You son of a bitch!" Riley screamed at him.

Daniel opened his eyes wide in surprise.

The look of shock on his face almost made Riley laugh, but she had to compose herself. She always laughed when she was upset; it was a nervous habit. "You were having an affair with Siobhan; one of my best fucking friends," she yelled.

Daniel fell silent. He felt like the earth was crumbling beneath his feet, and he was about to fall straight down into hell. He had to think fast. "What are you talking about?" he asked, pretending to be completely miffed.

Riley rolled her eyes. "Daniel. I. Know!" she said.

"That's absurd!" Daniel protested.

"Argggg!" yelled Riley, in frustration.

Daniel grabbed Riley's arm. "Please calm down Riley. Tell me what you think happened," he said, trying to sound like he was in complete control.

Riley repeated what Blair had told her. To her complete surprise, Daniel burst out laughing. "Oh my god, you don't actually believe that psycho bitch, do you?" he asked.

Riley was dumbfounded. "Jeff confirmed it," she said, angrily.

"Jeff is a dickhead. He's a jealous, twisted man who couldn't satisfy his wife. He thought everyone was having an affair with Siobhan. Remember that guy that they were friendly with who looked after their boat in the marina in Brighton? He thought Siobhan was having an affair with him and the next thing, the poor fella's body was found washed up on the beach," said Daniel.

Riley couldn't speak. She stared at her husband, trying to comprehend what he was telling her. She remembered seeing the story on the news and how upset Siobhan had been. But surely Jeff wasn't capable of doing something like that. "I know you think Jeff is all sweetness and light, but he has a tough East End criminal family background behind him that you know nothing about," Daniel said, leaning up against the worktop.

"Siobhan was our friend, Riley. You made me go to her to help with my back. She helped me with my nightmares about James too. Surely you don't think she would have done anything to hurt you? She loved you like a daughter," he said.

Riley felt totally confused now. May be Daniel was telling the truth.

"You know me, baby, better than anyone else. I would die for you. You are my 'everything'. We are Daniel and Riley; we're meant to be together. I would never do anything to hurt you," Daniel said, as he walked towards her and reached for her hand.

Riley felt hot tears spring to her eyes. She really didn't know what to think anymore. "Blair heard your conversation though," she said.

Daniel rolled his eyes. "Blair hears what she wants to hear. I was comforting a friend of ours who had just told me she was dying from cancer. Yes, I was upset and so was she. Yes, I probably told her I loved her, just like you would have done. She even told me to make sure I looked after you. Is that a woman who would betray you?" he said, reaching over and gently wiping away the tears rolling down her cheeks.

Riley suddenly felt foolish and stupid. "I'm so sorry, Daniel," she said as she started to sob.

Daniel pulled her into his arms, and they held each other tightly. "It's okay," he told her.

Chapter 92
February 2017

Blair vigorously scrubbed the white marble coloured tiles on the kitchen floor. She had already descaled the kettle and given the oven a good going over too. She threw the cloth down and leant back against the cupboard, cross-legged on the floor. Her back and neck ached.

To take her mind off the constant memories of her life with Daniel that was playing on a loop in her head, she had decided to throw herself into cleaning the, already sparkling clean, apartment. She then burst into tears. The apartment felt empty and soulless, just like her. Riley had been ghosting her since her revelation about Daniel. Blair assumed she had forgiven him.

Knowing Daniel, he probably would have said Blair was making it all up. She was looking forward to going back to work. Selena had been surprisingly sympathetic and told her to come back when she was ready. Now, Blair felt it was the right time to go back. She needed distraction, and she also happened to love her job and was bloody good at it. She needed to feel like her old self again and forget about Daniel bloody Fairgate.

The new Fairgate Flight Centre and Flying School was up and running, and Daniel was excited. His business was thriving, he had a great business partner whom he trusted completely and his father was also involved, so they got to spend lots of time together, which they both loved. Since finding out Gordon was his biological father, Daniel had felt even closer to him. He also loved how it had put Joe's nose out of joint. His lazy, idle, good-for-nothing older brother would have to step up his game now if he was going to have any sort of relationship with their father. Things were also great with Riley; she seemed to have put all the Siobhan nonsense to one side and concentrated on them being a proper family again.

Annalisa walked into the hanger. "Hi, what are you doing?" she asked Daniel.

Daniel turned and smiled at her. "Just having a look at my new baby?" he said, admiring the new plane he had just bought.

"She is beautiful, I have to admit," Annalisa said, stroking her hand down the nose of the plane.

"This place is amazing, Anna. What a great find!" Daniel had been delighted when he heard the new airfield had eight grass runways and two tarmac ones for bad weather conditions. That was more than they had previously had and the new briefing and exam rooms were more modern and pleasant. Even the cafe was bigger and could cater for more people. Jeff Deakin did him a favour by buying that land; it had forced Daniel to go 'bigger and better' and he certainly loved a challenge.

It was unusual for Diana to still be in bed at midday. Carmelita had handed in her notice and Diana was distraught. Carmelita was like part of the furniture. Diana had got used to her being there and doing everything for her. How she was going to cope without her?

But it was what her housekeeper had said that had flummoxed Diana. She said, she was a woman of high morals and couldn't live in a house with people who didn't share the same morals as her. Diana had asked her to explain what she meant, but all Carmelita said was, "I'm sorry, Mrs Fairgate, I don't want to insult you or your family, but I must leave and go back home to my family." After overhearing her husband's conversation with his mistress on the phone at Christmas, Carmelita felt it was time to leave her employer's house and move on.

Riley wanted to speak to Blair. She had ignored all the texts that Blair had bombarded her with after their last meeting when she had accused Daniel of having an affair with Siobhan, but then Carrie Matthews had called her, out of the blue. She had begged Riley to reconcile with Blair as she was worried Blair was heading for another breakdown. She needed her friend, Carrie told her and could she possibly find it in her heart to forgive Blair. She hadn't meant to cause trouble for Riley apparently, but she had been confused and was still grieving for her father.

So Riley had given in and contacted Blair. They had both been through a lot in their lives and both done and said some stupid things, but Riley wasn't the sort of person to hold grudges, and they both decided to finally put the past behind them.

It didn't take Blair long to get back into the flow at work. Selena called her into her office one evening, just as Blair was packing up to leave. "I've lined up some great interviews for you and a trip to Paris in a few months for the first anniversary of the reopening of the Ritz. As you may know, the hotel has undergone a four-year; multimillion dollar renovation, and we are devoting a whole issue to the Ritz and everything Parisian. Cara Delevingne is going to appear on the cover, and you are going to be in charge of the whole shebang," Selena told her.

Blair stared at her, stunned. She then burst out laughing. "Oh, Selena, thank you so much. You have no idea how much this means to me," Blair said excitedly as she grabbed her boss and hugged her tightly.

Chapter 93

Ricky's thumb hovered over the send button on his phone. He had been thinking about Riley over the past few days and decided to text her. He re-read his message and then shook his head at the absurdity of it and swiftly deleted it. What was he thinking? Riley was a married woman; he needed to just leave her be.

Ricky had made a name for himself and was doing well. His design company had grown almost overnight, and their services were always in demand all around the world. His model looks also hadn't gone unnoticed and rich housewives everywhere were hiring him to work on the interiors of their palatial homes. He was finding it hard to accommodate all of them as they mostly asked for him personally to work on their houses. The women often approached him with indecent proposals, which at first, Ricky agreed to as it was such a novelty for him, but after a while, he got bored being a gigolo designer to a bunch of frustrated housewives and turned down their advances and concentrated on expanding his business instead.

Riley saw her husband sitting in the dark as she walked into the kitchen. She put her keys down, leant against the worktop and stared at him. He was so damn handsome. He was wearing his comfy loungewear and looked totally relaxed.

A bottle of whisky and a family sized bag of Tortilla crisps were on the table beside him. He heard Riley walk in and turned to look at her. His eyes glistened in the moonlight, and Riley's heart skipped a beat, like it always did when he looked at her that way. They didn't say a word to each other; they didn't need to. Their desire for each other was always there, it was a known fact between them.

When they were together, they were Daniel and Riley, and nothing else mattered. No matter how many times they drifted away from each other, the connection they had always brought them back to each other. Daniel held out his arms to her, and Riley slowly made her way over to him and climbed into his lap. She loved the feeling of his strong arms wrapped around her. He always made her feel loved and happy. She kissed him and his lips felt warm on hers.

Daniel ran his hand up her lower back, and then he slowly started undressing her. Riley lay down beneath him on the soft, white rug by the window, and he moved her hair away from her face and gazed at her whole body which glistened in the illuminating moonlight. "You are so beautiful," he told her, entranced.

She reached for his thighs and pulled him closer to her. Arching her back in pleasure she felt him enter her, but she kept her eyes open, so she could watch the ecstasy spread across his face. Daniel looked into his wife's eyes. Something about the way she was watching him at that moment made him feel vulnerable; like he was an open book, and she knew every chapter off by heart.

Chapter 94
June 2017

Riley threw her hands up in the air and pretended to scream in frustration like one of those actresses in the black and white silent movies. Her daughters were driving her mad, and she was late for work. She had a race that afternoon and liked to go to the kennels early and feed the dogs herself and then give them some gentle exercise before they left for the stadium. It was also her way of preparing herself before a race. Today, however, everything was going wrong. "Daniel!" Riley shouted.

Daniel bounded into the kitchen. "Sorry! Sorry!" he apologised.

"Please take your daughters to their swimming lesson. Now!" she demanded. Daniel and Riley both froze. The Saturday Morning Show was on in the background on the giant-sized TV mounted on the wall of the lounge area of the kitchen. They both recognised the voice of the guest who was on the programme that morning.

On the screen talking to the presenter was Ricky Berg. "So, Ricky, tell us how we should be preparing our homes and gardens for the summer months," the tall, glamorous blonde woman asked him, while flicking her long hair behind her, seductively. Riley was shocked to see her childhood sweetheart on national TV. He spoke confidently and looked polished and professional, but his blonde messy hair and moss-green eyes made Riley feel a tiny bit excited as a pang of nostalgia crept up on her.

Daniel turned his attention from the TV screen to Riley, trying to interpret her reaction. She looked as shocked as he did, but he was looking for a sign of emotion or a little telltale look of lust. The familiar jealousy was descending on him like red mist. *Would this newfound fame and fortune make Ricky more desirable to Riley?* he wondered? *What if he got in contact with her again? Would she be tempted?*

Riley felt Daniel's eyes boring into her. She turned to him and smiled. "Wow, good for Ricky," she said, matter-of-factly. "Now, can you get our girls to their lesson, so I can get to work," she said and lifted her head towards him to give him a kiss. She made sure the kiss was longer than their usual goodbye kiss because she knew he would be feeling weird after seeing Ricky on TV.

"Yuk!" Patsy and Rose shouted and then made exaggerated vomiting noises.

Riley and Daniel both laughed.

"Come on, girls," Daniel said as he picked up their swimming bags. He was satisfied that Riley hadn't been overly impressed at seeing her ex again. "Good luck, babe," he shouted to Riley as he left the house.

Riley switched the TV off and put Ricky to the back of her mind. She needed to focus on that afternoon's greyhound races and helping her dogs to win.

Chapter 95

The sun was beating down through the open window, and Daniel leant back in the black leather chair and closed his eyes. The warm rays on his face felt comforting. He had taken to sitting alone in his office at the end of the day and relishing the peace and quiet. He needed this quiet time to unwind. Echoes of his past had started plaguing him again and the nightmares had returned to haunt him.

Now, they were more vivid and psychotic and were, frankly, making his life hell. He dreaded going to sleep and stayed awake as long as possible, watching TV or checking his mail, but as a result, he was exhausted during the day. He had contemplated speaking to his doctor about going back on the pills he was prescribed in the past, but it would just be admitting his weakness. He was Daniel Fairgate. How could he admit to having nightmares, like a young child? He rubbed his face as if that would snap himself out of his misery.

Annalisa stared at Daniel through the full-length window of his office before walking in. She was wearing a white trouser suit and her black hair was tied back in a sleek ponytail, which swung from side to side as she walked into the office. Daniel admired her petite figure as she sat down opposite him. She leant across the table and pushed a small clear packet of white powder towards him. He threw back his head and laughed.

Annalisa looked at him with a glint in her eye. "Wanna share?" she asked. "It'll help get rid of all those lines you've acquired across your forehead."

"You're a star, Anna. This is just what I need," said Daniel. "How about dinner at my house? There's more where that came from," she said, pointing at the cocaine on the table. "I'll let Riley know I'll be late home," Daniel said, suddenly feeling lighter and more at ease than he had in ages.

Blair rushed round her apartment, ticking things off on her list. The room began to spin, so Blair sat down quickly and had a few sips of ginger tea. She had felt nauseous earlier, probably from all the stress of the Paris trip and the fact that she hadn't eaten properly for a couple of days. She sent Riley a text: *'The car will pick me up first and then collect you in about half an hour'.* Riley replied: *'Great I'll be ready. Can't wait!'*

"Rose baby, you have to get out of the suitcase now, Mummy needs to zip it up," Riley pleaded with her daughter.

Rose shook her head and pulled an angry face. "I don't want you to go!" Rose said, tearfully.

"I don't want you to go either," said Daniel, sitting on the edge of the bed.

"It's only one night, babe. Blair wanted me to go to support her. I'll be back before you know it," she said. She got up from the floor and wrapped her arms around her husband. She didn't want to go and leave Daniel; she had spent too much time apart from him over the years, but she couldn't let Blair down either; she had done too much of that over the years too.

Daniel carried Riley's suitcase downstairs for her. He was holding back the internal torment that had been simmering inside him since she had told him Blair invited her to Paris. He felt like he was going to implode. What if Blair let it slip about their night together? It was just a stupid mistake, but Riley would never forgive him.

Chapter 96

There was something exciting about being at the Ritz Paris. Riley imagined Princess Diana walking along the red carpet at the entrance just like she was now, just hours before she passed away. "I bet the Coco Chanel suite is unbelievable. Coco Chanel lived here for over 30 years," Blair told Riley.

"Would you like to see the Suite?" came a voice from behind Blair. She turned round and was face to face with an extremely tall, dark-haired, man. Blair guessed he was Louis, the general manager. "Hi, I'm Blair," she said, holding out her hand to shake his.

"Yes, Miss Matthews, I know who you are," he said. "The offer is still open if you would like to look round the Coco Chanel suite," the man said, in a strong French accent, which Blair found intoxicating.

"Yes, we would love to see the Suite," Blair said, excitedly.

"So this is the famous Suite," he said as he threw open the door.

Blair and Riley gasped as they stepped inside. They were both completely spellbound. "This is bigger than my whole house," Riley exclaimed.

Blair walked round the room stroking the sofa in front of the fireplace and the gilt-framed mirrors. The bathroom was enormous with an incredibly deep bathtub and plenty of neatly folded soft peach fluffy towels on the side. Louis then opened the huge window which exposed a breathtaking view of The Place Vendome. "Wow. That is The Vendome Column," said Blair.

"Did you know that was the inspiration for the octagonal stopper on the Chanel No. 5 perfume bottle?" Louis said, delighting in Blair's enthusiasm.

"No way?" she said. Blair gazed out of the window and imagined Gabrielle Chanel looking out at the Column and coming up with the idea. Riley noticed the way Louis kept gently touching Blair at every possible opportunity; on her back, her arm and even her shoulder. If Riley walked out of the room, she was sure the two of them wouldn't even notice she had gone. She glanced down at her phone, hoping Daniel might have sent her a message. She was shocked at how much she was missing him.

Back in the lobby, Louis gushed excitedly about the success of their first year after the reopening. Blair and the other members of staff were all pursed with their note books open, ready to take notes. "Everything needed upgrading. There was a tiredness here, which was sad, so we had to close the hotel down to be able to restore it to its former glory. As you can see, it has lost none of its essence and identity. Our residents have said the hotel has a lighter, fresher feel. See the reception area here?" he said, leading Blair, Riley and Blair's entourage further into the hotel. "This area is now flooded with light as the ceilings were heightened and windows were added; just subtle changes but modernising it too, which is important," he said, throwing his hands around theatrically.

Just then, Selena waltzed into the hotel dressed in a full-length electric blue satin duster coat and matching stilettos which complemented her bright red bobbed hair. "Hello, everyone! Shall we get some cocktails?" she called out, interrupting Louis while he was in full flow. Blair tried not to look surprised.

"Selena, what are you doing here?" she asked.

Riley noticed the slight agitation in Blair's voice. She obviously hadn't expected her boss to turn up and steel her thunder. Blair had worked hard arranging this trip for everyone and ensuring all the writers were very clear about what topics they were covering. Riley was relieved to hear Blair's phone ringing to defuse the awkwardness of the situation. "Hello," Blair said, abruptly. "What? Well, what else can we do? We'll just have to wait for her then." Blair was furious. "Cara Delevingne is going to be at least two hours late," she said.

Selena didn't look very happy, and Blair was starting to panic.

A short time afterwards, the suite, that the magazine was allocated for the day, was buzzing with activity. Stylists were flying around making last minute alterations to garments, models were tucking into tiny tubs of salads while their hairdressers were blow-drying and curling their hair. Cara, the star model, turned up two and half hours late, but Blair was so relieved to see her she burst into tears.

Riley was in one of the rooms rifling through a rail of clothes searching for a dress after Blair had told her to take her pick. She stopped midway as one of the dresses caught her eye. *Yep, perfect,* she said to herself.

Selena was sat cross-legged on one of the leather-topped barstools in the Bar Hemingway, soaking up the atmosphere. She knew she could trust Blair to do a good job, but she wasn't going to miss out on a free trip to Paris so had decided to invite a few friends and stick it on the company's expenses. She deserved this; she devoted every part of herself to the magazine and had sacrificed her personal life too. Now, she was too old to have children and surrogacy had never appealed to her, so she would carry on with her career and enjoy every perk that came with it.

Blair walked into the heavily wood panelled bar while the photographers got to work organising the models. The shoot would take a couple of hours which left time for Blair to relax with Riley. Selena beckoned for her to come over and sit with her. Blair sighed. She wouldn't be able to clock off just yet then as she would still have to be on her best behaviour with Selena.

Riley gazed up in awe at the magnificent painted ceilings above her and couldn't take her eyes off the huge bohemian chandelier. Gentle, relaxing music floated around the lobby as she made her way to the bar to meet Blair. She really wished Daniel was here to enjoy all this with her, she knew how much he would have loved it.

"You look fabulous," Blair told her.

"Thank you so much. I feel like a celebrity," laughed Riley as she did a little spin around in the emerald green, slinky, floor length, Alice Temperley dress she had chosen.

Blair had gone for a more subtle loose and floaty, brightly patterned 70s-style dress. The bartender slid two mocktails over to them and pointed to the one he had made for Riley; it was called Feuille and was a pale green colour which complemented her dress perfectly. He smiled at Riley, feeling very chuffed with himself.

"Thank you," Riley said, smiling back at him.

The photo shoots had been successful, and the models and their attendants packed up and got ready to leave in their chauffeur driven cars and limos. Blair, Riley and the rest of the staff from *Today Magazine* were staying for a well-deserved after-party. The music was still wafting around the hotel and the beauty of the place changed Riley's mood. "I love this hotel," she told Blair.

Blair nodded in agreement.

Riley's phone started ringing. Her face lit up as she answered the call. "Daniel!"

"Hi, darling. How's it all going? Are you having a good time?" he asked her.

"Yes, but I would be having an even better time if you were here," she said.

"I miss you too, babe, but I'll see you soon," he told her.

"Yes. See you tomorrow," Riley said, holding back the tears. She put her phone back in her bag sadly and turned around as she felt someone tap her on the back. For a moment, she thought she was hallucinating; then her face lit up, and she burst into tears. "Daniel!" she gasped.

He pressed his hands along the small of her back and hugged her tightly. After what seemed like an eternity, Riley pulled away, and Daniel gently wiped away the tears running down her cheeks. "You've no idea how happy I am right now," she told him in-between sobs.

Across the room, Blair's eyes were glued on them with wary intensity. *This really was the stuff of nightmares*, she thought.

"Well, well, well. So this is *the* Daniel Fairgate?" Selena said as she walked up the steps towards them. She held out her hand, and he shook it politely.

Riley reluctantly prised herself off her husband.

"Won't you join us for dinner, Daniel?" Selena asked.

"Thank you so much, but I've actually got plans for myself and my wife tonight," he said, looking mischievously at Riley.

"I've booked us a room here for the night. I hope you don't mind, Blair?" he said.

Riley grinned like a Cheshire cat. She was bursting with happiness. This was exactly what she had been dreaming of since she arrived; to be able to share Paris with Daniel. Blair felt like she had been stabbed in the heart and felt her legs wobble and then give way beneath her. Daniel reached out and caught her before she hit the ground. Riley gasped and Selena shouted for a member of staff to fetch some water.

"I'm okay, really. I feel so silly," Blair said as she was surrounded by worried hotel staff. "I'm just very tired. I think I should go back to my hotel and rest," she told them all.

Louis had arrived just after the drama had unfolded and looked puzzled to see Blair sitting on the bottom step of the staircase, surrounded by onlookers. "Is everything okay, Miss Matthews?" he asked, concerned.

Blair nodded. "Yes, really I'm fine," she insisted.

"Miss Matthews is going to return to her hotel. Could you organise transport for her?" Selena asked Louis.

"Actually, I'm just leaving for the evening, I am happy to drive you," he told Blair.

Before Blair had a chance to answer, Selena responded. "Thank you, that would be wonderful," she said and quickly helped Blair up to her feet.

"You go back and rest, Blair. I'll take care of the rest of the evening's schedule," Selena said, bossily.

Blair was too exhausted to be angry. She resigned herself to the fact that the rest of the day was a write off now that Daniel had turned up and was about to whisk Riley away. She was grateful for Louis's offer to drive her back to her hotel and smiled at him, gratefully.

Chapter 97

Riley woke up to find her body intertwined with Daniel's. As she listened to his soft, muffled snores, she smiled to herself. She was in the most romantic city in the world with the man of her dreams. Daniel rolled over and slowly opened his sapphire blue eyes. "Good morning, beautiful," he said, sleepily.

Riley leant over and kissed his forehead. Being with Daniel felt as natural as breathing. They had made love all night, and now, she wanted more. She pulled his face towards hers, and he kissed her lips softly then shifted his body slightly so his lips brushed against her throat. Riley felt herself beginning to tremble as her whole body cried out for him.

As he moved his mouth expertly around her body, she clutched the crumpled sheets around her tightly and could hardly breathe as her body ached in anticipation. Daniel was taking his time that morning which was sending Riley into a frenzy. She felt like she was in an erotic movie and about to explode with lust at any second. When Daniel eventually hit the spot, Riley groaned in relief and thought she had died and gone to heaven. Before long, she had switched places and was working her magic on him, and soon, he was crying out in ecstasy too before they both rolled back exhausted and fell back to sleep.

Daniel and Riley checked out of the hotel and decided to take in a few of the sights before heading back home. They strolled along the cobbled roads along the little lanes and boulevards, hand in hand. "I feel like we're in a perfume advert," said Riley.

Daniel laughed. "Yes, I know what you mean. Everything feels so perfect," he said. "Actually, I've been thinking about something for a while," he said.

"Oh, I'm intrigued," Riley said, squeezing his hand, playfully.

"How do you feel about renewing our wedding vows?" Daniel said. Riley stopped suddenly.

"Really?" she asked.

"Why not? We've had a few blips in our marriage which we've sorted out now. I think it would be nice," Daniel said, wondering if Riley thought the idea was crazy.

"I think that's a great idea, darling," she said, excitedly.

Blair gasped as she sat up in bed and saw Louis asleep on the sofa in front of her. The events of the day before slowly started to trickle into her mind. He had given her a lift home and ordered her some food from room service. She must have fallen asleep after eating, but why was he still there?

As if he sensed her staring at him, Louis groaned and started to wake up. Blair pulled the covers up to her neck, self-consciously. It must have dawned on Louis where he was, and he jumped up in a panic. "Oh, I'm so sorry, Miss Matthews. I didn't mean to fall asleep. I just wanted to make sure you were okay; you looked unwell last night," he was talking so fast and seemed so nervous, his apology sent Blair into a fit of giggles.

There was a very tall French stranger in her bedroom with his hair sticking up all over the place. Soon, Blair was in hysterics. He looked at her, puzzled, which made her laugh even more. Soon, Louis joined in the laughter. He had no idea what they were laughing at, but it was funny all the same.

Daniel and Riley walked happily around a local market. There was an overwhelming array of stalls selling everything from tomatoes to sofas, and Riley was having the time of her life flitting from stall to stall. "Oh my goodness, Daniel, look at those cakes," Riley said as she stopped to look in the window of a patisserie. "That lemon meringue and pistachio cake is calling out to me. Can you hear it?" she said.

Daniel laughed. "Yes, I can, and I think that huge baguette over there is calling out to me," he replied, leading her into the little shop.

As they walked through the door, they heard a loud throaty laugh which they both recognised immediately. They looked to the back of the dimly lit cafe and to their astonishment they saw Gordon having coffee with an elegant blonde woman. "Dad?" called out Daniel.

The couple's conversation stopped in mid-flow as they turned round abruptly. Gordon let out an incredulous gasp, while Madeleine remained perfectly composed and slowly drew her hand away from Gordon's. The four of them stared at each other not knowing quite what to say. Riley was the first to speak. "What are you doing here, Gordon?" she asked.

Gordon had kept his clandestine meetings concealed for many years, but now, the skeleton had well and truly fallen out of the closet. Daniel's face was livid. It took Riley a while to catch up, but then it dawned on her; her father-in-law was having an affair. Gordon and Madeleine exchanged a brief conspiratorial look, and then Gordon turned to his son. "Could I have a chat with you outside?" he asked with slight trepidation.

"What is there to talk about Dad? You're in Paris, cheating on your wife; my mother!" Daniel's voice was flat and calm even though inside he was full of rage.

Madeleine fixed Daniel with an icy glare. "Shall we leave, Gordon?" she asked, not wanting any part in the drama that was about to unfold.

"Yes, I think you better had, Dad!" Daniel spat the words out as his father stared at him in shock.

"I think we should go, Daniel," Riley told her husband, as she started to pull him towards the door. Daniel let Riley lead him out of the cafe before he was tempted to go over and beat seven bells out of his father.

Chapter 98

Blair sat on her favourite bench under the shade of a willow tree beside the river and watched the families and couples walking past. It was her new favourite past time on a Sunday afternoon. She usually took a book to read and sometimes a packed lunch too. She loved the gentle calmness of the water until every now, and then a canal boat would go past and interrupt the peace and quiet.

An email flashed up on her phone. She looked at it in irritation, expecting it to be from Selena. She had been hassling her for the Copy for the Paris edition of the magazine, but Blair knew it didn't need to be in for another week and had made the decision to stop working at weekends; it was making her tired and irritable. She was surprised to see it wasn't from Selena but from Louis. '*Hello, Miss Matthews, it is Louis from the Ritz Paris. I hope you do not mind me contacting you; I was wondering how you were? Since you left Paris I have not been able to stop thinking about you*'. Blair smiled.

She had enjoyed the brief time she had spent with him and appreciated how kind he was towards her. She also guessed he liked her. She typed back: '*Hello, Louis. I am very well thank you; it is very kind of you to ask. I am currently enjoying an afternoon beside the river where I live. I hope you are well. Best Wishes, Blair*'.

Daniel had refused the invitation to the Fairgate Sunday lunch and his mother was not pleased. "What excuse are we going to give?" Riley asked him.

"We'll just have to say I'm not well or something," said Daniel. Riley was secretly pleased. She wouldn't have to put up with the sarcastic remarks Diana usually threw at her and since Carmelita had left, the food was usually cold by the time it got to the table. Diana tried her best, but she never managed to get the timings correct, and there was always something she had forgotten to cook; one Sunday it had been the roast potatoes. The family pretended it wasn't a big deal, but Rose, being Rose, looked at her grandmother in horror and said, "We can't eat a roast without potatoes."

Diana had fled the table in tears, and Daniel had rushed off after her in an attempt to console her. Riley had to stifle a laugh and caught sight of Joe doing the same as he put his napkin up to cover his face.

Daniel's phone rang. Riley saw Gordon's name come up on it as she handed it to him. Daniel looked at it for a couple of seconds, contemplating whether to answer or not and then put it on 'loud speaker' so Riley could hear too. "Hello," Daniel said.

"Daniel, you're not coming for lunch?" Gordon asked.

"That's correct," said Daniel, indignantly.

Riley was waiting with bated breath; she knew Gordon wasn't going to let this go.

"You know, Daniel… People who live in glass houses shouldn't throw stones! We'll see you at 1:00 pm."

Gordon then hung up.

Riley looked puzzled. "What is that supposed to mean?" she asked.

Daniel had his back to Riley, so she couldn't see the shock on his face. "I don't know, but I think we better go," he told her. Daniel knew exactly what his father had meant. Like father, like son, he thought to himself.

Chapter 99

Diana had set the table in the garden for lunch. The theme today was pink! Fresh pink roses were strewn centrally along the length of the table. It was Diana's attempt at 'shabby chic' and she was delighted with the result.

As the table layout had taken so much energy and time, Diana decided she would get the caterers in to prepare the lunch, that way she could enjoy the day too; she hadn't seen the family in a while and wanted to savour every moment. She looked at her watch. She had just enough time to shower and get ready. She heard a pigeon shuffling about in the branches above her, and she glared up at it. "Don't even think about it!" she said. The last thing she needed was pigeon poo on her freshly decorated table.

Before long, the caterers emerged from the kitchen with the food. Everyone around the table sighed silently with relief. They wouldn't have to endure Diana's half-hearted attempts at a Sunday roast today. Gordon went round the table pouring out more wine for everyone as they all tucked into their meal. He paused when he came to Riley, knowing she wouldn't want any. "How's work, Riley," he asked.

"Good thanks Gordon. We're getting ready for the Derby next week," Riley told him.

"Ah yes; the pinnacle of the greyhound racing calendar," he said. "Well, I shall be there to cheer you on, my dear."

"Thank you, Gordon; I appreciate your support," Riley said.

"Will you definitely be in the country next weekend?" Daniel asked, sarcastically.

Gordon noticed the edge to his tone. "Of course, I'll be in the country. Family means everything to me, just like it does to you, son. I will be supporting my beautiful daughter-in-law, just like you will be," he said, not taking the bait that Daniel had thrown. As far as Gordon was concerned, what he got up to was nothing to do with his son or anyone else. There were some things in life that were too complicated to truly understand and his relationship with Madeleine was one of them.

Chapter 100
July 2017

Riley had been awake for most of the night, tossing and turning. She felt like she had an army of frogs leaping around in her stomach. She couldn't believe she had got to this stage; finalist in the English Greyhound Derby. It had been a long journey of competition and elimination to finally reach this 6-dog final. If only her dad was there to see it, he would have been so proud of her.

All the work he had put in to patiently teach her all he knew, had finally paid off. She couldn't wait to get down to the kennels and see her beautiful Blaze. She had complete faith in him and didn't care if he wasn't the favourite to win. Punters had lost faith in him after his injury, but Riley had worked hard to get him back to full fitness. If she had had any doubts she would never have entered him in the competition. Blaze was ready for this. He was born for this.

She picked up her bag and double checked she had everything she needed. Daniel had brought her tea and toast on a tray earlier, but she was too nervous to eat. "Right, I'm off," she said before kissing each of her girls on the cheek. She hugged Daniel tightly.

"You'll smash this, darling," Daniel said, confidently.

"Not me! Blaze," said Riley.

"We'll see you down there," he told her, kissing her on the forehead.

Riley jumped out of the car and ran down to the paddock. The kennel staff had already taken the dogs down, and Riley could see Blaze leaping around with his tail wagging furiously. It was as if he knew he was going somewhere special. Blaze spotted Riley in the distance and his eyes lit up. He sprinted across the paddock towards her, and Riley burst into tears as he leapt up into her arms, knocking her on to the ground. She laughed hysterically while Blaze whipped her with his tail in excitement. "You are going to win this for us Blaze. I love you so much. I know you can do it," Riley told him.

Blaze licked her across the face, frantically.

"Okay, my big beautiful boy, are you ready for this?" Riley said, pushing him off her.

Blaze jumped up and howled.

"I'll take that as a yes then," laughed Riley.

When they pulled up at the stadium, Riley was surprised to see that the place was already heaving with people, even though it was still early. She walked around with her team, who had come down with her, soaking up the atmosphere. They were in Towcester this year; it was the first time the Derby had been held outside London. "The crowd are in a good mood," said Liam, one of the trainers in Riley's team.

Riley nodded. Her whole body was shaking in anticipation. She watched the punters and bookmakers walking around, talking quickly into their phones. The owners and their guests were dressed up to the nines in the VIP areas, sipping champagne. "Time to go get Blaze," said Riley.

As the trainers came out with their dogs, a load roar erupted in the grandstand. Riley looked down at Blaze and smiled. He was nice and calm. His coat was glossy and his eyes were bright. She was dressed in the obligatory blue coat featuring the name of the Derby sponsor on it.

Nearby, a group of men watched Riley in awe as she strode along with her endlessly long legs and thick dark hair blowing gently in the evening breeze. They now understood why she was known as the sexiest greyhound trainer in the country. The light was beginning to dim, and there was great excitement as the stadium became atmospheric.

Riley's pre-race nerves had disappeared, and she felt confident and composed. She spotted Daniel with the girls who waved wildly at her. They were on their way to one of the food stands. She also saw Gordon coming up behind them. She hoped he and Daniel had put their differences aside today for the girls' sake.

Daniel stopped and looked at his wife. He felt a surge of love and pride, seeing her walking around with the other trainers. He knew that winning this Derby meant everything to her. Ever since he had known her, she had talked about this day. He hoped and prayed Blaze would do it for her. "Okay boss, are you ready for this?" asked Liam, shaking Riley out of her thoughts.

"As ready as I'll ever be," Riley said, taking a deep breath.

Riley knelt down to stroke Blaze at the back of his trap. He had his black and white striped jacket on and was still calm. "Do this for Terry," Riley whispered in his ear. Blaze went into his trap obediently. Some of the other dogs were putting up a bit of a fight and had to be coaxed in by their owners. Riley walked over to the side so that she could get a good view of the race, but her eyes were transfixed on trap number 6. She looked up and blew a kiss to the sky; she knew her dad would be there watching.

"Six of the nation's finest canine athletes are ready, but there can only be one winner of the 2017 English Greyhound Derby," shouted the commentator. "Good luck to all the teams. All set? Ready to go?"

The crowd went wild. The flag was raised. The bell was rung and as the electronic hare flew past the traps, the trap doors were raised and the dogs came flying out, to deafening cheers. Blaze was out like a bullet.

The roar of the crowd sent shivers down Riley's spine, and she glanced over at Daniel and the girls, who were screaming. She looked back but had lost sight of Blaze. Her eyes searched the track desperately, and then she spotted him in his striped jacket in-between a flurry of long furry limbs. He forced his way round the 4th bend with an electric turn of speed. Her heart leapt, and she felt like she was going to explode. Blaze had great spatial awareness and was in complete control.

Riley watched him almost glide through the air. She knew he had nailed it. She heard the commentator shouting excitedly, "He's had a rough time lately, but he's charged up on the inside and closed in from behind." He continued, "It's unbelievable; the rank outsider of the field is weaving his way through to victory, but can he do it? Yes, he can! Blazing Zippy has pipped Balymo Jim to the finishing line."

Riley thought the commentator was going to combust with hysteria.

"What a great test of speed, perseverance and stamina. Blazing Zippy is the sensational winner of the 2017 English Greyhound Derby!" shouted the, now almost hoarse, announcer.

Riley screamed, jumped up and punched the air in victory. "We did it, Dad," she shouted up to the clouds. Her team ran over and grabbed her, and they all hugged each other as they danced around the track.

"Well done, Riley!" Liam shouted with tears in his eyes.

Riley ran over to Blaze as he bounced around triumphantly. She heard one of the pundits describing him being a 'jewel in the crown'.

"You have made my dreams come true," Riley told Blaze in-between sobs as she put the winner's blue jacket on him, and then she led him to the podium.

Riley stood on the podium feeling completely overwhelmed, unable to take in the enormity of what they had just achieved. She was asked to explain how it felt to win. "I can't quite explain it," she said, hardly able to breathe. "It is what I have dreamt of since I was a little girl and today seeing my Blazing Zippy roar to victory as he crossed the line was indescribable. I am so proud of him. To watch him make such a comeback after suffering a fractured wrist not so long ago, which threatened to end his career, was incredible."

Daniel and the children ran over to be with Riley. She bent down to squeeze the girls and then kissed Daniel. "I'm so proud of you babe," he said as his eyes glistened with tears.

"The atmosphere here today was electric. What a crowd!" Riley continued, "I want to dedicate this trophy to my dad, Terry Mulligan, the most incredible greyhound trainer ever." Riley held the silver trophy up as high as she could and everyone around her clapped wildly. The sponsors of the Derby came over to congratulate her and told her they were delighted to see a woman win this year.

A Sky Sports journalist fought her way through the crowd who were gathered around Riley. "Could I just ask you Ms Matthews, what is your advice to all the young women out there who dream of being where you are today? Greyhound racing has predominantly been a male dominated industry hasn't it and women have been accused of being too soft and affectionate with their dogs?" Riley paused.

"People have told me throughout my career that I have been too affectionate with my dogs and that women can't compete with men in this industry. Well, frankly, that's a load of rubbish. If the dogs are happy, they are going to perform at their best. My track record proves trainers have more success by treating their animals well. To all the young female greyhound trainers out there; follow your dreams. I am the third woman to have ever won the Derby, so it just goes to show anything is possible if you want it badly enough."

"Blazing Zippy was the outsider in this race, wasn't he?" The woman asked.

"Yes, he was, but I have always had complete faith in him. Today, he has shown durability, stamina and guts," said Riley.

"So what is next for Blazing Zippy?" asked the presenter.

"He is now going to enjoy his retirement in his new home, with me and my family," Riley said, happily.

The woman turned back to the camera and said, "What a wonderful evening it has been here at Towcester. Riley Matthews has been chasing the Derby dream since she was a young girl and today, the dog she has hand-reared from a pup, Blazing Zippy, has earned legendary status. Congratulations to Ms Mulligan and her team for a superb win."

"Is Blaze going to live with us now, Mummy?" Patsy asked, excitedly.

"Yes, he is," said Riley.

"Dudley will be happy," Rose said as she stroked Blaze.

Chapter 101

It was the day before the wedding vows renewal ceremony, and Riley woke up with a huge grin on her face. She was still buzzing from the Derby win, Blaze had settled in well in his new home with them, and now, she was re-marrying the man she loved. Riley didn't actually believe that it was necessary to have a whole ceremony and reception afterwards, she would have been happy just going away somewhere with Daniel and doing it in private, but for some reason, Daniel was excited about the whole day.

Riley never would have guessed Daniel would even have known what a wedding vow renewal was, let alone suggest they have one; however, she was happy to go along with it if it made him happy. He had even had a word with his mother to ask her to try and get along with Riley from now on, for his sake. She agreed, slightly reluctantly, but said she would do it for Daniel and her granddaughters, whom she adored. When Daniel told her about the ceremony, light bulbs lit up in Diana's mind. "Let me organise it!" she said, excitedly.

Daniel hesitated for a moment, not sure how Riley would feel about it, but his mother was so thrilled at the idea that he didn't want to disappoint her. "What a great idea, Mum. I'm sure Riley will be thrilled!" he said.

"Are you sure you don't mind that Mum is arranging it all?" Daniel asked Riley as she got out of the bed and stretched, sleepily.

"No, not at all. One thing your mother is good at is throwing a party, and it's saved us a job," she said, crawling back over the duvet to give Daniel a kiss. As she got up to go, he pulled her down towards him. "I've got to get showered honey; my dress will be arriving in half an hour," she told him as she dragged her arm away from his grip.

Daniel groaned. He desperately wanted to make love to his wife.

"You could always join me in the shower," Riley said, with a wink.

Daniel didn't need telling twice. He leapt out of the bed and chased her into the bathroom.

Riley tipped her head back as the warm water trickled down her face and splashed onto Daniel's tanned stomach. He turned her around, so she faced the shower wall and moved his hands down to her waist. Riley's hands were firmly up against the wall as she revelled in the touch of his strong hands caressing her body. She moaned softly as his fingers moved up and circled her nipples, and she raised her hips up towards him, waiting to feel him inside her. Daniel moved himself into position, and they moved slowly back and forth rhythmically in time with each other as sprays of water cascaded down them until they both cried out at the same time in a moment of pure bliss.

Blair was sitting on her bed looking at the choice of dresses hanging up that she had picked out for the wedding renewal. Whoever came up with such a stupid idea? If you're married, then you're married! Why would you need to go through it all again. It wasn't as if it was even a legal ceremony. It was a complete waste of time, and Blair didn't want to go.

Of course, she had to go because Riley was her best friend, but Daniel was the love of Blair's life so how was that fair? She wasn't even sure she would be able to get through the day without bursting into tears. It was one thing knowing that Daniel and Riley were a couple, but she wasn't sure she was strong enough to watch them drool over each other right in front of her. She was suddenly overcome with sadness and felt the tears start to roll down her cheeks. A knock on the door interrupted her misery.

Blair didn't want to see anyone and contemplated ignoring it, but whoever was out there was persistent and carried on knocking. "Oh for fucks sake!" Blair shouted, angrily as she dragged herself off her bed.

Carrie was standing on the doorstep when Blair answered the door. "Mum," she said, surprised. "I'm not stopping love. I just wanted to drop this off for you," her mum said as she reached inside her bag for a small package. She held it out for Blair.

"What is it?" asked Blair, frowning.

"You'll see when you open it. Now, I must go, or I'll miss my train," Carrie said.

"Where are you going?" Blair asked.

"Oxford Street. I'm going on a shopping trip with a friend from work. Must go! Bye!" she said as she hurried off down the road. Blair stared at the white package in her hand then went back inside the apartment and shut the door.

Chapter 102

"Is that your new wedding dress?" Rose asked as Riley took it out of the wardrobe.

"Yes, darling, it is. Do you want to see it?"

"No thanks. I already know what it looks like. We saw it in the shop," Rose said, matter-of-factly as she skipped away.

"Can I see it, Mummy?" asked Patsy.

Riley smiled at her other daughter. "Of course, my darling," she said. Riley shook out the dress, which was hanging on a red velvet hanger, and held it up in front of her. "What do you think?" she asked Patsy.

Patsy beamed at her mum. "You will look like a princess," she said, admiring the knee-length, cream silk dress. Riley had refused to buy a wedding dress but had chosen a pretty, elegant dress which she found on the high street that fitted her perfectly.

"Cuddle?" Riley asked.

Patsy smiled and leapt on top of her.

"I love you to the moon and back. You know that, don't you?" said Riley.

She caught a glimpse of Patsy's bare feet and saw her slightly twisted little foot, and a wave of guilt washed over her, as it did every time she looked at her daughter. They were assured that in time, as Patsy grew, the foot would realign, but Riley would never be able to forgive herself for what she did. "You know, baby, your foot will get better; I promise you," Riley said, ruefully as she gently stroked the soft skin on Patsy's foot. "I wish I could go back and change things. I would never have got in that car and caused that accident. It is entirely my fault that you can't walk properly, and I'm so sorry I crashed the car."

"You didn't crash the car; Daddy did!" said Patsy.

Riley moved Patsy round, so she could look at her face. "No, darling, don't you remember? I was driving the car the night we had a crash," Riley corrected her.

Patsy shook her head hard and rolled her eyes. "No, silly, Daddy opened the door and pushed you over to the other side, and he drove the car, but you kept shouting, and then Daddy didn't see the man. The man fell on the car, and Daddy drove into the tree."

Riley sat rooted to the spot in shock. For a fleeting moment, she believed Patsy, but then remembered that Patsy was very young at the time, and she must have got confused.

Patsy got up when she heard Rose calling her downstairs and scurried out of the bedroom. Riley shook the thought quickly out of her head and hung her dress back on its hanger.

"Rodriguez, I said red roses! Why have white roses turned up on my doorstep?" Diana said angrily down the phone.

"Well, that's not good enough, I'm afraid. Take them away and send the ones I ordered. I need them here by the end of the day."

Diana shook her head in despair.

Gordon handed her a gin. "Don't stress, darling; it will all be fine," he assured her.

Diana wanted to scream. "Why do you always say that? It is not fine, Gordon! They have sent the wrong flowers and the catering company can't get hold of the Siberian Caviar I wanted for the canapés; apparently, there's a problem in Poland," she said, grumpily.

"Just take ten minutes and sit down and have a drink with me," Gordon said, trying to calm his wife down.

"I haven't got time to sit down, Gordon," Diana yelled and marched off in a huff.

Riley's head was spinning from her daughter's revelation, which was now firmly stuck in her head, and the words were going round and round in circles. She knew it was a mistake, but why was she having doubts? Something didn't seem quite right. Riley closed her eyes and tried to remember that fateful night. She had blocked the events out of her mind like she did with everything traumatic that had happened in her life, but now she had to dig those memories back up because things didn't add up. She remembered the row between her and Daniel clearly. She had stormed off with Patsy while Rose was still in the house. The next part was a bit of a blur. She remembered Daniel running after her, shouting at her not to drive because she was over the limit.

Slowly, fragments of the rest of the night started to fuse together. She watched it play back in slow motion in her mind. Daniel had pulled open the door and pushed her over into the passenger seat. She had got her leg caught but managed to pull it free while Patsy was crying hysterically in the back seat. *Oh my god!* Flashbacks started to come flooding back.

Daniel got into the driver's seat of the car. He was livid and shouting at her, and then he slammed his foot down on the accelerator, and the car shot forward. It was pitch black outside, and somebody came out of nowhere and landed with a thud on the windscreen. She remembered putting her hands over her face as she screamed in horror. Then she must have blacked out because the only thing she remembered after that was being outside the car and talking to a police officer.

Riley slumped down on the floor and leant against the wall for support. The shock stunned her, and she felt totally numb. After what seemed like an eternity, she managed to pull herself up off the floor as she heard her children calling her. She felt like a zombie on autopilot as she walked down the stairs. Soon, the numbness started to fade as reality hit her.

Her husband, the love of her life, had let her take the blame for the car accident. He had let her go to prison for a crime she didn't commit. He had let another woman come into her house and be a mother to her children. He had also made her live with the guilt and shame all these years. She was married to a monster.

Blair was stunned. "Are you sure?" she asked when Riley phoned her.

"Yes. It was Daniel who crashed the car, not me," Riley cried angrily down the phone.

"Maybe Patsy made a mistake?" Blair said.

"No, Blair, I remember," insisted Riley.

"What are you going to do?" asked Blair.

"I need time to think. Can I drop the girls over to you?" asked Riley.

"Yes, of course," Blair told her. Blair closed her eyes and silently winced. She had kept Daniel's secret all this time after she overheard Patsy talking in her sleep after one of her nightmares. At the time, Blair hadn't mentioned it to Daniel because she didn't want to worry him, so she just kept it to herself.

"Thanks. I'll see you soon," Riley said and hung up. Her body was quivering with rage as she quickly packed two bags for the girls.

"Where are we going?" asked Rose.

"To stay with Aunty Blair for the day," Riley said.

The girls looked puzzled. "It's only for a little while. Mummy's got some important business to sort out. You can take Dudley and Blaze with you if you like; I'm sure Aunty Blair won't mind," she said, rushing around scooping up jackets, colouring books and coloured pencils.

Annalisa walked with Daniel to the plane they were going to use that afternoon. It was going to be another glorious afternoon, and flying conditions would be perfect. "Let's quickly go through it again," she said.

"We stop off on the flight path on the way to Belgium to make the pickup. They will be waiting in a black Range Rover. The blocks will go in the tail section of the plane, and the Border Control guys will be waiting to let us through at this end."

"Correct!" said Daniel.

"And the money?" she asked.

"I'll pick it up tomorrow when I drive to the warehouse to deliver the goods," said Daniel.

"And we definitely won't end up in the bottom of a canal like that, Dooley guy?" Annalisa asked.

"I bloody hope not," laughed Daniel.

"Okay, I'll see you in half an hour then," she told him.

"Oh. By the way, I never did thank you, did I? That was a great idea about renewing the wedding vows," Daniel told her.

Riley raced across the airfield as Daniel was walking around the aircraft doing his pre-flight checks. Startled, he looked up and was shocked to see Riley's car heading towards him. She stopped the car and yanked up the handbrake. She then got out and slammed the door behind her.

"Is everything alright, darling?" he asked.

"No, Daniel. Nothing is alright!" she said coldly.

"What do you mean?" Daniel asked, disconcertingly. The colour drained out of his face as he stood opposite his wife.

Riley looked at him with disgust. "You were driving the car on the night of the crash; not me," she said, trying hard to remain calm and composed.

Daniel shuddered. He was speechless for a few seconds, and then said. "Don't be silly. Of course, I wasn't."

Riley laughed in disbelief. "I can see the lies in your eyes, Daniel," she told him. "You let me take the blame and live with the guilt. How could you do that?" she asked. She could feel the tension emanating from his body.

"It's not that straightforward." Daniel's voice started to crack. He was about to lose Riley. He couldn't deal with this now; he had a drug-run to concentrate on. "If you hadn't got in that car in the first place, Riley, none of that would have happened," Daniel said weakly.

Riley shook her head. Her eyes didn't leave his. She couldn't believe he was twisting it around as if she was still to blame. "The villain isn't necessarily the one who lit the match, Daniel, but the person who chose not to put out the flame," she said, without emotion. Daniel felt the panic rise in his stomach.

"I had no choice, Riley," he cried.

"Life is all about choices, Daniel. We always have a choice," she said, feeling strangely calm all of a sudden.

Annalisa frowned as she walked towards the plane. Daniel couldn't afford to get into a domestic situation with his wife right now; he needed his wits about him to get this job done properly without putting them both at any risk. "Everything okay?" she called out.

Riley turned round to look at Annalisa. She looked incredibly elegant in a black jersey trouser suit with her hair pulled back into a bun at the nape of her neck. Her dark olive skin glistened in the sunlight. "Hello, Riley. What brings you here?" Annalisa asked breezily.

Riley stared at her and wondered if she had been in on the secret. She and Daniel were as thick as thieves, and it wouldn't have surprised Riley if it had actually been Annalisa's idea to blame her for the accident to save precious, privileged Daniel Fairgate from getting into trouble. It suddenly all made sense to her. Jeff had been telling the truth about Daniel and Siobhan, Daniel always did what Daniel wanted, regardless of the consequences. "I thought I knew you, but I never really knew you at all," Riley said, sadly and then turned and walked back towards her car.

"Riley. Please, wait," begged Daniel.

Annalisa stood in front of him to prevent him from chasing after her. "We've got a job to do, Daniel. Focus!" she said, sternly.

He nodded, reluctantly. "Riley! We'll talk when I get home," he shouted after her.

"Diana, will you please stop stressing and sit down and have a drink," insisted Gordon.

Diana sighed. She was exhausted but pleased that the flowers had finally arrived and the caterers had found a suitable substitute for the caviar. The tables were all set up for tomorrow, and the stage was erected, ready for the band that would arrive in the afternoon. She slipped off her shoes and flopped into the chair beside her husband. She reached for the TV remote control and turned on the news channel. Gordon handed her another gin.

"That's Daniel," she exclaimed, turning up the volume. Gordon leant forward in his chair to get a closer look. A slightly blurred screenshot photo of Daniel was shown behind the newsreader.

Chapter 103

Riley pulled up in the driveway and thumped the steering wheel in anger. She started to shake uncontrollably from the wave of hurt and devastation that engulfed her, and then she sat back in the seat and succumbed to the wails of grief and rage that poured out of her as the tears poured down her face.

The silence was deafening as Riley walked into the empty house, feeling completely exhausted, and threw her keys onto the side table by the door. She felt gut-wrenchingly sad and wanted to curl up in a ball and go to sleep and never wake up. Instead, she decided to make a phone call. "Hello, Riley," said a voice. "Are you busy?" she asked.

The newsreader looked at the camera solemnly as he said, "Concern was raised when the aircraft failed to reach its destination. It is believed that the private plane belonging to Daniel Fairgate from the Fairgate Flight Centre in Hertfordshire went missing over the English Channel. Helicopters and lifeboats are scouring the area after an alert from Air Traffic Control reported that the plane had disappeared from the radar at approximately 4:00 pm." The glass slipped from Diana's hand and shattered into tiny pieces as it hit the stone-tiled floor.

Riley sat on the wall at the end of the drive and smiled as she heard the deep, throaty rumbling sound of the Harley-Davidson as it came flying around the bend. She got up as it stopped in front of her. "Where to, my lovely?" asked Ricky.

"Anywhere, away from here," Riley said as she put on the helmet he handed her and climbed on behind him. She wrapped her arms tightly around his waist as he revved the engine and roared away.

Blair reached into the back of the cupboard for the pancake mix as the girls chatted away happily beside her. As she pulled the packet out, she remembered the pregnancy test stick on the side of the worktop that her mum had bought for her. She picked it up for what must have been the tenth time that day and stared at the two lines in the little window. She caught a glimpse of herself in the mirror, and she gently stroked her stomach as Rose and Patsy laughed and chased each other around the table. Blaze and Dudley were stretched out on two blankets, lazily lapping up the sun's rays on the balcony outside. Blair smiled to herself; she had never felt so content. Life was about to get very interesting!